CW01628819

MURDER IN THE GARDEN

A completely unputdownable cozy mystery

VERONICA HELEY

The Ellie Quicke Mysteries Book 5

JOFFE
Ostara
CLASSICS

Revised edition 2023
Joffe Books, London
www.joffebooks.com

First published by Severn House in Great Britain in 2004

This paperback edition was first published
in Gret Britain in 2023

© Veronica Heley 2004, 2023

This book is a work of fiction. Names, characters, businesses, organizations, places and events are either the product of the author's imagination or are used fictitiously. Any resemblance to actual persons, living or dead, events or locales is entirely coincidental. The spelling used is British English except where fidelity to the author's rendering of accent or dialect supersedes this. The right of Veronica Heley to be identified as author of this work has been asserted in accordance with the Copyright, Designs and Patents Act 1988.

Cover art by Dee Dee Book Covers

ISBN: 978-1-83526-126-2

CHAPTER ONE

She couldn't understand what was the matter. Her legs refused to hold her up. She clung to the door frame.

Her tongue was being lazy, too. 'What did you put in my drink?'

'A mild sedative to help you relax. I have brought your suicide note with me. Where is it? Didn't I put it in my wallet? See how you have upset me. I am shaking with nerves. I have never killed anyone before, you see.'

He unfolded a piece of paper, and held it up for her to see. She read the words aloud.

'I can't bear the shame any longer. My husband did kill the girl.'

She knew it wasn't really funny, but for some reason she wanted to laugh. How absurd! No one would believe it for a minute!

It had been stupid to laugh, because it made him angry.

His face darkened. He caught hold of her arm and swung her back into her chair. The sticky liquid from the overturned bottles swelled into pools and began to move slowly to the edge of the table. One drop fell on her skirt. Another on to her leg.

'Make yourself comfortable,' he said, producing a sharp knife. He lifted up her right hand. She tried to pull away. He was much stronger than her.

He closed her fingers around the knife.

He laid her left hand palm upwards on the table. He forced her right hand — still holding the knife — to hover over her left wrist.

'No!' She tried to scream. No sound came out.

'And now, dear lady, let me help you slash your wrists . . .'

* * *

Ellie Quicke couldn't concentrate. The noise of the mechanical digger was driving her insane. She covered her ears, pushing her fingers through her short, prematurely silvered hair. She couldn't even complain to her neighbours about it, because she was responsible for the digger being there in the first place.

Kate and Armand were a lovely couple but they couldn't tell a gladiolus from a nettle. They'd copied Ellie's new conservatory at the back of her house, intending theirs to be a dining and living room.

The view from the back of these semi-detached houses was spectacular, as the gardens sloped down to an alley and then up to a pretty Victorian Gothic church surrounded by mature trees. That view — added to the nearness of a decent row of shops, a primary school and a library — kept up the price of these undistinguished but well-built three-bedroomed houses. It was a most desirable neighbourhood, usually.

But not today.

The noise was an assault on the ear. Midge — Ellie's marauding tomcat — didn't like it, either, but plopped out of the cat flap and disappeared over the garden fence.

Kate and Armand had asked Ellie to mastermind a makeover for their neglected garden, and she'd been delighted to do so. They were happily out at work when the machinery started up, but Ellie wasn't.

For the third time she tried to add up the monthly accounts and for the third time failed to agree a total. If only her dear husband Frank had allowed a calculator in the house, she could have resorted to one. A memory came up and hit her; Frank was standing beside her saying, 'Only the mentally deficient need calculators.'

She winced.

So there wasn't one in his desk. She still thought of it as 'his' desk, in the same way as she still thought of the computer as his, even though he'd died some time ago.

She eyed the PC with misgivings. She'd been told that she only used a tiny fraction of what the machine was capable of doing. She was pretty sure there'd be a facility for adding a column of figures on it. But where? And how? She could run off the occasional letter on it. Yes, it allowed her to do that when it was in a good mood. But add figures? No.

The noise was appalling, even though she was in the study at the front of the house. There was a hatch from the study into the kitchen, so she shut that. The noise abated from a hungry howl to a moan. Better.

She squared her elbows. She would not be beaten by a column of figures. If necessary, she'd ask Kate next door to check them when she returned from her highly paid job in the City. She wouldn't ask Armand, who was a teacher but had a short fuse.

She tried again, and reached a fourth figure which didn't match any of her preceding attempts.

She threw up her hands and set the ledger on one side. There was a great muddle of papers on the desk, not to mention an ancient cigar box containing some pieces of undistinguished family jewellery which her aged aunt Drusilla had insisted on giving her. Ellie hadn't worn any of it yet, or even had it insured. She pushed the box to the back of the desk and drew some bills towards her. At least she could pay those. At the back of her mind she could hear Frank snorting, 'How can you work in such a mess?'

She shook his voice away.

He was right, of course. The muddle of paperwork was a sign that she was not coping. Frank had left her very comfortably off but she didn't want everyone to know it, so she'd set up a trust fund to give money away to deserving causes. To her dismay, that also took a lot of time to administer.

Then there was her difficult daughter Diana, whom Ellie did not class as a deserving cause. Diana was expecting

Ellie to back her latest money-making project, which Ellie was declining to do. Then much of her time at weekends was taken up with the care of her grandson, little Frank, who was much loved but a little too active to be an easy charge for someone in her fifties. There was also her aged aunt Drusilla, and her cousin . . . and friends . . . all demanding time and attention.

She raised her head from her paperwork. Something was wrong.

Ah, she had it. The noise had stopped.

Had they finished already? They'd had their elevenses some time ago. True, they had to dig out two fairly large holes in the ground to accommodate the water feature which Kate and Armand had specified, but . . .

It was rather like the silence you get after a child has fallen and hurt itself. If machinery stopped and men then shouted at one another, that was all right. If it stopped and there was a horrible hush, then it wasn't.

She went through the kitchen into her new conservatory to have a look, but couldn't see properly into next door's garden for the shrubs between. She opened the back door, telling herself she was being silly, but would just have a look to satisfy herself. Halfway down the path there was a natural break in the hedge, and she could see through.

Billy the handyman was standing by the earth digger, looking down into the hole that had just been dug. His mate was sitting on the seat of the digger, also staring down.

Ellie said, 'Anything wrong?'

Billy wiped his arm across his forehead. ''Fraid so. Don't you come no nearer, now. You don't want to see this.'

There is nothing more irritating to a grown woman than to be told 'you don't want to see this', so naturally Ellie hastened down her own pretty garden, into the alley, and up through the gate into Kate's. The untrimmed bushes, brambles and saplings which had covered the garden for the last umpteen number of years had been crudely scraped off and dumped in a skip. Halfway up the garden, a pit had been excavated to form the top pool of a new water feature, and the topsoil from that hole had been dumped in the skip on top of the vegetation.

Kate and Armand had wanted a small upper pool, with a trickle of water from a large bamboo pipe feeding a larger lower pool, which would then be recycled back up the slope via a pump. There had evidently been no problem cutting out the upper pool, but the machine had just started on the lower one when . . . something white had appeared in the grab.

Billy's mate got down from his seat. 'I never dug up one of them afore.'

'This'll cost us,' said Billy. 'Put us right behind.'

Ellie thought that the skull looked exactly like the ones which they sometimes found in her favourite television programme on archaeological digs. It looked quite clean and not at all alarming.

'Have you found a Saxon burial, then? Are there any gold rings in there?'

'I can see the ribs,' said Billy. 'Don't think it's Saxon, though.' He exchanged a man-to-man look with his mate. 'Perhaps you'd best go back your side of the fence, Mrs Quicke. We'll have to report this. Don't suppose they'll let us get on with the job for a while.'

'No, I don't suppose they will,' said Ellie, her mind still running on archaeology. 'Would you like a cuppa?'

They both nodded. On her way back up to her own house, she heard Billy on his mobile asking for the police, to report finding a body.

'What nonsense,' thought Ellie, amused rather than perturbed. She began to speculate as to whether the present church had been built on the site of a much earlier one, and if so, whether there were more burials to be found in the locality. What happened to the grave goods that were sometimes found with such burials? She'd read of gold rings and daggers and, oh, all sorts of interesting things that usually ended up in museums. She wondered if Billy would be able to claim treasure trove if they found some gold coins or rings. She'd known Billy for years. She'd be pleased if he had found some.

She took a tray of mugs and some biscuits back down the garden and up through the gate, just as the police arrived. Two men in uniform, neither of whom she knew. 'Someone reported a suspicious death?'

'A body,' said Billy, taking a mug of tea from Ellie and adding sugar. 'Excavating for a pond. Turned it up in the grab.'

'It's exciting, isn't it?' said Ellie. 'Who would have thought it, a body in the garden. Would you gentlemen like some tea, too?'

Again a man-to-man sign passed between Billy and his mate. Billy said, 'Suppose you go back to your house, Mrs Quicke. Make yourself a cuppa in peace and quiet. No need for you to stick around, is there?'

One of the policemen stared at Ellie. 'You're that Mrs Quicke, are you? I've heard about you.' He didn't seem to have liked what he'd heard.

Ellie blushed, but tilted her chin at the policeman. She couldn't help it if the police had written her off as an interfering fool before, when crimes had been committed locally. She might not be a Great Brain, but she knew people and she'd proved the police wrong on a couple of occasions when they'd jumped to conclusions.

Bill took the tray off Ellie, and shooed her to the alley. 'Go on, now. The police will want to cordon the site off, I shouldn't wonder.'

'Ring it in,' one policeman said to the other, and called in to the station. 'Yes, they have found a body. A skull, anyhow. And some ribs, looks like . . .'

Ellie did as she was told. She made herself a cuppa and sat down in her conservatory, from which she could catch glimpses of the activity next door through the hedge. She had a better view when she went upstairs to the back bedroom, because then she could see right over the hedge. More police arrived. A tent appeared to be erected in the garden, even though the weather was set fine and warm. It could be cool in September, but they'd had good weather that month so far.

Tired of standing at the window and looking down on an all-concealing tent, Ellie returned downstairs. Standing in her living room, she could see down the garden and up to the church one way, and the other way she could look up through the bay windows of her living room to the road at the front of the house. She wondered how long it would take for people to gather in little groups . . . and yes, there was a group of neighbours across the road, all looking down at Kate and Armand's house.

She was just debating whether or not to ring Kate at work to tell her the exciting news, when there was an uproar in the road outside. Ellie recognized that voice, so rushed through her hall and opened the front door.

Yes, there was red-headed, foxy-faced Armand, just returned from a tiring day at school, and objecting like mad to being forbidden entry into his own house by one of the uniformed policemen. What fun! Ellie called to him to come over to her place, but the policeman wouldn't allow that, either.

Armand's face was an unbecoming red by this time, prompting Ellie to wonder how often he had his blood pressure checked. 'That's my house!' he was yelling. 'How dare you . . . !'

The policeman said something Ellie couldn't hear.

Armand looked shocked. 'What? You mean . . . in our back garden? But . . . I don't understand.'

A tall, well-built woman with badly dyed mahogany hair came out of the house, accompanied by a sandy-haired man who was also in plain clothes.

Ellie drew in her breath. Detective Sergeant Willis was no friend of hers, but Ellie respected her brains, if not her dress sense. Ellie had no opinion at all of the sandy-haired policeman whose manners, she felt, left a great deal to be desired.

It was at that moment Ellie began to wonder if she hadn't misinterpreted the situation. Perhaps it hadn't been a Saxon burial, after all. Perhaps the skull wasn't that old, though it had looked pretty clean to Ellie. Perhaps someone had been coming home from the pub, had fallen down in that deplorably neglected garden and died there. Then the brambles had grown over him or her. Oh dear. Poor man.

Or perhaps not.

Ellie let her tea grow cold while she thought about that. Armand had been neatly inserted into the back of a police car, still fuming. DS Willis had got into the car with him, but didn't drive away. Sandy Hair disappeared back into Kate's house, talking on his mobile. His mobile was usually attached to his ear. In Ellie's opinion, that mobile prevented him from having any meaningful communication with the rest of the human race.

Ellie could imagine Armand's rage and bewilderment. Rage probably winning out over bewilderment.

Suddenly he shot out of the police car and, pursued by DS Willis, thundered down the front drive to Ellie's house. Forgetting that there was a bell, he hammered on the door.

Ellie opened it and registered the annoyance on DS Willis's face as she in turn recognized Ellie. It was clear the policewoman welcomed the encounter as little as Ellie did.

Armand demanded, 'Tell this woman how long we've been living here, Ellie.'

'You moved in last August sometime. A couple of months before my husband died.'

'You see!' said Armand, whirling his arms around. 'We haven't been here long enough to have been responsible for that skull or whatever it is! And why would we bring in a digger to excavate for a pond, if we'd buried someone there earlier?'

'So you say,' said DS Willis in a flat voice which meant she'd really hoped she could have cleared up the case by arresting Armand for murder. 'So who did you buy the house from, may I ask?'

'I don't know, do I! Someone who lived abroad. They'd let it out to some woman with three kids. Her husband left her, she moved into council accommodation, the house came on to the market and we bought it.'

'Ah-ha,' said DS Willis. 'Disappeared, has he?' Meaning she thought the man who'd disappeared might be the body in the garden.

Ellie was doubtful. 'I don't think a body could become a skeleton quite so quickly, could it? I suppose it depends on the soil . . .'

'Acid soil, you want for that,' said Armand, the schoolmaster.

'Is clay acid?'

DS Willis raised her voice. 'So what was this woman's name?'

Armand shrugged. 'Moved out before we ever saw the house. Try the estate agents. Jolley's, in the Avenue.'

Ellie raised her eyebrows, but of course it would be Jolley's, who had almost a monopoly of house sales in the district.

'Yes?' said DS Willis, noticing Ellie's reaction and swinging round on her.

'It's only that my daughter Diana has moved in with Derek Jolley, the estate agent. She's turning a big house into flats which he's going to let.' And taking advantage of her in other ways too, thought Ellie, with some distaste. It occurred to her that Diana hadn't been pursuing her for money lately. Could it be that her daughter was avoiding her?

DS Willis looked grim. 'Oh, I remember her. Do I remember her!'

Most people remembered Diana, who was tall, dark and handsome, with the disposition of a bully. Armand's flashes of temper were as nothing to Diana's prolonged bouts of ill humour.

Armand was interested. 'Is Diana still with Derek Jolley? What on earth does she see in him? He must be twenty years older and not exactly the Body Beautiful.'

DS Willis called him to order. 'If you don't mind, I'm trying to conduct a murder investigation here. Shall we move indoors? No, not into your house, sir, but into Mrs Quicke's.'

Ellie led the way into her big sitting room, but didn't offer tea or coffee, as perhaps she ought to have done. Well, she would have done, if she'd liked the policewoman better.

'Now, Mrs Quicke, can you tell me the name of the woman who last lived next door, and her husband, and where they went when they left here?'

Ellie suppressed a grimace. She hadn't liked the woman, or her children. In fact, it was hard to think of anything positive to say about them. The whole neighbourhood had sighed with relief when the family had at last moved out. But there was no need to go into detail now.

'I hardly knew them. My husband didn't want me to get involved. The man and the woman weren't married, and I don't think one of the children was his, either. His name was . . . no, it's gone. I'm not sure I ever knew it. I think he came from Nigeria and went back when he got fed up with her.'

Armand was beginning to enter into the spirit of things. 'Or disappeared when she got fed up with him? Can they tell if the skull is European or not?'

'Once the pathologists have done their job . . .'

'When will we know?'

There was a screech of brakes and a cry of alarm as Kate drew up in her car outside. Seeing a policeman standing beside her front door, she jumped to the wrong conclusion.

'What's wrong? My husband! Something's happened to him!'

Armand ran outside to clasp his wife in his arms — which took some doing as she was a trifle taller and heavier than him.

'I'm perfectly all right. It's just that they've found a body in the garden. Come into Ellie's. The police won't let us into our own house at the moment, and I've got a ton of marking to do.'

'What?' Kate went pale. 'You mean . . . in our garden? No! I can't believe it! Who? How long?'

Ellie was aware of yet more neighbours gathering on the opposite side of the road. She said, 'Come on in, and we'll tell you all about it.' Between them Armand and Ellie got Kate seated on the big settee.

'Calm down,' said Ms Willis, flashing her badge at Kate. 'Detective Inspector Willis.'

'Really?' Ellie was interested. 'You got promotion? Congratulations.'

'Thank you,' said DI Willis, looking anything but pleased at being interrupted. 'Now . . . Kate's your name, isn't it? It's probably nothing for you to worry about, but we need some details of the people who had the house before you.'

Kate was frowning. She had heavy eyebrows which made strangers think she had a sullen disposition, which she hadn't. 'Never saw them. They lived abroad, I think. Ask the estate agents. All I can say is, their tenants left the place in a right old mess. We had to have all the wallpaper stripped, the woodwork, everything. And a completely new bathroom and kitchen. You wouldn't believe that two small kids could do that much damage. Now, wait a minute. I must have seen the owner's name somewhere.' She concentrated. 'Chater. That's it. Chater. But what do you mean, a body in our garden?'

Ellie nodded. 'I was trying to think what it was. Chater, that's right.'

'And their tenants' name?' asked DI Willis.

Kate shrugged. 'Never heard it. There wasn't even any mail coming for them when we bought the house. There was stuff for the Chaters, bills mostly. I dumped them at the estate agents. When can we get back into our house?'

'I'm afraid,' said DI Willis, 'that we won't be able to let you back into your house tonight. We have to regard it as a crime scene, you see. Have you any friends who could put you up?'

* * *

'Where have you been? Your mobile's been switched off and your wife said she expected you back hours ago.' An educated voice.

Another educated voice. 'An emergency meeting. You know how it is, I have to keep my eye on so many business affairs. What's so important that—?'

'They found the body!'

A pause. 'What? What are you talking about?' Cautiously.

'They were excavating for a water feature or something. I only heard by chance. One of our old neighbours thought my wife might be interested.'

'She knew about it? How could anyone know about it? You've been talking . . . ?'

'Of course not. No, it was just gossip. Her husband and I were at the same hospital, before I moved up here. Our wives were friends and kept in touch. She heard about it when her son brought the news home from school. It seems that a couple of students came in late. They'd had a study morning off . . . you remember how it was in the last year at school? They took the alleyway that runs along the bottom of the garden to get to the bus stop and saw the police there. Naturally the news was all round the school by lunch time. So, this evening my friend's wife rang to tell my wife the news, thinking she'd be interested.'

A long pause.

The businessman said, 'I don't see any need to panic. They can't trace anything back to us.'

'Will you warn Father?'

Another long silence. 'What good would it do? He's not well, hooked up to oxygen most of the time, especially at night. Surely he doesn't need to know?'

'Let's hope not. Will you find out what you can?'

'Yes, yes. I can go round that way, see if there's police still there, ask at the shops, perhaps. The local paper doesn't come out till Friday but perhaps there may be something on local radio. I will go out to my car and listen. It would be remarked upon as strange if I listened at home, because I never do.'

'It would be best if the women did not hear about it.'

'Agreed.'

'I'll ring again tomorrow evening.'

CHAPTER TWO

Kate stared at the policewoman in horror and disbelief. 'You want us to move out of our house?' said Kate. 'But . . . I need . . . can you do that? A warrant. Don't you need a warrant?'

'Move in here,' said Ellie. 'Of course.'

Kate glared at her. Kate was, like Diana, tall, dark and good looking rather than handsome, but she had a capacity for warmth and friendship which Diana would never have. Kate could be sharp, but she would never be unreasonable. However, she'd never been thrown out of her own home before.

'Ellie, that's my home. Our home. I can't just . . . then there's clothes and things. I've got this meeting in Birmingham tomorrow. How could I have forgotten about that! I'll need some papers and my new suit, undies, and . . . I can't think straight!'

Ellie patted her shoulder while Armand patted her arm. Ellie said, 'Kate, dear. We'll manage, somehow. You can see that the police have to investigate. I'm sure they'll be as quick as they can.'

DI Willis got to her feet. 'We'll make as little mess as we can. Considering. But I must ask you to stay in London, cancel your meeting.'

'What? No, I can't do that. You don't understand . . .'

DI Willis raised her voice. 'Under the circumstances . . .'

Kate got to her feet. She was vibrating with rage and bewilderment. An explosive mixture.

Ellie got between the two women. 'Inspector Willis, you have to agree that whatever happened to that poor man out there, it has nothing to do with Kate and Armand, because they've only been here just over a year. Of course you have to look at their house as if it were a crime scene, but that's no reason to inconvenience my friends more than is necessary, is it? No belongings of theirs can have any bearing on the tragedy.'

'That may be true, but—'

'So let them go into their own house. They can go one at a time and accompanied by a police officer if you wish, so that they can pack some things for an overnight stay here. Right?'

'I'll have to think about . . .' DI Willis hated to backpedal, but even she realized that Ellie had offered a reasonable solution. 'Oh, very well. Stay here while I arrange it.'

She left. Kate subsided on to the settee again.

'Tea, anyone? Sherry?' asked Ellie.

'Coffee,' said Kate, and then, 'No, nothing. Armand, did you see the body? Is it very much decomposed? I can't believe it. This *cannot* be happening!'

Ellie was soothing. 'Here's a pen and some paper. Why don't you both start making lists of what you need out of the house tonight, while I go and make up the bed in the spare room. Do you have to do your marking tonight, Armand?'

'What? I don't know. Yes, of course I do. But . . . well, I suppose not.'

'Then we can all go out to supper somewhere, have an early night.'

Kate took the pad and pen. 'What do I need? I left my briefcase in the car and that's got nearly all the papers I need in it, but . . .'

'Overnight things,' said Ellie, trying to be practical. 'Anything special you want for breakfast, anything special you'd planned for supper?'

'We were going to phone for a pizza and watch a video,' said Armand. 'I picked the video up on the way home. I suppose that's still in my car, too.'

Kate began to laugh. 'Do you think they'll want to take our cars away to be examined? They wouldn't do that, would they? I mean, mine's new since we moved in.'

Ellie pressed Kate's shoulder. It was unlike Kate to give way to hysteria.

Kate coughed, blew her nose, and began to make her list.

DI Willis rang the doorbell as Ellie finished making up the bed and seeing to clean towels. Ellie let her in and stood aside as the policewoman pushed past her to confront Armand and Kate.

'If you've told us the truth you're in the clear, because it seems the body has been in the ground for some time. However, it doesn't appear that death was accidental, so you must understand that we now have to regard your house and garden as a crime scene. You will be allowed to take away such items as you need for tonight — under supervision.'

'And tomorrow we can get back in?' said Armand.

To give her her due, DI Willis looked uncomfortable at this. 'It might be as well for you to consider moving out for the time being. We'll be as quick as we can, but we have to be thorough.'

Kate stared at her. 'You mean, a murder was committed in our house? That we'll have to find somewhere else to live?' She shuddered. 'But we've only just got it as we like it, and built the extension and . . . I can't bear it!'

Armand was looking hollow-eyed. 'I couldn't live in a house where there's been a murder. Who'll want to buy a place where there's been a murder? We'll practically have to give the house away, which means we won't have enough to buy another!'

* * *

Kate began to recover over supper at the Carvery. Ellie recognized the signs. Kate wasn't used to being ordered about; she was the one who usually did the ordering. Kate was beginning to get angry.

Armand was a Celt and subject to mood swings. He was depressed and unable to lift himself out of it.

Ellie appreciated their problem, and hadn't a clue how to help. A quick prayer to God didn't seem to come up with any helpful hints as to how to deal with the situation. Practical help she could give: a bed for the night, a little bit of cossetting, finding an extra table lamp so that Armand could start on his mountain of marking, polishing Kate's shoes for the presentation she would have to make on the following morning. But more than that, what could she do? She felt so helpless.

It occurred to her for the first time to speculate about the poor man who'd gone missing. Had he been a 'gentleman of the road'? Someone who'd long since dropped out of society? A pitiful end. She wondered if he'd once had family and friends, perhaps held down a good job and lived in a house like hers. Whoever he'd been, he hadn't deserved to die alone and lie unburied in the undergrowth. Presumably the rains had gradually washed soil down the slope to cover him. Perhaps he could get a proper burial now.

Ellie grieved for the young couple who'd sunk so much of themselves into what they'd thought would be their long-term home.

The Carvery had been a bad choice, for they were almost certain to run into people they knew. Roy Bartrick — who was her aunt Drusilla's son and therefore Ellie's cousin by marriage — was wining and dining across the room with a man wearing a good suit and an air of disdain. Who was Roy's guest? Normally Ellie's curiosity would have led her to wave to Roy and give him an opening to tell her what he was doing. But not tonight. Roy saw her and waved cheerfully. It seemed likely that his business meeting — for surely that was what it must be — was going well.

Kate allowed herself just one glass of red wine, while Armand sank the rest of the bottle. Kate was going to explode with fury if she weren't diverted in some way.

* * *

DI Willis hadn't supplied any comfort for Armand and Kate, and before she left, had added to Ellie's worries. 'Mrs Quicke, I believe you've lived in this house for some years. What year did you move in? You must have known everyone who lived next door. I'd like you to make a list of them, please. And is there anyone else in the road who's lived here longer than you?'

Ellie thought about it. 'The woman in the end house on the other side of the road was here when we came. She's confined to the house now with arthritis.'

'What year did you arrive?'

Ellie shrugged. 'Oh dear, I'm hopeless at dates, I'm afraid. Frank always said . . . well, as you know, he's dead. I could look up my old diaries, but . . .'

'Perhaps it won't come to that. Now I believe the people in the house on the other side of the murder scene have only been here a short while . . .'

'They moved in that very hot summer we had, the year our daughter was married. Her little boy is two years old now. Does that help?'

Ms Willis sighed. 'Would you please make a list of all the people you know who've lived next door, and I'll pick it up tomorrow morning, right?'

* * *

Over coffee at the Carvery, Ellie said, 'I wish I had the sort of mind which remembered dates. I can remember faces, but not all the names. Or dates.'

Kate allowed herself to be diverted. 'What, no scandals?'

Ellie could see that Kate needed to think about something different, so tried to oblige, racking her memory for details. 'You want a scandal? Oh, well . . . perhaps. There was this nice man who lived there some years ago, died of cancer, poor dear, had to wear the most awful wig, which he hated, and I don't blame him for that. His wife was distraught when he died. She even stopped Frank on his way back from work, asking for advice about something . . . I don't know what. Frank was livid because, as he said, it was none of his business and she oughtn't to accost people like that in the street . . .'

Kate produced a smile. She was trying to smile, anyway. 'Your husband was a very private person, wasn't he? I remember . . .' Her voice died. 'Oh, well, it doesn't matter.'

Ellie reddened. Frank hadn't had any sympathy for people who broke down and cried in public. He'd been a great admirer of the stiff-upper-lip type. He'd been that way himself, never giving in to his ailments, carrying on long after he should have gone to the doctor, by which time it was too late. Ah well. Water under the bridge.

Armand pointed his finger at her. 'What was the scandal, then?'

'Oh, not really a scandal, I suppose,' said Ellie, remembering. 'The widow was rather quickly consoled by someone who said he'd been a close friend of her dear dead husband's, though she'd never heard of him while her husband had been alive.'

'So Victorian,' said Kate, with an acid laugh. 'Clinging widow finds someone else to cling to and marries him within . . . what? Three months?'

'Four, I think,' said Ellie. 'He got her to sell the house and they emigrated to Australia on the proceeds. There was some talk at the time, but . . .' She shrugged. 'Frank said the new man would probably ditch her and go off with the money as soon as the sale of the house went through. Maybe he did. I wish I could remember their name.'

'In our house?' said Kate. 'Fancy that. You don't think of who's lived there before you. You just think of your future there. Did her husband die in our bedroom, do you know?'

'Oh no, dear. In hospital, just as he should.' Ellie could so clearly see Frank coming home, angry that the little widow next door had waylaid him, wanting to pour out all her troubles to him. Suppose Frank had listened, had perhaps even brought her into the house and sat her down, asked Ellie to make them a cup of tea and let the poor creature talk herself out . . . would she then have fallen into another man's arms so quickly? And been persuaded to sell up and move away from everything she'd known, to go to Australia?

'I wonder if it was Australia. It might have been New Zealand,' said Ellie. 'I'm afraid the detective inspector is going to find me a poor sort of witness. All I can remember now is how odd the poor husband's wig looked, rather like a ginger tomcat perched on his head. No wonder he hated it so, poor thing. I remember he grew tomatoes in Gro-bags on that patio of yours, but the rest of the garden was rather neglected even then.'

Armand drained the last of the wine in his glass. 'When was the garden last a proper garden?'

'I don't think there's ever been anyone there who really looked after it, which was why I was so pleased when you two decided to do something about it.'

'And now we wish we hadn't,' said Kate.

Ellie nodded. 'I don't blame you.'

Kate shot up out of her seat. 'I left my laptop and briefcase on the front seat of the car, in full view! I never gave it a thought when . . . Suppose someone's pinched it! The meeting tomorrow!'

They'd come in Armand's car, of course.

Ellie was soothing. 'No one would pinch something from a car with a policeman standing outside your front door.'

Kate was fumbling into her coat. 'You don't understand. It's brand new, and all the data for the meeting . . . we must go back at once!'

'Hi, Ellie!' Roy Bartrick had got rid of the man he'd been dining with, and now walked up to them, all smiles, six foot of charm, with black brows under silver hair and startlingly blue eyes. He knew Kate and Armand, of course. But on seeing Kate's face, he said, 'What's up?'

'Sorry, must go! Emergency!' Kate whisked Armand out of his seat while Ellie was still signalling to the waiter for the bill.

Kate realized she was being rude and dashed back to the table. 'Look, do you mind, Ellie? So sorry. I'll settle up with you later.'

'Key!' said Ellie, extricating one from her handbag and handing it to Armand. 'I'll pay and follow on, get a cab home.'

Roy seated himself in Armand's chair. 'No such thing. I'll run you home in a while, Ellie. It would be good to have a chat.'

Ellie tried to switch her mind away from Kate and Armand, into consideration of Roy and his problems. Why did everyone she meet have problems? Well, there it was. People did. Some problems were bigger than others. At the moment Roy's seemed small compared to Kate and Armand's, but still needed to be listened to. She couldn't imagine he'd ever be able to help Kate and Armand with theirs, because he'd not even been as long in the neighbourhood as they had.

She switched. 'Everything on course for the big move on Saturday?'

Ellie's husband had left her a huge house on the other side of the shops. His aunt had been born in the house and hadn't the slightest intention of moving, although it was far too large for her and needed a lot of work doing to it.

Ellie's ambitious daughter Diana had planned to push her great-aunt into a home so that she herself could pull the house down and develop the site. Ellie had somehow found the courage to oppose Diana, saying she'd never dream of turning Aunt Drusilla out of her home.

Then Roy Bartrick had arrived on the scene, and turned out to be Aunt Drusilla's long-lost illegitimate son. What was more, he was also a respectable and respected architect. Despite hostility from Diana — who thought him a fortune-hunter — Roy had learned first to value and then to love his mother. He'd also proved himself a good friend to Ellie and occasionally asked her to marry him.

Ellie always said no to Roy's offers of marriage. Being fond of a man didn't mean you wanted to marry him . . . and anyway she was nowhere near ready to marry again.

In recent months Ellie had been forced to learn a great deal more than she wished about builders' regulations and tantrums, since she'd at long last persuaded Aunt Drusilla that changes had to be made to the big house. Thank goodness the project was nearly finished now, but what a job it had been!

The great house had been stripped, remodelled and repainted. Inside, there was new plumbing, central heating and wiring. Aunt Drusilla retained the great reception rooms and two large bedrooms above, with the addition of a new kitchen and two new bathrooms. A connecting door led into what had once been the servants' quarters but was now a separate two-bedroom house with new kitchen and bathroom.

Ellie's dear friend Rose had thankfully moved into these new quarters from her council flat, and enjoyed looking after her new employer and friend. To everyone's surprise, Miss Quicke had taken to Rose, which made life a lot easier for everyone who came into contact with the cantankerous old lady.

The drawings for these conversions, and that of the huge garage with its wooden-floored loft, had of course been done by Roy. Originally it had been planned to make two flats out of the garage space, but Roy had sold his old house in the country and decided to settle in the parish, so he had created a superb modern maisonette and office for himself out of the garage and outbuildings.

Aunt Drusilla was currently developing a large site on the Green, in partnership with Roy. Aunt Drusilla, a wily and wealthy old bird, never backed a loser.

The carpets and curtains had already been fitted in Roy's new quarters, and on Saturday his furniture would be delivered from store, so that he could move in. He'd asked Ellie to help him settle in and Ellie had agreed while saying no to yet another offer of marriage.

* * *

As Kate and Armand disappeared, Roy brushed aside Ellie's polite enquiry about moving, and asked if he'd interrupted something important, as Kate seemed to be acting the Tragedy Queen even more than she usually did. Roy was wary of Kate, who was one of the few women who didn't appreciate his charm.

Ellie was happy to tell him what had occurred, while Roy summoned some more coffee for both of them.

Roy whistled. 'Nasty. Who do the police think it was?'

Ellie shook her head. 'They want me to make a list of everyone who's lived in that house, but Frank wasn't exactly gregarious. He always said people should mind their own business, and he didn't want me hanging around gossiping when I had more than enough to do at home. Which was true, of course. About my not having time to gossip, I mean.'

Roy leaned back in his chair. 'I like to know my neighbours and keep on good terms with them. Frank was the opposite of me, for all we were cousins. Do you think we'd have liked one another if we'd ever met?'

Ellie went pink. She didn't think they would have done, no. But she wasn't going to criticize Frank to anyone. He'd been a good husband to her, and she owed everything to him, including the fortune he'd left her in his will.

Roy was amused. 'My mother talks about him sometimes. She was fond of him, she says, but I think she's much fonder of you, dear Ellie.'

Ellie went even more pink. 'Well, I'm very fond of her, too.'

'Yes, she's a nice old trout. I rather like her myself.'

Ellie tried to look scandalized, then gave in and laughed. 'Oh, you! You know you'd do anything for her.'

'As I would for you, dear Ellie. Particularly as you've made my move here so easy. Was it you or dear Rose who cleaned my new kitchen and bathroom as soon as the tilers had finished?'

'We did it together. But Roy, aren't you going to miss the house you had in the country?'

'I thought I would, but I've discovered rather late in life that I'm a sociable animal and really enjoy living in a community. I put the best of my furniture in store when I sold the old place, and I've had fun buying some modern pieces to go with it. From time to time I've created modern environments for clients, and I'm looking forward to trying a mix-and-match look in my new quarters. Besides—' he looked away from her and tried to sound off-hand — 'it makes me feel as if I've really got a family now.'

'I must warn you that your mother plans to have you over for a special welcome dinner the night you move in. Best bib and tucker, please.'

He groaned. 'I'd thought I might pop down to the golf club . . .'

'That's why I'm warning you. Leave the golf club for another night.'

He pulled a face, then said, 'Well, I'm glad I saw you this evening, because I happened to see your darling daughter in the Avenue this morning. We've never been on the best of terms, so I was surprised when she took the trouble to cross the road to speak to me. I'd just come out of that estate agents at the end of the shops, you know it? She — er — harangued me at the top of her voice, accusing me of disloyalty . . .'

Ellie winced. 'I suppose her boyfriend, Derek Jolley, hoped to get the sale of your new houses on the Green.'

'The silly thing is, it wasn't anything to do with the new houses that took me to that estate agents. I was only dropping off some stuff for my mother, concerning the flats she owns down by the river.'

Ellie waited. He still wasn't meeting her eye, so there was more to come.

'Diana seemed angry . . .'

'She's always angry,' Ellie said, more to herself than to Roy.

'She ordered me to give the Close development to Derek to sell. I told her we'd already made arrangements with a big estate agents near the tube station, which didn't improve her temper. She said . . . various things which I won't repeat.'

Ellie sighed. 'I wonder what's happening there. Usually she's on to me two or three times a week, but I've just realized I haven't heard from her for a while. Oh, she dumps little Frank on me at weekends, but she hasn't stayed for a chat recently, or even pestered me to put money into that big house she's doing up.'

Roy was looking down into his cup of coffee, which was empty. 'I wondered if she was, perhaps, not well?'

Ellie braced herself. It crossed her mind to wonder if her daughter could be pregnant. She couldn't ask Roy if he thought so. But if Diana were pregnant, it opened a nice can of worms. Diana had always been selfish, ambitious, and able to wind her father round her little finger. She'd married pleasant but middle-of-the-road Stewart because he'd agreed with her that she was something special. Motherhood and unrealistic ideas of what she was worth had lost Diana various good jobs; she'd set up as a developer and interior designer against Ellie's advice, chucked Stewart for Derek Moneybags Jolley . . . and now was pregnant again?

Roy was pouring himself some more coffee, but Ellie refused another cup. She'd never sleep tonight if she drank more than one cup of coffee so late in the evening.

Ellie thought it highly unlikely that Derek Jolley would want to marry Diana. Why should he? He was getting a decorative mistress for nothing at the moment. Her little boy lived with her husband Stewart and his girlfriend during the week, and Diana only had him at weekends when Derek was out and about, selling houses. And most of the time at weekends, Frank was dumped on Ellie, anyway.

Would Derek even want her to have his child? One could never be sure what men would do in such circumstances, but . . . probably not.

Ellie did not want to think about it.

'Well, Roy. The last time I was over at your new place, the carpets were being laid, but there were no curtains or blinds up. Are you leaving those till you're in?'

'Workmen! I added a couple of weeks to my original schedule, knowing what they're like, but even so, the carpenters only finished on Monday. Curtains and blinds are supposed to be delivered and hung tomorrow. Rose is going to let them in. You are going to be able to help me settle in on Saturday still? No other calls on your time? I know you, someone's in trouble and you drop everything to help them.'

'I promise I won't let anything else distract me.' Not even finding a body in the garden next door, which was nothing to do with her, anyway. 'I'll be there bright and early to help, and maybe Rose will come across to lend a hand — and I'm sure Aunt Drusilla will come to inspect your furniture . . .'

He laughed. 'She's promised to give me some of the family china, provided I keep it behind glass and get Rose to wash it up every time I use it. I told her I'd be honoured, but a large pottery mug suits me best. Which gave her an opportunity to tell me I've no taste!'

The bill came and she paid it. Roy helped her into her jacket, and took her home.

CHAPTER THREE

Thursday morning brought nothing by way of consolation. Ellie got dressed in a hurry, wanting to be downstairs before her guests. She had a feeling the day was going to be difficult, so she asked for a little extra help, please Lord, and a good dollop of patience to help her cope.

Kate went off early — luckily nothing in her car had been disturbed while they were out at the Carvery. Armand didn't want to leave his house in the hands of the police but he was due at school, so Ellie managed to soothe him off to work . . . leaving her to clear up the house, make a shopping list, and refuse to think about the activity in the garden next door.

At intervals she tried to remember the names of people who'd lived there, but didn't get very far. When she concentrated certain faces came to mind, but she couldn't get them in any proper order. A woman with dyed blonde hair, who never spoke but always shouted? No, wait a minute . . . wasn't that the one Ellie'd nicknamed the Shrieker? A plumpish man, very quiet and pale. Ah, she could remember him better. But what was his name?

She couldn't really give the police a list which read:

- *A middle-aged man and his wife, can't remember their first names. Surname Chater (Kate says it's Chater, and I think she's probably right). No children. Noisy parties which used to drive Frank scatty. No idea when they left, but think it was midsummer, some years ago. They went to live in Spain, I think.*

- *A woman with two children and an African boyfriend who went back to Nigeria.*
- *A refugee family (Bosnian?), housed by the council on behalf of the Chaters, who still owned the house but lived abroad. The father used to come round and ask me to light his boiler when it went out, but Frank told them to get a builder in.*
- *A nice man with a ginger wig, and his wife who married someone else and went to Australia or New Zealand.*
- *An elderly couple. He died and she broke her hip and died.*
- *A tramp? Someone who strayed into the garden after having too much to drink, and died there?*

Ellie liked the idea of the tramp best of all and gave it a couple of stars.

She looked at the list in despair. The police would want names and dates and she hadn't got any. Her mind had never coped well with dates or indeed with figures in general. That was one of the things which had made Frank treat her as if she were a second-class citizen. Well, not that, precisely. But he'd always been clever with figures and he hadn't perhaps quite understood that people had different skills.

She knew of people who could carry whole lists of telephone numbers in their heads, who never needed to take address books away with them when they went on holiday and needed to send picture postcards to their friends.

She could normally add up columns of figures and keep household accounts. It wasn't that she was illiterate or innumerate. She could spell much better than most, but she could not retain numbers in her head.

She could remember — if she concentrated — the year in which she got married, which was . . . nineteen seventy-three. Diana had been born eighteen months later, in nineteen seventy-four. Diana was now thirty, nearly thirty-one years old, and little Frank was nearly two.

When she'd met Frank — at the tennis club — Ellie's mother had just died, making her an orphan, since her father had died when Ellie was a child. Frank was also an orphan, having been brought up by his aunt Drusilla. Frank had had a good job but no savings, so Frank and Ellie had sold her mother's flat and used the money for a deposit on their present house. They'd been hard up in those early years, not even being able to afford a car or central heating, because they'd also been supporting Frank's Aunt Drusilla, who'd fooled everyone into believing she was vicarage poor.

Even now the thought of how she'd scrimped and saved and run around after Miss Quicke made Ellie grind her teeth. Perhaps if she hadn't had to work so hard, she wouldn't have suffered all those miscarriages after Diana was born, wouldn't have been so tired all the time, would have had more time to think about herself. Think *for* herself.

But there it was, Ellie had done typing at home till Diana went to school, and had then gone out to work as a shorthand typist in various local businesses to help pay the mortgage and supply treats for Aunt Drusilla, until she'd become something of an automaton; going to work, shopping, returning; providing home-cooked food and clean clothes.

She'd cleaned the house, looked after the garden; polished Frank's shoes, found his pocketbook, his car keys . . . pandered to Diana's every whim, walked her to and from school, to dancing classes, to friends' houses for tea, made and mended clothes (Ellie's), bought clothes (Frank's and Diana's), took Diana to have her hair cut, cut and washed her own . . . ordered a taxi to take Aunt Drusilla to the dentist's, the chiropodist's, the hairdressers. Sat with her. Did her shopping. Made her aunt's tea as she liked it, scrubbed out the larder for her when the cleaner hadn't done it properly . . .

She'd lived in a state of exhaustion. When she'd gone to church she'd leaned against a pillar and dozed off, soothed and relaxed for an hour. When she got into the back of the car after they'd managed to buy one — Diana had always sat at the front — she dozed off again.

She'd never learned to drive, because Frank had said she would never be able to cope. Perhaps he'd been right about that, since she certainly felt too timid to take a car out on the busy London roads nowadays. She'd taken some driving lessons, but had given up when the driving instructor told her she was wasting her time. Perhaps she ought to have tried harder?

Neighbours? Yes, she'd noticed them come and go over the years. Sometimes she'd stopped and smiled at someone new, passed the time of day. But Frank hadn't wanted her to get involved with other people, especially with those next door. On the whole she'd agreed with him. She simply didn't have the time or the energy.

Even after Frank began to do well and they were able to do without her wages, she was kept busy as a volunteer in the charity shop in the Avenue. She'd made some good friends at the charity shop including dear Rose, which had turned out to be a major blessing when Rose took on the task of looking after Aunt Drusilla.

It was only after Frank had died that Ellie'd really become aware of Kate and Armand next door to her. She knew lots of other people in the community slightly, if not well. The last vicar and his wife had become great friends of hers, and had coaxed her into joining the choir, so she knew more people in the neighbourhood now than she ever had done while Frank was alive.

But names and dates . . . oh dear.

* * *

The phone rang: the imposing Mrs Dawes, she of the jet-black hair and earrings, had just finished giving her flower-arranging class in the church hall, and wondered if she might drop round to have a word with Ellie about Sunday. Ellie translated this as: Mrs Dawes had a good enough reason to call on Ellie on church business, but was really hoping to pump her about the police presence next door to her.

'Why not?' said Ellie. 'Perhaps you can help me out, as well. You know how stupid I am about names and dates. The police want a list of everyone who's ever lived next door. You always know everyone hereabouts. Perhaps together we might—?'

'Of course, my dear. Five minutes. Put the kettle on.'

Ellie grinned. Knowing Mrs Dawes, she put the sherry bottle and a couple of glasses out in the conservatory instead.

Mrs Dawes was wearing a navy-blue Tricel blouse with self-embroidery on the collar, over a pleated skirt which could have done with a better underskirt, as it didn't hang well over her ample frame. She was, as usual, carrying an enormous tote bag containing all the tools of her flower-arranging trade. Mrs Dawes was a well-known judge at flower shows in Middlesex and the west of London.

As usual, Mrs Dawes demurred at the idea of drinking sherry in the morning, and as usual accepted a schooner full. As usual she leaned over to test the dampness or otherwise of the soil in the flower tub nearest her, which was planted with a four-year-old orange tree. Beside it stood a lead tank in which ten goldfish swam — Ellie counted them every morning, hoping one day to see some baby fish. Frank would never have considered such an extravagance worthwhile, but it gave Ellie enormous pleasure. In fact, the whole of the conservatory, filled with geraniums and stephanotis and bougainvillea, plumbago and climbing ivies, gave her enormous pleasure.

Ellie waited for Mrs Dawes' comment on the compost in the tub. It would be either, *Too dry!* or, *Too wet!*

Mrs Dawes frowned. What criticism would now fall from her lips? 'You've done well in here, Ellie.'

Ellie blushed, warmed by these rare words of praise. 'You've taught me a lot.'

Mrs Dawes inclined her head graciously, her earrings swinging. 'I came back across the Green. They've put incident tape across the bottom of next door's garden and erected a screen. Lots of men there, trying to hump the skip out of the way. Could have told them they were wasting their time. You can't move a skip full of earth without a proper crane.'

This oblique opening was enough to start Ellie off. 'You heard they found a skeleton when they started digging up the earth for Kate and Armand's pond? The police think it's been there some years and wanted me to give them a list of everyone who's lived in that house, but I haven't got very far with it.'

'Ah,' said Mrs Dawes, setting down her empty glass beside the sherry bottle. 'You haven't been here as long as I have. I was born in the next road, you know. My sister and I went to the school across the Green, and went to Sunday school in the church, too. I've seen some changes in my time.'

'Yes, indeed,' said Ellie, pouring a refill for Mrs Dawes. 'We only came in seventy-three. My mother and I had a little flat on the other side of the Avenue, so I went to school up by the Common.'

Mrs Dawes was gracious. 'A good enough school, they say.'

Ellie nodded. 'So do you remember the people who lived here before us? Frank found this house and got the mortgage, and I can only remember seeing it once before we bought it, and that was in the dark after work one day. I seem to remember there was a man and his wife, quite young, and his elderly mother and a child . . . ?'

'A little boy. Yes, I remember him. He was not very well behaved in Sunday school and the vicar then — not our dear last vicar, but another one, before your time — he had to speak to the parents about his behaviour . . .'

Ellie smiled. 'Boys will be boys.'

'Not that kind of behaviour, dear.' Mrs Dawes sipped sherry in silence, her eyes far away but very aware that Ellie was dying to ask what sort of behaviour might have brought about the intervention of the vicar. 'Baring his bottom in public, dear.'

'Oh.' Ellie hadn't expected that.

'I'd been married some years and been teaching in the Sunday school for some time, but even I . . .'

'Of course. Understandable,' said Ellie. 'So was that what caused them to sell up and go?'

'No, no. His father had a chance of a better job somewhere up North. Although . . .'

Ellie nodded. 'I can see it might have made it difficult for the boy at school.'

Mrs Dawes nodded, too. 'That's what we all thought. But you wanted to know about next door. Well, I can't tell you much—' reluctantly, she had to admit this — 'because the people who've lived there recently have hardly been the type to go to church, and never joined in any of our local activities.' She sniffed. 'Not that we would have wanted them . . . though of course the church doors are always open to . . . well, you know what I mean.'

Ellie knew exactly what Mrs Dawes meant.

'We're talking about the people who owned the house, of course. Not those they let the place to afterwards. Now, what was their name?'

'Chater? I seem to remember they were a bit loud.'

Mrs Dawes snorted. 'A bit? The whole neighbourhood suffered when they moved in.'

'Oh, surely it wasn't as bad as that. Frank started complaining about them almost straight away, because they'd come back from the pub at all hours, slamming car doors and shouting. But it wasn't so very bad at first, was it? It was quite a long time before they started having all-night parties.'

'Torture!' proclaimed Mrs Dawes. 'Karaoke! Those big amplifiers. I could hear it from my little house at the top of the next road! Once a month they had those nasty noisy parties, keeping us awake until the small hours, and if anyone complained they got screamed at and threatened . . . and well, dear . . . you must have suffered, too, being next door.'

'Frank got terribly distressed. He always slept so lightly. I did go round and try to talk to the woman once about it, but she said her husband had a stressful job and if they wanted to have a party, who was going to stop them? Frank did get on to the noise people, and they did come round and have words, but nothing happened. I got Frank some earplugs in the end, because he used to get so mad he'd go round there and ring the doorbell and shout at them, but . . . as you say . . . they took no notice. It was lovely and quiet when they went. Do you know why they left?'

'I think he retired from whatever it was he did. They said they wanted to go and live somewhere in the sun.' Mrs Dawes sniffed. 'I met her in the queue in the supermarket one day and she said they couldn't get away quickly enough, that they'd hated living here and were going to live in Spain, in some expat community, great big villa, enormous cars, getting cancerous lesions because they were in the sun so much.'

Ellie snapped her fingers. 'Now I remember which one she was! Didn't she wear lots of jangly bracelets? And short shorts with halter-neck tops?'

'Bottle-blonde hair, very dry. Too many perms, if you ask me.'

Ellie tapped her forehead. 'What was her name? Sonia? No. Shirley. Yes, that was her name. And he had a pot belly, wore those bright shirts with short sleeves and sandals, even in winter. Ronald, Donald? Wasn't he a car dealer or something?'

'So he said.' Mrs Dawes laid a finger to her nose. 'So he said.'

Ellie's mind sharpened on the word 'drugs'. Perhaps she should tell the police this? Although really it was only a rumour, wasn't it? She certainly hadn't heard it before . . . but then, she'd not exactly been friendly with them. 'Shirley and Donald Chater,' she said, to herself, trying to work out when they'd arrived. 'When did they arrive, do you know?'

Mrs Dawes thought about it. 'It would be early in 1994; I should think very early. There was a fine camellia bush in their front garden, which they hacked out so that they could drive their car off the road. But they never got the council to alter the kerb, so they still had to keep the car out in the road. That big flash-looking car, not English, do you remember?'

'I do. Now the thing is, did both of them actually go to Spain . . . ?'

'Or could one of them be the skeleton in the garden? Sorry, dear. They both went. They didn't want to sell the house outright in case they didn't like it out there, and that's why they let social services rent it out. I don't think he lasted too long — liver, I think. She — Shirley — was friendly with a woman up the road, divorced, one little boy, you know him, don't you? Used to have him in for tea after school at one time, didn't you?'

'You mean Tod's mother, Mrs Coppola?' After Diana had married and left home, a neighbour's boy called Tod had filled a gap in Ellie's life. Tod had used her as a surrogate mother because his own was out at work all day. That had been fine until, inevitably, Tod formed a friendship with a boy of his own age and ceased to need her. Ellie and Mrs Coppola didn't see eye to eye about anything, and yes, it was very likely that Mrs Coppola would have attended parties at Shirley and Donald's.

'That's the one. He's growing fast, little Tod, isn't he? Not so little nowadays. Well, his mother used to go to their rowdy parties. She was their sort, if you know what I mean. I was behind her at the bakery one day and heard her saying she'd just come back from visiting her friends in Spain, so she probably knows how they got on. Why don't you ask her?'

'Thank you, I will. So that disposes of the Chaters.' Ellie made a mental note of their names and dates. 'Now who . . . ?'

'Is that really the time, dear? I must be getting on. I'm due at my friend's this afternoon, our weekly get-together, you know.'

Ellie did know. Someone at church had once called them the Three Witches, meeting weekly to stir gossip. She stood to show Mrs Dawes out. 'Will you ask them if they know of anything else which might help? And was there something you wanted to ask me?'

'Oh, will you help out with the coffee on Sunday at church, dear? Someone's had to drop out, and they're short-handed.'

Ellie smiled and nodded as she was expected to do. Some day she'd say something extremely rude when asked to wash up and do the coffee . . . and wouldn't that cause a fluster! But not today.

Ellie showed Mrs Dawes out and checked the answerphone, which registered three phone calls.

One: Diana had rung, impatient as ever. 'Mother, pick up the phone! I've got something to tell you, important. Oh, and can you have little Frank on Saturday afternoon, as I'm showing some people round the new apartments . . .'

Ellie hoped Diana wasn't about to confess she was pregnant, but . . . it might not be that. As for Saturday, she'd told Diana ages ago, and repeated earlier that week, that she was not going to be able to babysit this Saturday. Not that Diana ever listened.

The second phone caller left no message.

The third was from Stewart, her nice but slightly dim son-in-law, who'd been discarded by Diana only to be picked up by charming Maria Patel, who ran the Trulyclean domestic cleaning services.

'Mother-in-law . . . I mean, Ellie! Maria wanted me to check that it's still all right for us all to come to supper tonight? Half six? We'll pick little Frank up from the childminder early, feed him, give him his bath and see him settled with the babysitter before coming on to you.' Pause. A clearing of throat. 'And, er . . . don't be too shocked, will you, but we might have some news for you soon. Diana wants . . . well, we can talk about it tonight.'

Oh. Now what? Ellie's first thought had been that perhaps the delightful Maria had also got herself pregnant, which wouldn't come as a great shock, considering how neatly she and Stewart had fitted into one another's lives.

Ellie had been a virgin till she married and had always taken her marriage vows seriously. Ellie didn't approve of divorce. Of course she didn't. But, with a heavy heart, she could see that that was where Diana and Stewart were heading, and she couldn't really blame Stewart for wanting out of a bad marriage and into a more suitable one.

On the other hand, Ellie thoroughly approved of Maria, who had restored Stewart's self-esteem after the battering he'd got from Diana, and had taken over little Frank during the week as to the manner born. Stewart was now doing very well, managing part of Aunt Drusilla's empire of flats and houses to let, even though he still didn't know that it was she who owned them.

Ellie could worry about three things at once, but this time she decided not to worry about Diana or Stewart, but to offer up a little prayer for them and concentrate on what to get for supper.

Only, she didn't know if Kate and Armand would still be staying with her that night, and where she'd put the pen which normally lived by the telephone in the hall.

Ellie's ginger tomcat. Midge, appeared at the top of the stairs and sat, checking out the house for intruders. His ears swivelled and one second later both the doorbell and the telephone rang. Midge had an Early Warning System to die for.

Ellie let the phone ring and opened the front door. Her most unfavourite sandy-haired policeman was standing there, hands in pockets. Behind her she could hear the answerphone record the crisp enunciation of a woman brought up to 'speak properly'. Aunt Drusilla was demanding something or other. Ellie ignored the phone to concentrate on her visitor.

She tried to put aside her prejudice against this man, and made an effort to smile at him. It *was* an effort. From the first moment that he'd mistaken her for a cleaning woman and called her 'ducky', she'd disliked him. He in turn treated her as if she were a lower form of pond life.

She decided to try once again. 'You've come for the list of people who lived next door?' She opened the door wide and let him into the hall. Aunt Drusilla was still talking into the phone, but Ellie ignored that to lead Sandy Hair into the living room.

'I'm afraid I haven't got very far with it. I was asking one of my neighbours this morning, and—'

'Is this all you've managed to produce?' he asked, picking up her piece of paper from the table. He quoted in a sarcastic voice, '"A middle-aged man and his wife, can't remember their names . . ." Oh, really! And not a single date! This is going to help us find Jack the Ripper, isn't it?'

'I did have some dates, but . . . you don't mean that poor creature out there was mangled by a Ripper, do you?'

'No, of course not.' Impatiently. 'I was speaking metaphorically, which means, in case you haven't come across the word, that . . .'

Ellie took a grip on herself. She wanted to shout at the man. She wanted to hit him, preferably where it would hurt a great deal. She took a deep breath, and closed her eyes, counting . . . praying . . . Lord, please help me not to lose my temper, which won't help that poor soul out there.

'Wake up, dearie!' said Sandy Hair, none too amiably. 'Or have you got a bad headache and need to take a pill?'

Did his wife need to take a headache pill every time he approached her?

Ellie opened her eyes wide, and tried to work out how they'd got into this situation. Every time they met, things seemed to deteriorate. She had a mental vision of them both sitting down with a cup of coffee, talking over what she'd learned. She'd ask him about his life, and he'd thaw and smile at her, and they'd get on famously and solve the case together.

His bad-tempered expression — almost vicious — brought her back to reality. She had another mental picture, of Frank dealing with this man. Icy disdain would have been the way of it. No, that wouldn't do, either. Sandy Hair was only doing his duty, though really they ought to send him on a Relationship Course or to Charm School or whatever they did with such incredibly maladroit men.

She made an effort. 'Do you know, I don't think I ever heard your name. Detective Constable . . . ?'

'Detective Sergeant Cartwright.'

'So you've been promoted, too. Congratulations. I'm sure you deserved it.' Actually she wasn't at all sure he'd deserved it, but his superiors must have found his work satisfactory, or he wouldn't have got his promotion. 'Would you care for a coffee, and I can fill you in on what I learned from—'

He folded her inadequate list and stowed it in a pocket. 'They wanted me to pick this up straight away, not that it'll be much help. They'll be very disappointed.'

'Don't you want to know what—?'

He was on his way out, but stopped. 'Tell your friends from next door that they can move back in — for the moment, anyway, though the garden's still out of bounds. Our Jane Doe's been in the ground for quite a few years, they tell us.'

'Oh, but—'

He was out, slamming the front door behind him.

Silence.

Midge came and pushed at the back of her legs with his head, which was meant both to remind her of his existence and as a gesture of affection to a worried woman. Midge wasn't a naturally affectionate cat; he didn't like being petted, but he considered it part of his duty to look after his provider of food and creature comforts. He butted the back of her legs till she bent down and stroked him, which he suffered for a short while till he could feel that Ellie was no longer angry. Then he charged off into the kitchen and leaped on to the table — which was strictly forbidden territory — waiting for his dish to be replenished.

Ellie scolded him. 'You bad cat, you know you've been fed once this morning already.' But she gave him some treats, which he accepted with kingly dignity. And then departed to enjoy the sunshine in the conservatory.

Ellie listened to the message her aunt had left on the answerphone, left a message at the school for Armand and went shopping.

CHAPTER FOUR

Ellie arrived back home to find several unexpected items on her doorstep. One was a box of spring bulbs she'd ordered, and the other was Detective Inspector Willis in her usual state of suppressed annoyance, plus a spare policeman in plain clothes who looked as if he'd rather be elsewhere.

Ellie was burdened with bags of shopping, which she had to set down to get at her front-door key. Midge appeared from nowhere and wound round her legs. He'd be in the house first, no matter who tried to stop him.

DI Willis produced a painful-looking smile and picked up the box of bulbs to carry inside. 'I was on the point of giving up again.'

Ellie didn't explain her absence. Why should she? 'Come in, then. Put the box down in the hall somewhere. I hope you don't mind talking in the kitchen, but I've got people coming for supper.'

Ellie ignored the flashing light on the answerphone and allowed the policeman to carry some of her bags through into the kitchen. Midge leaped on to the table, so Ellie fed him even before she took off her jacket — it had looked like rain when she went out, but the sky was clear again now.

She glanced out of the window, but couldn't see or hear any activity in next door's garden.

'Can I help you with anything?' asked Ms Willis, seating herself unasked at the kitchen table. She jerked her head at the accompanying policeman and he faded away into the hall.

Ellie blinked. The woman must want something pretty badly. 'No, thanks. I'll just put things away and start supper. A cup of tea?'

'Thank you.'

Wonders would never cease. The woman was actually being civil for a change. Ellie flicked the kettle on and packed away most of the stuff she'd bought, leaving out potatoes, fresh beans and a nice piece of white fish which she proposed to make into a pie for supper.

She sprinkled salt and pepper on a baking dish, added a dash of milk, put in the fish, covered it with foil, and popped it in the oven to cook. She made a pot of tea, and laid out mugs, milk and sugar. 'Help yourself.'

Ms Willis said, 'Shall I be mother?' Meaning, should she pour out the tea?

'Yes, please do.' Ellie started to peel potatoes with rapid efficiency. 'So, what can I do for you?'

Ms Willis seemed to be choosing her words with care. 'We've been doing a house to house, asking about the people who lived next door, but people don't seem able to tell us very much.'

'There's a very good reason for that,' said Ellie. 'Nobody socialized, because — if I can speak frankly — we couldn't talk to them. And I mean that both ways. Some of them didn't want to communicate with us, and others couldn't speak English.'

'I gathered as much. Now this list . . .' Ms Willis produced Ellie's list from her bag.

Ellie couldn't apologize quickly enough. 'I'm so sorry, I know it wasn't at all what you wanted. I'm bad at remembering dates. I did have some more information on the Chaters, but your sergeant didn't have the time to listen.'

'We can get names and dates from various sources, power suppliers and the like,' said Ms Willis, passing a mug of tea back to her silent companion in the hall, and providing herself with a mug of almost black tea. 'What we can't get is a feeling of what these people were really like. I can trust you not to fob me off with all the politically correct talk about "making allowances" that I've been getting from other people.' She scrabbled in her handbag, produced some painkillers, and took two. Had she got a headache?

Ellie was embarrassed. 'Well, we did all make allowances. I can't tell you much about them, because I hardly knew them. In those days I didn't have the time to talk to them, even if they'd been the sort who liked a chat, which mostly they weren't.'

Ms Willis produced another painful-looking smile. 'So tell us why they didn't want a chat. You're a really shrewd judge of character. Everyone says so.'

Ellie blinked again. Was she a good judge of character? She wouldn't have claimed that for herself.

'Look,' said Ms Willis, 'the woman in the garden . . .'

'Woman? Oh dear, I did hope it was just a tramp who'd died of natural causes. Though you do get some women who take to the streets, don't you?'

'It was a woman, that much we're sure about, and it was definitely not natural causes. Afterwards she was stripped and buried. We think she's been in the ground for some years. They're doing more tests, but they'll take time, so . . .'

'Not a tramp, then. Oh, I am sorry. Poor thing. How terrible.'

'Until we can — hopefully — narrow down the time of death, we've not the slightest idea who she was. Thousands of women go missing every year. There's no clue as to identity. So you see, we need to account for any woman who might have gone missing from next door over the last few years. Absolutely anything you can tell us would be helpful.'

That was a shock. Thoughtfully, Ellie put the potatoes on to cook, added milk to the tea which Ms Willis had poured out, and reached for her list. What did she really know about these people? Not much. But if she could help to narrow the time down, then she supposed she must try.

'Well, now. What I was going to tell your sergeant — why don't you send him on a relationship course, by the way?'

'He's been on one.' Ms Willis met Ellie's eyes with a bland stare.

Ellie shook her head. 'It hasn't taken, has it? Though, to be fair, he didn't sink so far as to call me "ducky" again today. What I was going to tell him was that I had a word with a friend today about these people—' and here she placed her finger on the list — 'the Chaters, husband and wife. Names: Shirley and Donald . . .'

She repeated what she'd learned from Mrs Dawes and what she'd remembered of her own accord.

'. . . and I think I might know someone who's been in touch with them more recently. Another neighbour. I was going to pop out and see her when I'd got the supper on, and before my guests arrive. Which reminds me . . .'

She put some marge in a heavy pan and let it melt, added flour, stirred, added milk and kept on stirring while she talked, till the sauce thickened.

'. . . but if you like to go round there and have a word with her . . . does this need salt, yes, just a little? Yes. Then you could find out from her if both Shirley and Donald left here alive. Mrs Dawes seemed to think one of them died out in Spain, and I suppose that's why the house was put back on the market and not rented out to social services again. My neighbour's name is Mrs Coppola, a couple of doors along.'

DI Willis turned her head to the hallway, from which a disembodied voice said, 'I tried her a couple of times, but she's been working late, and there was no one there. A neighbour said the boy was staying over with a friend down the next road. I checked, and he was.'

Ellie sighed. It was par for the course. Mrs Coppola enjoyed her occasional flings with an admirer, and who was to say she shouldn't? The boy Tod was perfectly happy staying with friends. Probably happier, because then he'd get a proper meal after school instead of junk food.

DI Willis nodded. 'So, Ellie. What about the people who've lived here since? Is there anyone else you can think of who could have been a candidate for murder?'

Ellie rescued a packet of peeled prawns from the fridge, and stirred it into her sauce. 'Well, the refugees came next. I think they were Bosnian. They didn't speak any English at all. There were a lot of them, and the number varied. The father was in his late forties, maybe, and his wife was a bit younger, not Muslims, no. At least so far as I know they weren't, because the women didn't wear headscarves. Then there was the daughter. I should think she was in her early twenties, but she looked older. No husband. I think he'd been shot or otherwise disappeared and that's why they came here, for safety.

'The daughter had two tiny children. Then there was Grandma; she was tiny with black, black eyes. There seemed to be lots of uncles and aunts and cousins all coming and going and . . . I don't know. Sometimes it was just the nuclear family — is that the right word for it? Just the two grandparents, the mother and two children, anyway. And then there'd be lots of others. How they all fitted into that house, I really don't know. They left . . . now, let me think . . . about three years ago, in the summertime?'

'Did you see them go?'

'No, I was at work — I was putting in a lot of hours at the charity shop then, because . . . well, you won't be interested in that. Frank was at work, too. When I came back, I noticed that the front windows were hanging open, and there was a fresh lot of mess, cardboard cartons, discarded children's clothing, that sort of thing, in the front garden. And that it was very, very quiet. It hadn't really been quiet all the time they were there.'

'So you don't know how many women were living there at that time, or whether they all left with the rest or not?'

Ellie had been staring out of the window. She started. 'I was just wondering who cleared the place out between lets?

I wondered if they'd notice anything wrong. If there was anything wrong, I mean.'

'Social services are responsible for returning a house to its original condition after a let.'

Ellie nodded. It had occurred to her to wonder if Maria Patel's cleaning service had done that job. Maria had told her that she used a team of men to clear and clean a house at the end of a tenancy. Perhaps it would be a good idea to ask if her agency had been responsible for clearing the house next door.

Ellie retrieved the cooked fish from the oven, flaked it, removed one or two bones, and tipped it into a large oven-proof bowl, stirring the prawn sauce into it.

'What were their names?' asked Ms Willis.

'I ought to know, oughtn't I? But I don't. They had the radio on all the time, full blast, and when they shouted at one another, it was hard to understand them. I must have heard their names. Of course I must have heard them, but they didn't sound like English names, apart from the two women who were both called Maria something. Not plain Maria, but Maria hyphen something. Like Maria-Joseph, all run into one.

'They hardly ever spoke to us, unless it was to ask for directions to the shops, or the tube. Then they'd hold up a piece of paper with a picture on it, or a word, and say, "Please?" If anyone tried to talk to them, they'd sort of fade back into the house. Looking back, I suppose they were scared of us, but at the time we thought they weren't interested in being friends. They didn't go to our church or come to any of the social events in the neighbourhood, and the children were too young to go to school here.'

'So you can't tell us whether all the women left when they vacated the house?'

Ellie shook her head. 'Perhaps . . . perhaps one of them was sick and died, and they wouldn't know what to do about it, and were afraid they'd be blamed for it in some way. I can see how that would happen. Suppose one of them had an accident, fell downstairs, or suddenly went into labour and died. They might have been scared to report it, have buried her in the garden and hoped for the best.'

'It's possible,' said Ms Willis. 'Yes, that is a possibility, though . . . but we'll follow it up and see what happened to the family. What happened after they left?'

'Well, you have to allow about a month for the house to be cleared out and made ready for the next lot. Next was a woman with her two children and her man, who was not her husband. I think he was Nigerian. He had a long name with lots of consonants in it, and a gap between his two front upper teeth. He was rather charming, though idle. Frank said he smelled. I think Frank meant that the man smoked cannabis, although I can't be sure because I don't think I've ever smelled cannabis myself. He used to drink beer out of the can and throw the cans into the road, into our garden, anywhere. The woman was quite dreadful.'

She could see that her words surprised Ms Willis.

Ellie firmed her mouth. 'I'm sorry, but she was. I used to call her the Shrieker; to myself, you know. Not to others, of course.'

She'd been on good if distant terms with all their neighbours through the years — except for that one person. She'd kept up a facade of politeness even with the noisy Shirley and Donald. She had tried — now and then — to communicate with the Bosnians by smiles and nods. But that one last neighbour had defeated her.

She drained the potatoes, tipped in some milk and a knob of marge, and mashed them. 'Let me explain. In the first place, the woman had a voice like a parrot. That sounds awful, but you didn't hear her. We all said Shirley was noisy, and she was. Shirley shouted at everyone, but it was a sort of full-bellied good-natured shout, if you know what I mean. This last woman whined and shrieked in a most unpleasant way. I can't describe it, except by saying it set your teeth on edge.

'She shrieked at the kids, she shrieked into her mobile phone, she shrieked and whined at her boyfriend and actually screamed at their pet animals. She had the television on all the time, turned up full pitch. The boyfriend's name was . . . Aymo? No, I don't know how you spell it.

'She was home all day, smoking, drinking instant coffee, eating takeaway food, shrieking at the kids, who were really not very nice kids, though I suppose I shouldn't say that. We all thought—' she reddened — 'well, naturally we discussed them. They were so noisy and their behaviour was antisocial in the extreme! We all thought the elder child ought to have been at school, because he certainly looked old enough, but when I asked her once she said he was big for his age and what business was it of mine, anyway. The two boys used to throw stones at anyone who used the alleyway, they upset the litter bins on the Green and played rather nasty tricks on elderly people. They'd wait for you to come along the pavement and they'd spit on the pavement just in front of you and laugh.'

Ellie shuddered. 'I tried to give them some biscuits once. I thought they looked as if they could do with someone to give them a bit of loving care, but . . . the woman shouted abuse at me . . . ugh! Frank said, "What did you expect from that sort?" They weren't very clean, either. Also, I saw nits . . . lice on one of the children. Just the once.'

She spread the mashed potato on top of the fish mixture, sprinkled some Parmesan cheese on top, and popped the dish back into the oven to keep warm and to brown the top.

'I suppose we were bad neighbours, really. I mean, nobody liked to go near to either of those families, not because they'd come through the social services, but because they didn't live the way we did. The litter, the graffiti, the noise, the loud arguments. The neglect of the house and garden. They say you can never tell what goes on in a house behind closed doors, but I think now that those people did everything in the open.

'Perhaps we ought to have made more of an effort. I think now that I should have tried harder, particularly with the Bosnians. Perhaps if I'd taken round some cooked meals for them, or offered to babysit with the children? But I didn't.

It never occurred to me even to try. You see, I was pretty busy with my own family and Frank. Frank didn't think it was up to us to . . . well, to try to civilize them. That's what he said. If it happened again now, perhaps I'd be better able to cope.'

Ms Willis finished her tea in silence. Ellie washed up the pans she'd used, and started slicing some runner beans.

Ms Willis said, 'As far as you know, the woman you call the Shrieker left this place safe and sound?'

Ellie snapped her fingers. 'Jade! That was her name. It was on the tip of my tongue all the while. It never occurred to me to think there could be anything wrong when she left, but the answer is, I really don't know. I'm trying to be accurate, to tell you what I know for certain, not what anyone else has told me, or what I assumed. What I do know is that after Aymo left, things went from bad to worse. One day he was there, and the next he wasn't. It's not him at the bottom of the garden, is it?'

Ms Willis shook her head. 'Definitely not a man. What do you mean, things went from bad to worse?'

'He knew right from wrong. He tried to keep the kids in order. He'd cuff them if he caught them throwing stones, that sort of thing. One day he bought the children a dog. I suppose he thought it would be a humanizing element in their lives, that they'd learn to play with it, and look after it. But he was the only one who had time for it. It was he who used to feed it, play with it, and take it for walks. Give him credit for that. Probably he only went down to the pub and back, but he did use to take it out.

'He left the dog behind when he went, and Jade tied it up in the back garden. I could hear it howling and scrabbling. I do wish I'd done something about that dog, but Frank said we couldn't interfere, so naturally I didn't. I did ask her one day if she was going to keep the dog now that Aymo had gone, but she said it was good for the kids to have a pet and she was going to get them some hamsters or rabbits to keep the dog company, and if Aymo wanted his dog, he should come back and . . .'

Ellie shook her head. 'I'm such a coward when people start swearing at me. I ran away, and Frank said . . .' Frank had said that it served her right for interfering. Perhaps he'd been right.

With an effort, she resumed. 'Aymo didn't return, but after a while she had men visiting her, day and night. Frank wondered if she were selling drugs but I think she was just selling her body, because they usually stayed an hour at a time. She did get some more pets for the kids, but the children didn't look after them and after a while they stank. And the dog . . . I used to turn the radio on when I was in the kitchen, because he used to whine all the time, and when I looked through the hedge, I could see he was chained up, and the children used to tease him because he couldn't get at them, you see. And then they used to stand there and laugh at me because I got so upset.

'And the smell! That's what did it in the end. Frank called the council and they came round and took the animals away — some of them were dead. I don't think the dog survived. Then — you'll be able to find out about this from social services — I think the children were taken into care. Jade came round and shrieked that she'd pay us out for getting her into trouble, although she didn't do anything except throw things into the garden. And then one day, she'd upped and gone.'

'What happened to her?'

'I don't know. Someone in the charity shop said they'd seen her get into a big car driven by a man — someone they'd never seen before. That was the last anyone saw of her.'

'Who saw her? Can you give me a name?'

Ellie thought back. The charity shop was staffed by volunteers, some doing two days a week, some doing only one afternoon. Gossip went round and round. 'I think it was Anita who told me, but she might have just been passing on what she'd heard from one of the others. You could trace the family by looking up the case with social services, couldn't you? Those poor kids. I wonder what became of them?'

'I'll do that. Anything else?'

Ellie shook her head. 'The men came to clean the house out. It was in a bad way, toilet overflowing, kitchen wrecked. They did what they could, and then the For Sale notice went up. Jolley's, in the Avenue. Kate and Armand bought it, and had to pretty well gut it before they moved in. End of story.'

'We'll check it out. Meantime . . .'

'I'll see if I can find out anything else from the people who are coming to supper, and if I do, I'll let you know, shall I? But my money's on an accidental death in the Bosnian family.' Which was a comforting thought, though sad for the woman, of course.

She saw the police out, and as she did so, young Tod walked by on his way home from school with a friend. Since he'd started at secondary school, he'd not come by her house for the occasional snack so often, but they were still on good terms.

Now he stopped and waved at her. 'I told my mate you'd found a body in next door's garden and he didn't believe me, but it's true, isn't it?'

'I'm afraid so, yes.'

'I wish I could stay off school to see what's happening. Did they dig it up with one of those earthmovers? I really fancy a go on one of those! You wouldn't ask them if I could have a go, would you?'

'Tod!' his friend protested, laughing.

'Oh, go on with you!' said Ellie, also laughing. She wondered if it was all right to laugh, when someone had just been found dead. But of course it was. It often happened after a funeral, too. People found release in laughter. And why ever shouldn't they?

* * *

Armand arrived back from school at six o'clock, and came straight in to see Ellie.

'I rang Kate and told her the police said we could go back in. I'm dreading it. Strangers treading all over our house, looking at our things. I keep wondering, in which room was that poor creature murdered? In our bedroom?' He shuddered. 'Kate won't be back till about eight. Ellie, would you do me a favour? Come in with me? I don't want to go in alone, imagining ghosts in every room.'

'It might not have been murder. It might have been an accidental death, and the others just buried her in the garden because they didn't know what to do.'

'Do you think so?' He revived. 'Well, that would make it a lot better. Although sad, of course. But, will you come in with me still?'

She went in with him.

The police had moved one or two pieces of furniture about — which he put back into place. Otherwise, the place was as they had left it. Only, their newly built extension and the garden had been cordoned off.

Armand turned his back on the garden. 'I'm all right now, Ellie. Thanks for coming in with me. And thanks for putting up with us last night. We owe you for that. Don't let me forget.'

'Join us for supper?'

'No. I've got to get used to it. Mountains of marking to do, anyway. I'll be all right.'

She was doubtful, but left him to it.

* * *

The businessman parked his car on the main road, near the public library. Daylight was beginning to fade, but there were still plenty of people about. There seemed to be something on at the primary school next door to the library. An open evening, perhaps? There were no free parking spaces around the church, and the church hall also seemed to be open for a meeting.

It was good that this was such a multicultural, multi-national area. His appearance didn't cause anyone a thought.

He walked across the Green, admiring the new houses which were going up where there had once been a tumbledown old mansion, very large and inconvenient. He thought they'd have no difficulty selling the new houses.

He turned into the alley that ran along the back of the gardens, and tried to remember how far along . . .

He saw it at once.

Incident tape was stretched across the gateway into a steepish garden, which had been scraped clean of its all-concealing undergrowth. A mechanical digger had been removed to one side of the site, and a large white tent erected over the spot where, long ago, they'd buried the body.

A policeman was on duty, but currently occupied with an elderly couple who were walking their dog along the alley, and asking questions about the body. There were lights on in the house, which boasted an extension which was new since his day.

The man hesitated, and then walked on, along the alley away from the incident tape and the tent and the policeman. Nobody thought anything of it. People walked that way all the time.

So it was all true, and the whole horrible business was going to be opened up again. They were all in danger.

He flicked open his mobile and phoned his brother.

CHAPTER FIVE

Stewart and Maria arrived on the dot of half past six. Ellie liked people who arrived exactly when they said they would, as it saved so much anxiety about getting meals ready to serve on time. She was all ready for them, with the table laid in the big bay window at the front of the house. She'd even had time to change into one of the pretty blue dresses Kate had urged her to buy — hideously expensive but rather becoming, she had to admit.

'Stewart! Maria!' She went on tiptoe to kiss both of them. 'Lovely to see you. And little Frank is all right?'

'He's learned two swear words this week,' said Stewart, with mingled pride and annoyance. 'Betty, the childminder, thinks he picked them up at the supermarket. The more I tell him not to, the more he says them.' Stewart was looking relaxed and healthy.

Maria was wearing a soft cream-coloured two-piece in some silky fabric which suited her. She'd always been a handsome girl, but now there was a glow about her which made Ellie wonder if . . . Was Maria pregnant, too? No, no. She was imagining things, as usual.

'Your conservatory is a picture,' said Maria. 'And your garden, too.'

Ellie suggested, 'A sherry?'

'Not for me. I'm driving,' said Stewart.

'Nor me,' said Maria.

The idea that Maria might be pregnant strengthened in Ellie's mind. 'Then let's eat before we talk, shall we?'

She suddenly thought how much her husband would have disapproved of her inviting their daughter's discarded husband and his new girlfriend to supper. When Frank was alive, this meeting would never have happened. But now it seemed absolutely right.

The food disappeared fast. After the fish pie and beans, Ellie produced a home-made fruit salad with the banana sliced into it at the last minute, plus cheese and biscuits. Stewart cleared the table while Maria tried to start on the washing-up, but Ellie would have none of it.

'Dump everything on the kitchen table, I'll make us some coffee, we can take it into the conservatory and you can tell me all your news.'

Stewart sighed, sinking on to a cushioned bamboo chair, and passing a hand across his eyes. 'It's not bad news, exactly.'

Maria said gently, 'Ellie might think so.'

Stewart held out his hand and Maria put hers into it. He said, 'We've got a date for the divorce hearing. Neither Diana nor I want to hang about, so that's good news from our point of view. But I'm sorry, Ellie. I know you don't approve of divorce.'

Ellie sighed. 'I was brought up to believe that marriage was for life. That's what the Bible says, too. Stewart, I know you stuck by Diana even after she'd broken her marriage vows. I know you struggled to think the best of her, even after she'd left you. I know you love little Frank, and are a good father to him. I know that you love Maria . . .' She sniffed and reached for her handkerchief. She blew her nose. 'I'm sorry. So stupid. I wish you well. And Diana, too, of course.'

With one part of her mind she could hear her husband shouting, 'Tell them they are breaking God's laws. Tell them what you really think!' But she had. Of course she deplored the break. It was not right to break vows made before God. But this was a far from perfect world, and people had somehow to struggle through it as best they could. Ellie really did wish them well.

Stewart tightened his clasp of Maria's hand. 'There's more. Diana wants custody and care of little Frank. Obviously, so do we. We have him from Monday morning till Friday evening, and he's settled down nicely. He loves Maria and Maria loves him.'

Maria smiled at him. Yes, she did.

'Of course,' said Stewart. 'We can't offer him a live-in nanny and foreign holidays, as Diana can . . .'

Ellie's attention sharpened. How could Diana afford such things? Had she got Derek Jolley to provide them?

'. . . and Diana's right in pointing out that our flat is rented and we haven't even got a garden, though we're hoping to do something about that. But we can provide Frank with love and a quiet, regular routine. Of course, we both work during the week, but little Frank's very fond of his childminder, and she's excellent with him. You know yourself that he's growing fast, and sleeping well. Next week he's starting at a toddlers' group. Diana's convinced the court will give him to her. She says . . .' He nerved himself to say this. 'She's going to call you as a witness to speak for her.'

Ellie felt as if she were about to be crushed between two enormous stones. On the one side, her daughter, who surely had first right on her loyalty, and on the other, two people who were not even her own flesh and blood.

'I'll speak up for you,' she heard herself say. 'I trust him with you.'

Stewart and Maria relaxed. Maria said, 'We're looking for a small house to buy, somewhere near here. Or even a ground-floor flat with a garden. Twice we've found something suitable, and twice been gazumped. We've visited every estate agent in the neighbourhood and left our details, but house prices keep rising and we don't want a complete wreck which needs a lot spending on it, because we're both working. We've enough for a deposit, with half the money Stewart has from the sale of their house, plus the sale of my little flat. My father will help us, if necessary . . .'

'So will I,' said Ellie, banishing her husband's furious face from her mind. 'I don't suppose one of Roy's development of town houses on the Green would be suitable for you, would they? They've no garden, only a patio. And they're hideously expensive, too.'

'We might have to go further out of London,' said Stewart. 'We don't want to, because Frank's childminder is here, and the toddlers' group, and both our jobs. Maria did suggest asking Miss Quicke if she had anything suitable to let . . .'

Ellie started. It was supposed to be a secret that her aunt Drusilla owned a lot of property in that part of London. Miss Quicke had taken on Stewart to manage some of the properties for her, on condition that he didn't know who owned them. So how had he found out? Ah, but Maria had dealt with Aunt Drusilla for many years, as had her father, who had founded the Trulyclean agency. Maria must have put two and two together and told Stewart who really employed him.

'. . . but,' said Stewart, 'I don't like to ask her. She's been good to me, giving me a job and letting me keep it even when Diana and I split up. I can't ask her.'

'*You* may not be able to ask her,' said Ellie, 'but I can. If she thinks it a good idea, she'll say so. If she doesn't, she won't. She doesn't usually sell any of her properties, but she might let you have a long lease on something. I'm seeing her tomorrow, and I'll ask her then.'

'Thank you,' said Maria. 'But won't that make Diana angry with you?'

'That's my worry, not yours. Now precisely what is it you're looking for?'

Only when they were ready to leave did Ellie think to ask Maria if her firm had handled the cleansing of the house next door.

Maria shook her head. 'No, it wasn't us. There's a firm up by the supermarket who do that sort of thing. You could try them. It must be horrible for your neighbours. I don't think I could face living in a house where a murder had taken place.'

'Armand almost didn't go back in there, and I don't know how Kate will cope.' Kate's car was there now, nudging up to the back of Armand's, as usual. There were lights on in their house now, but they'd drawn the curtains at the front. They'd probably drawn them at the back, too, because they wouldn't want to look out on their desolate garden any more.

* * *

As Maria and Stewart were leaving, one of Ellie's neighbours stormed down the path.

Mrs Coppola, on her high horse and extremely high heels, bottle-blonde curls bobbing.

'You! Ms Quicke! I want a word with you!'

Ellie blew a kiss to Stewart and Maria and invited Mrs Coppola into her house.

Mrs Coppola's colour was high, even through her make-up. 'I'm not coming in, you needn't think I will, because I wouldn't dream of it!'

Ellie drew Mrs Coppola into the hall and closed the door behind her. 'Has something happened to Tod?'

'What? No, of course not! He's completely grown out of that silly phase of his, when he always wanted to hang around with you, and I blame you for that, too! It was quite ridiculous, a woman of your age, enticing a boy in to—'

Ellie flushed. 'I don't think you really mean that, Mrs Coppola.'

'I won't stand for you gossiping behind my back, making out I consort with criminals and murderers . . .'

'What on earth are you talking—?'

'Can you deny you sent the police round to ask me about my friends? No, of course you can't!'

'Oh, you mean that they asked you about—?'

'My friends are absolutely innocent! How you dared to throw suspicion on them! Fancy suggesting that either Shirley or Donald could have been guilty of—!'

'Do come in and sit down for a moment. All I said was that—'

'I know what you said! You told them—'

The phone rang.

Ellie lowered rather than raised her voice, thinking that might calm Mrs Coppola. In the background she could hear that Diana was leaving yet another message on the answerphone. Tough!

'Mrs Coppola, there's a body in the garden next door. It didn't get there by accident. Someone was killed and the body left there, ages ago. If it were someone you knew . . .'

'How ridiculous! Are you accusing Shirley of having killed Donald? Is that it?'

'No, the police said it was a woman out there.'

'So you think Donald killed Shirley? Well, that's even more ridiculous! Won't she laugh when I ring her and tell her that . . .'

'So she's still alive?'

'And kicking. Of course she is. It was Donald who turned up his toes. I blame the doctors, myself. He should have got a liver transplant, but there, Shirley says he was too far gone, poor beggar, only lasted a couple of years. I thought she'd take to the bottle herself, but no, she's made of sterner stuff, as I told her when I went out there for the funeral. "You've still got your looks," I said, "and a nice little pension to keep you warm."

'It wasn't long after that she met her second husband, who's another Don, would you believe? A fine, generous man, and they suit one another down to the ground, as I should know, having been invited out there every year since. Not that I take the boy with me. That wouldn't be at all suitable. But there's always times when he's going away with school parties and such.'

Mrs Coppola had run herself down a bit, but now geared herself up again. 'So I think you'd better apologize, don't you?'

'I'm really glad to hear Shirley is doing so well. Give her my regards when next you speak to her.'

'Yes. Well. No thanks to you, if the Spanish police are set upon them.'

'I shouldn't think that will happen if you tell Ms Willis what you've told me.'

Mrs Coppola huffed and puffed herself away while Ellie went to feed Midge, who'd sneaked in the front door as Mrs Coppola eased herself out.

So, it wasn't poor noisy Shirley in the garden. Ellie discovered that she was rather pleased than otherwise. They'd never had anything in common, but Ellie didn't like to think of anyone she knew lying out there, lifeless . . . perhaps with open eyes staring up at the sky.

Best not to think about it. She set to work on the washing-up, wondering if dear Rose were right and she ought to think about buying a dishwasher, not for herself but for the times when she was catering for others.

There was a soft tap on the front door and a tentative ring on the doorbell.

Kate and Armand, both looking subdued. 'For looking after us,' said Kate, handing over a bouquet of flowers.

'You were great,' said Armand, delivering a bottle of wine.

They weren't immediately taking themselves off, so Ellie invited them in. She said she'd open the bottle and they could all relax and have a drink. Once they were seated in the living room, she asked, 'Was there much mess?'

Kate eased off her high-heeled shoes and settled herself back with a sigh, closing her eyes.

Armand ruffled his ginger hair. 'No, not really. You could see they'd been all over, looked into all the cupboards, even. They said they were coming back tomorrow, with some heat-seeking equipment, to run it over the garden . . .'

'. . . and possibly dig up the extension floor,' said Kate, still with her eyes closed.

What? Dig up all those beautiful tiles, and the underfloor heating? Ellie could understand they must be feeling shattered. She poured wine for them all in silence.

Armand rubbed his eyes. 'Kate tells me I'm imagining things, and I suppose I am, but it's as though there's a dirty grey mist hanging around the house . . .'

'You're imagining things,' said Kate, still with her eyes closed.

'Yes, I expect I am,' said Armand. He stared out into the conservatory. Dusk was upon them, and the street lights were beginning to turn cherry-red. Ellie switched on a couple of low lights and drew the curtains to shield them from curious eyes in the road outside.

Kate made an effort to sit upright and sip her wine. 'Tell us about the people who lived there, Ellie. I never wanted to know before. It seemed to me that whatever the house was like before, Armand and I could make it a happy home. I don't believe in atmospheres and all that nonsense.'

'I still think there's something,' said Armand.

'You never mentioned it before.'

'I did, when we first moved in. That back bedroom had a—'

'That was the damp patch,' said Kate. 'Tell us the worst, Ellie.'

Ellie sipped her wine. 'If you don't believe in atmospheres — by which I suppose you mean ghosts — then why do you want to know?'

Kate shivered. 'Armand's been letting his imagination run away with him, thinking of bodies hidden under the floorboards.'

Armand groaned. 'They want to dig up where the patio was. I told them, no one could bury a body in our garden without someone noticing. Could they, Ellie?'

'I wouldn't have thought so, no.' But now he'd raised the point, Ellie wondered if they could have done, given that next door's garden had been so heavily overgrown. At the top, for instance, unpruned hedges had almost met over the place where the patio had been, and the lower part of the slope near the alley had been a thicket of shrubs and sapling trees.

'It's a nice little house,' said Kate, evidently trying to convince herself of the fact. 'Armand says that if people are happy in a place, you can feel it. Like you, Ellie, in this house; I come in here and feel, well, serene. I think we make our own atmosphere, but just to satisfy him, Ellie, tell us about the people who lived here before.'

Ellie thought about the Shrieker and Aymo, and the animals dying on the patio. Had one or more been buried there, perhaps? Under what was now Kate and Armand's extension, built with such high hopes?

She thought of the Bosnian refugees, their numbers always fluctuating . . . the young mother grieving for her husband, who'd been killed in the troubles. Was it her body which had been buried in the garden? How very sad it all was.

She thought of Shirley and Donald, heavy drinkers, noisy neighbours.

None of them had been happy, and certainly not serene.

She remembered that when they'd first arrived, Kate and Armand had spent a lot of time quarrelling and that Armand had even hit his wife.

Could feelings of violence and distress — even of murder — be left behind in a house, to be picked up by the next people who lived there? Was the house jinxed?

No, of course not. She was being fanciful. But she didn't really want to tell Kate about the people who had lived there.

She said, 'The police are following up all the leads I've been able to give them. All I can say is that the people who lived there before you were all very noisy. They had lots of parties, which were fun if you like that sort of thing. They used to shout at one another and the children and the animals. I don't suppose any of them liked the classical music which Armand plays, and they would have been amazed at all the lovely gadgets and modern furniture you've put into the house.'

She was saying the right thing. Both her visitors began to relax.

'And you're on the case, right?' said Kate.

Ellie demurred. 'I wouldn't have said that, exactly. I'm giving the police my impressions of the people who lived here, that's all.'

'I've always had an active imagination,' said Armand, trying to laugh at himself.

'So you have,' said Kate, smiling at him. But her smile was strained. 'Thank you, Ellie. I'm sure we'll sleep better tonight. Before we go, we must settle up for the meal last night. You were an angel to put up with us.'

'It was my pleasure,' said Ellie. 'And please, keep the key to this house, just in case. I don't suppose you'll need it, ever, but I'd feel safer if a good neighbour had a key, in the event of my mislaying mine.'

Kate saw through that, of course, though Armand didn't seem to. Kate was very tense as she kissed Ellie and thanked her, saying she'd keep the key safe, of course she would.

As Ellie let them out, she wondered how she'd feel if the body had been found at the bottom of her garden. She shuddered. How terrible! If Frank had still been alive, she would have been able to go to him, share her fears with him. He would have told her to stop worrying about something that had nothing to do with them. Perhaps he'd have suggested they have a glass of brandy to go to bed on. He might even have given her a hug and kissed her ear.

Or would he? Wouldn't he have told her roughly that that's what she got for poking her nose into someone else's business?

She was all alone in the house with no one but Midge for company. She double-locked the door, which she rarely bothered to do, and put the chain on. Then she went round the house making sure every door and ground-floor window was locked up tight, and the keys taken out and hidden out of sight.

She played back the message Diana had left on the answerphone and deleted it, sighing. What else would Diana demand? This time she wanted Ellie to use her influence with Roy, to let her prepare his show house for viewing. As Diana was into open-plan minimalism with candles, and Roy had very properly slanted the town houses towards the family market, there was no way Roy would agree. Even if he hadn't already asked a local firm to do the job.

She rang Diana back. Diana was not picking up the phone, and her answerphone was on. Ellie left a message that she'd rung and would no doubt be seeing Diana soon.

Ellie decided to do a little praying for everyone as she washed up the last of the supper things, and went up to bed.

* * *

The businessman sat outside his house in his car, making another call to his brother.

'You got the message that I rang earlier? Yes, I guessed you'd be in theatre all day. Well, you're right. They've found her. But I've been thinking. There's absolutely no way they can connect us with her. All we have to do is sit tight.'

'Have you told Father?'

'No. He really is most unwell. I told you.'

Silence.

The surgeon said, 'I have operations scheduled tomorrow at the private hospital. But afterwards I will come down to London. We must talk.'

'Of course, you are welcome, as always. My wife and daughter will be delighted to see you, but . . . is there any need? In my opinion, we should do nothing whatsoever to draw attention to ourselves.'

'If they find out, we'll be ruined.'

'There is nothing to find out.'

The surgeon persisted. 'We'd be arrested. Father would be . . . it doesn't bear thinking of.'

'What are you suggesting?'

'A diversion. We must point them in another direction.'

'What sort of diversion? I am against our doing anything at all.'

'We could tell the police about the man next door. We'll discuss it again tomorrow.'

* * *

Friday morning. Ellie woke from a hazy dream which faded as she sat up in bed, dislodging Midge, who'd arrived in the early hours after a hunting expedition. He smelled of fish; now how had he got hold of some fish? Or had he been raiding a goldfish pond somewhere? And did goldfish smell of fish?

The dream had faded, but something remained. A snatch of overheard conversation in a shop in the Avenue . . . one of the refugees speaking in her own language to a shop assistant in . . . the grocer's? The shop assistant was a dark-skinned woman who'd been there for ever. Ellie had never thought of her as being 'foreign' but it was true that her hair was very dark and so was her skin. She spoke perfect English, and was always very helpful to the elderly who fumbled with their change, and couldn't always put their own purchases in those flimsy plastic bags. A really nice woman. Ellie didn't often buy things in that shop, but perhaps today she should make an exception?

Mentally she reviewed the jobs lined up for today. She must see Aunt Drusilla and check up on the Gate House, as Roy wanted to call his new quarters.

She must shop for the weekend, take her library books back, because they were running out of time. She would also call in on the grocery shop and see if the woman there knew anything about where the refugees had gone.

Once there had been a very large Co-op store in the Avenue, but that had long since gone. Two of the newsagents had expanded their premises to include mini grocery stores, but most people still went to the slightly old-fashioned shop right in the middle of the Avenue. Especially if they didn't have a car and couldn't visit the supermarkets, which were some distance away.

Ellie was unlucky. The shop was full, and there was a queue to pay at the till. The manager was there as well, taking money, chatting away. It wouldn't be possible to have a quiet word with anyone. A pity, but the police should be able to track the family down much better than she could. She had plenty of other things to do that day.

* * *

Miss Quicke was enjoying herself, pointing out to the jobbing gardener that he hadn't cut the laurels in the driveway back hard enough. Miss Quicke appreciated order and symmetry. Perhaps, thought Ellie, Aunt Drusilla would have been happier with topiary, rather than shrubbery. This fancy led Ellie on to wonder what shapes Miss Quicke would have wanted to cut her bushes . . . perfect cubes, perhaps? With every edge sharp?

Although Ellie was not tall, she had to bend to kiss Aunt Drusilla's cheek.

'You're looking well, Ellie. Have you checked up that everything's all right for the dinner party tomorrow?' Miss Quicke left the chastened gardener to attack the offending bushes again, while she led Ellie indoors.

Ellie shuffled in her handbag for the menu. 'I just popped into the French restaurant in the Avenue, and everything's in order. Supper for eight, dishes as selected by you from their menu, to be brought in hot and ready to serve at half past seven. They will send someone to lay the table, serve and clear away. Neither Roy nor Rose is to know anything about it, except that you're giving a dinner party for Roy and that they're both invited. Yes, that's all arranged, but who else is coming?'

'You'll see when you turn up with Roy. Rose is pottering away in the back garden this morning, but she's left the coffee things out for us.'

Ellie made coffee and took it through into the enormous lounge at the back of the house. Miss Quicke had at first declined to change anything in here, but as new wiring had made redecoration essential, she'd allowed Ellie to get the walls repainted a lighter shade of cream and to replace the ancient lined velvet curtains with modern replicas. As Rose had a mania for polishing good furniture, the effect nowadays was rather more *Antiques Roadshow* than the abode of Miss Havisham.

Miss Quicke rested her stick against the arm of her high-backed chair. 'So you've found another body, have you?'

'Really, Aunt Drusilla. I didn't find it, and it's got nothing whatever to do with me. It happened next door.'

'So tell me all about it.'

This was, of course, the magic formula. Ellie relaxed, sinking into an equally comfortable high-backed chair, and closing her eyes for a moment. She was not quite sure how it had come about, but this fierce old woman, who had once been the bane of Ellie's life, had gradually become a trusted friend and confidante. What was more, as Miss Quicke's mind was as sharp as a tack, her comments were likely to be a help rather than a hindrance.

'Well, the earth digger turned up a skeleton in Kate and Armand's garden. It's upset them both.'

'And you, too?'

Ellie nodded. She sipped her coffee, looking out of the windows on to the once bare and uninteresting garden, which dear Rose was gradually transforming with a stone container for plants here, and a stand of herbaceous flowers there. Why, she'd even imported a sundial! Ellie reflected that Rose could probably humanize a municipal park, if she put her mind to it.

'I don't know how long the body's been there. Long enough to become a skeleton. The police say it was a woman, and they're doing tests. They want to know everything I can tell them about the people who've lived in that house before Kate and Armand came. It's . . . disturbing.'

Aunt Drusilla's eyes gleamed as she, too, sipped her coffee. 'Not a nice lot of neighbours, as I remember.'

'No. Frank used to say . . .' Ellie stopped. 'What's the point of looking back? It doesn't change anything. He's dead and gone. I hate remembering.'

Aunt Drusilla nodded.

Ellie put her cup down with a click. 'He's been gone nearly a year now.'

'It comes up and hits you every now and again, doesn't it?'

'You think you've got over it. Crying all the time. I've moved on, done lots of new things, made new friends.'

'But every now and then, you hear something or see something, and it all comes back, just as raw as when it first happened.'

Ellie dived for a handkerchief, and blew her nose. 'It's ridiculous!' She scolded herself.

'It happens,' said Miss Quicke, who never allowed herself to weep in public.

Ellie poured out more coffee, and they drank it in silence, watching Rose, hair all over the place, cardigan buttoned up wrongly, lovingly insert some miniature dahlia plants into containers which already looked full. The result was not just pleasant, but spectacular.

Miss Quicke said, 'I told Rose some of these plants will have to come in soon, or the frost will get them. She doesn't care. She's been spending her own money on buying them, would you believe? Now, Ellie, this is a secret, between you and me. Don't tell Rose yet, but I'm thinking of having a conservatory built on at the side of the house, so she can enjoy her plants throughout the year. I suppose I have to ask your permission, since it's your house? But I'll pay for it myself.'

Ellie blew her nose again. 'Of course I agree. It will add to the value of the property and please Rose enormously.'

'I used to think that this house was my shell, and that if it was taken away from me, I'd die.' She gave a cackle of laughter. 'Hark at me, being fanciful. I hated the idea that it didn't belong to me, but to my feckless brother . . . and then to my nephew. I suppose that's why I never did anything to it. It gave me a grim pleasure to watch it deteriorate around me. And then my nephew died and left it to you, and I was worried you'd turn me out . . .'

'No, you weren't. You knew I'd never turn you out.'

Miss Quicke gave a yelp of laughter. 'No, you're right. I know you better than that. I know you don't want to live here, and you've been left comfortably off. Then you found Rose to look after me, and made me put some money into the house, and now I'm actually starting to enjoy living here. What's more, since you've altered the layout, it's no longer a burden. I don't even have to worry about the cleaners any more, because dear Rose sees to all that for me.'

'Rose is good with people.'

'So are you, Ellie. So are you. It did occur to me to buy the house off you, so that I could leave it in my will to Roy . . . but who knows how much longer I've got left? It saves death duties to leave things as they are.'

'Do you want me to make the house over to Roy?' Ellie didn't know how she felt about that. 'I could do, I suppose. He'd never turn you out, either, but if it was in his name he could raise money on it, to fund his next development scheme.'

The development on the Green had been funded partly by the sale of Roy's house in the country and partly by Miss Quicke. They both stood to make a fortune from the development, which they planned to reinvest in another concern in future.

'Leave things as they are,' said Miss Quicke. 'Roy's good with the larger picture but not so good on detail, and it's in the detail that the balance lies between profit and loss. He may learn. He may not. But so long as he depends on me for financial backing, I can keep an eye on him. Which is not to say that I'm not very fond of him, because I am. And of Rose, too.'

'You've been good to her.'

'She's very good to me. That is one happy woman, Ellie. She actually likes doing things for other people. Little things that make all the difference. She's certainly changed my life for the better. And Roy, too. I wish you'd marry him.'

Ellie shook her head. 'I'm not ready for it, especially now when everything keeps reminding me of Frank.'

'Don't look back. Look forward.'

'I wish I could, but I must help Kate and Armand if I can. And don't say, "Leave it to the police . . ."'

'Leave it to the police.'

'. . . because they don't know the people involved as I did.'

'Did you, my dear? Now I thought you kept away from them as much as possible.'

'Yes, I did. Frank didn't want me to get involved, and somehow that makes me feel even more guilty. Suppose I had been on friendly terms with them, perhaps I'd have been able to help . . .'

'Families come first, and you put yours first, which was only right and proper.'

Ellie sighed. She picked up the coffee tray. 'I'll wash these up, and then pop in to Roy's place, see if the curtains and blinds are up yet. Moving day tomorrow.'

CHAPTER SIX

On her way back home she popped into the grocer's shop for this and that: a mayonnaise she fancied, another bottle of milk, some biscuits. But the shop was crowded and the manager was at the till instead of the usual shop assistant.

Ellie shrugged, thinking the police would surely soon discover the identity of the body in the garden, and that it was none of her business.

When she got back home, she dashed off a note to DI Willis, telling her what she'd learned about the couple who'd gone to Spain. That should keep the police quiet for a bit. The police had set up an incident centre in the church hall, which was convenient for them, but highly inconvenient for the toddlers' group which usually met there of a morning. Several disgruntled young mothers had removed themselves and their pushchairs to the Green around the church, to meet and moan about it. Ellie dropped her note into the incident room, and went back to change the sheets on the beds and do some housework. She always liked the place to be neat and tidy for the weekend.

She stood at her upstairs window for a while, watching men dig over Armand and Kate's garden. It didn't look as if they'd found anything interesting. It was distressing to think of them wanting to dig up the floor of the extension.

In her inner ear, she could hear Frank saying something sharp about people who spent their time looking out of windows instead of getting on with the housework.

She began to weep, softly. Why was it that everything she recalled about Frank nowadays somehow tarnished his memory and made her think less of him? She didn't want to think less of him. She wanted to remember him as he was, a man who loved his home and his family and worked hard to provide everything they needed. A successful businessman. Someone who'd worked hard for the church, and who'd put up with his aunt Drusilla's foibles year after year after year.

He'd been a good man, and if he hadn't had any time left for other people after caring for his family, that didn't make him any the less a good man.

She went downstairs to open the parcel of bulbs which she'd ordered. Some of them had been intended for Kate and Armand's new garden. She put them aside with a sigh, wondering how soon the police would let them get on with the garden . . . or even . . . *if* they would. Or even, if Kate and Armand would stay in that house now.

Some of the bulbs she put aside for her own garden, and some she put in a carrier bag and took across the Green to the church. Their vicar, Thomas — known to his intimates as 'Tum-Tum' because of his rounded figure — was often to be found, between tea and evensong, pottering around the flowerbeds against the church walls.

His Victorian Gothic horror of a vicarage had a dull garden of sorts, which their curate was supposed to look after but didn't. Tum-Tum preferred to work around the church. He said people in need of a chat would often come to talk to him if he was poking about in the flowerbeds outside the church, rather than formally walk the crunching gravel of the driveway and stand in the imposing porch to ring the doorbell at the vicarage, where everyone could see that they were calling on the vicar.

It had become something of a routine that Ellie would help him with the gardening at church on Tuesday mornings. One or two others would join them on a regular basis; others would come along when they could and lend a hand for half an hour, an hour — whatever time they could spare. And whoever was still there at twelve o'clock would end up having coffee at Ellie's house.

Yes, Tum-Tum was there as usual, on his knees, weeding among the annuals. Bamboo canes and string nearby showed where he'd been staking some Michaelmas daisies and rudbeckias.

'I'm delighted to see you, Ellie.' He got off his knees, with an effort. 'I was praying someone would come along and give me an excuse to stop.' He seated himself on a bench and beamed at her.

She handed him her bag of bulbs. 'What do you think of these? I thought we might plant them under the trees for next spring. Miniature daffodils of all sorts.'

'Brilliant.' He patted the seat at his side. 'OK for next Tuesday? If you're not too busy with your neighbours.'

Ellie relaxed. 'Of course you've heard, haven't you? I suppose everyone's talking about it, and speculating who died there. What's the latest theory? I'd love it to have been a tramp, but I don't think it is. It must be someone who lived there once. But who? I think and think and get nowhere. You're the only person who says I should spend more time with my neighbours than with my family.'

Tum-Tum produced a couple of bananas and handed one to Ellie to eat. 'A nice couple. How are they coping? It's enough to put them off living here.'

Ellie nodded. 'Armand's the sensitive one, talks about there being a grey mist in the house. Of course, he's only seen that since the body was discovered. Kate—' Ellie hesitated — 'Kate will be the one to decide if they move or not.'

'You're doing what you can for them? They're not churchgoers, or I'd pop round to see them. They'll be safe in your hands, though. Someone said it was a woman's body.'

'Mm. Doing further tests. The police want me to help them with information about families who lived there before. That's upsetting, because I can see so clearly that I ought to have been more neighbourly. I could have done a lot to help them, if I'd not been so bound up with my own family.'

'Don't be too hard on yourself. From what I've heard, it would have taken an archangel with the muscles of Hercules to have helped some of them. Besides, you had your hands full with your own family.'

She had to laugh. 'An archangel with the muscles of Hercules!'

'Did they ask for help?'

No, they hadn't. They'd actually repelled the small advances she had made in their direction. She sighed. 'I suppose you're right. I'm a terrible worrier, when I get going, aren't I?'

He knew what she needed better than she did. He fumbled in his pocket and produced a key to the church, laying it on the bench between them. 'Drop it back through the letterbox at the vicarage when you've finished, as usual.'

He gathered his gardening tools together, dumped them in an ancient wheelbarrow, topping the lot off with the bulbs she'd brought him, and trundled away, stopping en route to talk to an elderly gentleman who was also pushing a wheelbarrow, having just come from the allotments at the far end of the park.

Ellie slipped into the church, which was full of rosy light from the setting sun. On Sundays she sang in the choir but when she went in by herself she sat at the back, leaning against one of the great pillars that upheld the roof. She didn't know what to pray about in the present situation. God knew all about it, of course.

She spread her hands out, palm upwards, and bent her head.

'You know all about it . . . that poor woman, lying in that garden all those years . . . how terrible! How lonely! Please look after Kate and Armand and . . .'

She didn't know what else to say.

'Look after me, please!' That didn't sound right. What had she got to fear? Nothing. Except her own guilty conscience.

'Please forgive me. I ought to have helped them, somehow. I ought not to have let Frank stop me.'

She covered her face with her hands and sobbed, once. She didn't want to criticize Frank, not even in her heart. Tum-Tum had been right. She'd done what she'd thought best at the time. It was no good looking back.

She hoped the police would soon identify the poor woman, and they could all go back to being as they were.

To thinking as they had done. 'Please, Lord. Keep your eye on all of us. Comfort us, strengthen us. Forgive us our sins.'

* * *

The surgeon was driving down the M1, and using his hands-free mobile to talk to his brother. 'The last operation was cancelled, so I'm on my way down. Listen, I've been thinking. We can't risk doing nothing, with our father in such a bad way. Did you get the local paper? What does it say?'

'I got it. There's something in it, but nothing we didn't know already.'

'Good. So the police will be looking for a lead. Suppose we give them one? Suppose we point them in the direction of the neighbour.'

'You said that yesterday, but I'm reluctant to do anything. If the police know nothing, then why not leave it at that? They'll have to drop the case.'

'If they know nothing, they'll start digging around, asking questions of the people who lived there. We don't want that.'

'It's not the same people that we knew. The people in the newsagent's told me . . .'

'You talked to them about it?'

'No. Everyone else in the shop was talking about them, so I listened, and nodded and said how terrible it was. Even my wife has heard about it now. She and the girls were talking about it this morning. I warned them not to tell Father, said that he shouldn't be worried with bad news, but of course they don't understand.'

'I have a plan. We will divert the police so cleverly that no one will be able to trace the diversion back to us. We will discuss it this evening.'

* * *

Saturday mornings were always busy, even if Ellie were not helping someone to move house. Today was going to be frantic. What on earth had possessed Aunt Drusilla to give a dinner party today of all days? Ellie looked out her best blue with the low neckline which she'd always thought too low, but which Kate said showed her assets off nicely. That would do nicely for the supper party. She wondered for the umpteenth time who else Aunt Drusilla had invited. *Not* Diana, of course. Perhaps Aunt Drusilla's unknown solicitor? The old dear was getting on a bit, and might want Roy and Ellie to have at least a nodding acquaintance with her solicitor.

The phone kept ringing as Ellie tried to eat some breakfast, pay some bills, water the plants in the conservatory, feed Midge and tidy up the place before she left.

One call was from Jean, one of the church's busiest bodies, wanting to make quite sure Ellie would do coffee after tomorrow morning's service. As Mrs Dawes had already asked Ellie to do this and Ellie had agreed, she found Jean's double check on her annoying. But, sitting on an impulse to tell Jean to stuff her coffee, Ellie meekly returned the call and said that yes, she would certainly be there.

Then it was Diana, wanting to drop off little Frank at Ellie's that afternoon.

Ellie only entertained the idea for two seconds. Could she manage to look after Frank while helping Roy to settle in? No, she couldn't. 'I'm so sorry, Diana, but I did warn you I couldn't look after him today. Why don't you come over for lunch tomorrow?'

'Mother, really! You've always said I could always count on you, and I really can't have Frank with me this afternoon. I have clients coming to see the flats at three o'clock, and at four. Then I'm going out with Derek in the evening.'

'I daresay you are, dear. But I really can't look after him today. Sorry.'

'I'm sure you can rearrange your day, which is more than I can do. You know how important it is that I should—'

'No, dear. I'm sorry, but I can't.' Ellie didn't want to tell Diana who it was she would be spending time with, because Diana thought Roy a fortune-hunter after his mother's money, and never missed an opportunity to snipe at him. 'I really must go. I'll be late.'

'I don't believe this! I really don't! It's not as if I—'

'I really must go,' said Ellie, and put the phone down as the front doorbell rang. The local newspaper had sent a man snooping round for information. 'I don't know anything,' said Ellie, trying to think whether she had a clean pair of nylons for the evening, and where she'd put her spare pair of washing-up gloves to take to Roy's, because men never did think about such things. Frank always thought housework did itself by magic, because he didn't like seeing her doing it when he was around, so she had to cram it into the time he wasn't in the house.

She popped a pad and pencil into her overnight bag on wheels and made sure she'd got her mobile phone with her.

Armand was mooning around in his front patch — for garden you could not call it, being mostly under concrete. 'I suppose Kate's working?' He nodded. 'Dear Armand, why don't you go out for the day? You can't do any good here and you're better off not knowing what's happening in your house.'

Armand snarled, 'I can't leave. Suppose . . . it's a nightmare. No, I'll get on with my marking.'

She wondered if he would. 'You've still got my key, haven't you? I'll be over at my aunt's all day, so you can work at my house if you like.'

* * *

The businessman and the surgeon shut themselves into the study, to consider how best to send an anonymous message to the police. They'd talked late into the night and come to no satisfactory conclusion. Now they were at it again.

'No phones,' said the businessman, who knew about such things. 'They can trace calls from land lines if you're on for more than a few seconds. We could use a mobile — no, not yours or mine. The phone companies can trace what calls we make at what time. I suppose we could buy one, give a false name and address, use it and throw it away immediately afterwards.'

'Ridiculous! What a waste of money!'

'Agreed.'

The businessman paced the floor. The surgeon kept glancing up at the ceiling. In the room above, their father lay dying. Yes, the surgeon now realized that his father was dying. He hadn't wanted to admit it before.

The businessman had another idea. 'I've heard it's impossible to trace letters run off from a computer. We could use mine here, making sure not to leave prints on the paper, put it in an envelope and push that through the letterbox of the nearest police station. The only problem is that if we're ever investigated, the evidence would be on the hard drive of the computer.'

'That's running an unnecessary risk.'

'I agree. We could use someone else's computer . . . but whose?'

The surgeon snapped his fingers. 'I have it. Suppose we use one of the computers in the local library . . .'

The businessman shook his head. 'My youngest daughter uses one at the main library for research, but I don't think they have printers. You can photocopy from books of course. But that's different.'

'Send an email, then. Yes, that's the perfect answer. It will have to be you who does it, not me. You know I've never been able to deal with computers. Give a false name and address. No need to worry about fingerprints, because the machine will be used by someone else immediately after you, which will erase all your prints. Type a short message, send it to the police by email and then walk away, knowing it will be impossible for them to trace you.'

The businessman thought about that, and nodded. 'Exactly what will we say?'

* * *

It really was good to get out of the house. The cosmeas in Ellie's front garden were doing brilliantly this year. She'd had to stake them, otherwise the wind would batter them to the ground. She loved cosmeas. Or should it be 'cosmos'? Or possibly 'cosmi'? What did it matter, anyway?

There was a nice show of snapdragons in one of the gardens fronting on to the Green. The old-fashioned sort, not the new kind with the open trumpets, which you couldn't call 'snapdragons' any longer.

Roy and Aunt Drusilla's new development of town houses was coming on well. Roy had asked her to fill the narrow flowerbeds fronting the Green, and the strip of raised bed along the back wall, with some small trees and low growing plants, and she noticed that the beds there had now been filled with good topsoil ready for planting. She'd already asked her favourite nurseries to look out some sapling trees and well-grown evergreen plants for her. An old friend had said he'd take her out to make her final selection early next week; she must check to see if he could still manage it. Once the beds were planted, the whole development would look ready for sale. Perhaps people would be moving into the houses before Christmas.

She picked up some bits and pieces in the delicatessen on her way, aware that while no one ever thought about lunch on removal day until noon, it was the first thing men wanted at that point. That and tea. Probably dear Rose would be able to supply that.

There, the removal truck had arrived already. She greeted Roy with a friendly kiss on his cheek, dumped her purchases on the shining granite work surface in the brand-new kitchen, and started to unpack boxes marked 'kitchen'.

Boxes . . . boxes . . . men shouting at one another about the turn in the new stairs . . . dear Rose popping across with mugs of tea and coffee . . . lots of cupboard space, what a blessing. Perhaps some time she would have her own kitchen redone, because it hadn't been touched since dear Frank put it in himself soon after they bought the house . . . sigh . . . so many years ago. She remembered the difficulty he'd had with the shelf over the boiler . . .

And then she thought of that poor woman stumbling into the garden next door and dying there, alone. It had been comforting to think she'd been a tramp, perhaps someone who preferred to die alone under the stars. It was better to think she'd been a tramp, rather than one of the Bosnian family. Not that you could see many stars in the city nowadays. Light pollution, they called it. But still . . . the poor creature had been so close, and Ellie had never known.

If the woman had only chosen another garden to die in, perhaps someone would have noticed, would have gone out and helped her, got an ambulance, maybe. But perhaps it had been what she wanted, to die like that. God would have known, of course. Perhaps she'd been a Christian and had chosen that place to die, because of the church nearby. Perhaps her last thoughts might have been of God, asking for her sins to be forgiven, claiming God's love . . .

Ellie felt guilty that she'd never known the woman was in such need, dying just a few feet away from her house. Perhaps, if no one claimed the body — and if she'd been on the streets then probably no one would claim the body — Ellie could arrange for the woman to have a proper funeral service in the church, see that she was laid to rest in a decent fashion. It was the least she could do.

Roy's dinner service went in a glass-fronted cupboard — after it had been carefully washed and dried. His pots and pans went into a carousel in the corner cupboard, his mugs on a stand, spices into a fitted rack on the wall. He had a lot of rather beautiful cut glass, which again she had to wash before drying and putting in another glass-fronted cupboard. Cleaning materials . . . another bottom cupboard.

No ironing board? No vacuum cleaner? Perhaps they were still in the removal van?

Cutlery . . . in a drawer above the pots and pans. He'd hardly any groceries. Luckily she'd had the foresight to bring tea, coffee and milk with her for him.

Then it was time to draw breath and ask if anyone fancied a sandwich.

On the dot of twelve, here came Rose, twittering as usual, her brand-new smart jumper and skirt covered with a plastic apron with cats on it, bearing a huge thermos of hot soup.

Dear, dear Rose. She always got her priorities right.

Ellie, Roy and Rose sat round the dusty dining-room table, while Roy mourned the fact that he'd had to leave his furniture in store for so long, and wondered if it would ever look good again.

'Of course it will,' said Ellie.

'I'll just fetch some proper wax polish from home,' said dear Rose, already thinking of her new quarters in the big house as 'home'. 'Now, don't you fret, and don't try to use any of those spray cans on your furniture. Old furniture likes being treated to a bit of TLC, and that's what it's going to get.'

After lunch Ellie busied herself in the bedrooms — there were two, plus a bathroom and shower room — making beds, putting linen away, stowing Roy's clothes in the built-in wardrobe and helping Rose to dust and polish some very respectable antique furniture. Downstairs the men dropped something heavy and Roy yelled at them. But finally the last box was dumped in the huge living room, and the removal men drove away.

Silence.

Dear Rose said, 'Do you think we should say a prayer, perhaps? Or get our dear minister over to bless the place? This place hasn't had anyone living here for ever, has it, and somehow, I don't know why, I just think it would be more comfortable for dear Roy, banish the glooms.'

The glooms? What was Rose talking about? The Gate House — they'd have to stop calling it a garage — was bright and cheerful. Only Roy, nursing a bruised shin that he'd banged on a coffee table, was looking gloomy.

Ellie set to work on some bookcases which Roy — manlike — had placed, not quite straight, into the embrasures on either side of the fireplace. He'd acquired a Victorian fireplace, prettily tiled, from a salvage yard. It looked good. Some of his furniture was startlingly new, some old, but the combination worked. Boxes, boxes. Stacks of pictures still to be hung, books to be dusted and put in the bookcases. The vast living room, which occupied all the ground floor except for a small kitchen and study, was going to look great.

A knock at the door. 'Sign here!' Two mature bay trees in tubs were being delivered, and on their heels came Diana with little Frank in a pushchair.

'So there you are! I've had the devil's own job to find you, mother. Did you know that horrid little man from next door was in your house, and that there were workmen all over the place? What on earth are you doing here? What's going on? And . . . Roy? Is that you?'

'It certainly is, Diana,' said Roy, deciding to be charming in a detached way. 'But I'm afraid I'm not able to receive visitors yet.'

Diana was power-dressed in black, as usual. Ellie, scrutinizing her daughter's figure for clues, couldn't be a hundred per cent sure that Diana was pregnant, but rather thought she was. 'Diana dear, I did say I couldn't look after Frank this afternoon, and I really can't.'

'Of course you can, mother.' Diana unstrapped Frank from his pushchair and gave him a little shove towards Ellie. 'You'd better keep him all night, because Derek wants us to go up West.'

'I've already told you I can't,' said Ellie, as Frank made a beeline for her and clasped her around her legs.

Dear Rose swooped on little Frank and gave him a smacking big kiss. 'Oh, we don't really mind, do we, Frank? Come along and help Rose with the polishing. See, here's a beautiful yellow duster just for you.'

Roy said, 'I'll see if I can get the telly and video fixed up for him to look at.'

Diana hated to thank Roy for anything, but she managed some sort of mumble which could be taken as 'thanks' if you were charitably minded.

Quite without foundation for her belief, Diana had expected to inherit Miss Quicke's millions till Roy came on the scene, and was unable to accept that it had been her own shady morality which had lost her her great-aunt's favour, and not the advent of a long-lost son.

Wordlessly, Ellie waved Diana goodbye, even though Diana never looked back as she got into her car and drove away.

Roy manoeuvred the two bay trees into position, one on either side of his new, or rather reclaimed, front door. 'Workmen all over your house, Ellie? What for?'

'I suppose she means policemen. You remember the digger turned up a skull in next door's garden yesterday. The police are all over next door still, and I told Armand he could work in my house today.'

'Who was that?' A sharp voice from a sharp old lady. Miss Quicke had arrived at the precise moment the living room was ready to receive a visitor.

'Tea up!' Rose sang out from the kitchen. Frank was busy tearing the plastic bubble-wrap off a picture. Roy pulled the rest off, and showed the little boy how to pop bubbles, which made them both laugh uncontrollably. Miss Quicke seated herself in the best chair, and motioned Ellie to a seat at her side.

'I can see you've got a lot to do yet, but I won't have Rose worn out before this evening's party, so why don't we call it a day, and tackle the rest tomorrow?'

Roy couldn't rest, but began pushing furniture about, an inch here and an inch there, followed around by little Frank, squeaking with pleasure, especially when Roy put the little boy into a chair and began shunting him around the room, pretending to be a train. Rose and Ellie, smiling a little wearily, obeyed Miss Quicke and found themselves comfortable chairs in which to relax.

CHAPTER SEVEN

Ellie had almost fallen asleep. Aunt Drusilla was right, as usual. They had worked hard that morning and could do with a little rest. Roy had taken little Frank out into the garden to give him a run around. Rose was gently whiffling, almost snoring.

Someone pounded on the front door and all three of them started awake, looking around to see who'd made that noise. Roy came in from the garden carrying little Frank and got to the door first.

It was DI Willis, looking thunderous. Plus sidekick, also in plain clothes, who was luckily not the ill-mannered sandy-haired one, but the one who'd sat in the hall when DI Willis had visited Ellie before.

'Mrs Quicke. I've been chasing you all over the place. Why didn't you leave a message saying where you'd be today?'

'I did,' said Ellie, struggling to her feet. 'I think you know Miss Quicke and Roy Bartrick, her son, and dear Rose.'

DI Willis scowled. Roy grimaced and Miss Quicke lifted her chin so that she could look at the policewoman down her nose. Little Frank ignored her.

'Tea, dear?' said Rose, never one to hold a grudge. 'Hardly any milk, no sugar and strong, isn't it? And what for you, young man?'

The 'young man' smiled and said politely that he didn't want anything, thank you. He gave his name, which sounded like 'Honeywell' but surely couldn't be that.

Miss Quicke was not amused at this intrusion. 'To what do we owe the honour?'

DI Willis persevered. 'I need to speak to your niece, urgently.'

'Can't it wait?' said Ellie, worrying about all the unpacking that still needed to be done.

'No, it can't. This is a murder investigation, you know.'

Roy said, 'Never a dull moment around you, Ellie. Why don't you use my office at the back? There's a couple of chairs and a desk in there already, and it's quiet.'

His office had once been a large outhouse. It was quiet, peaceful and full of light, as Roy had replaced most of the roof with glass panes. It was also dusty, uncarpeted, and still contained unpacked cardboard boxes. But it did contain a couple of chairs and a desk.

Ellie made herself comfortable in one chair while DI Willis sat in the other chair behind the desk. The young policeman looked around for a third chair, but there wasn't one, so he sat on the floor and got his notebook out. Ms Willis looked around her, and addressed the other policeman. 'I need to take another pill. Can you get me a glass of water?'

He nodded, and left.

Ellie was impatient. 'So, what was so important it couldn't wait till tomorrow?'

'Tomorrow's Sunday. You'll be off somewhere, at church or looking after your family.'

Ellie nodded. So she would.

DI Willis said, 'There are still more tests to be done, but we've established that the body must have been in the ground at least fifteen years. Possibly more.'

Ellie blinked. So, it couldn't have been one of the Bosnians. 'So that rules out the woman who shrieked at everyone, the Bosnian family and the two who went off to Spain. Is that right?'

The young policeman came back with a glass of water and handed it to his boss, who took a couple of painkillers and downed half the water.

DI Willis saw Ellie watching her, and said, 'Toothache. Now. We need to go back much further. The Chaters — that's the people who went to Spain — arrived in 1994 . . . ?'

'They rooted out that beautiful camellia in the front garden. It had been planted many years before and was quite a sight in the spring. Ah well.'

'So tell me about the people before the Chaters. According to you, there was a man and his wife lived there before, but the man died of cancer.'

Ellie could feel reluctance building up inside her. She did not want to think about those days. Diana had been a stroppy teenager, throwing tantrums the moment she was thwarted. If she'd stayed in the state system, perhaps she wouldn't have been so demanding, but Frank had put her in a fee-paying high school which, together with Aunt Drusilla's demands, had kept them in penury for years.

DI Willis intoned, 'Come on, Ellie. You can do it. What do you remember about them?'

'Nothing,' said Ellie, feeling cross. 'They lived there. The man died. She got engaged to another man. She left. End of story.'

Ms Willis was tapping on the desk, impatient. 'You can do better than that.'

Ellie rubbed her forehead. 'It's so long ago. How long ago did you say the woman was killed?'

'Fifteen to twenty years.' Impatiently. 'Come on, you can do it.'

Ellie had never been that good at mental arithmetic. If she had the figures written down in front of her, she could do it much more easily. She made a mental picture in her mind of the figures '2004' Then took away fifteen. Which made it 1989. What had happened in 1989? She couldn't remember.

Furthermore, Ellie did not like being called by her Christian name by this woman. She did not want to look back into the past. She definitely did not want to think about what Diana had been like in those days. Wild, that's what. A constant anxiety. And foul-mouthed, though luckily she'd grown out of that eventually.

Relax. The DI didn't want to know about that bad time which Ellie had been having. Or her family.

'Concentrate, Ellie. Fifteen years ago. 1989. You would have been — how old? Thirty-five?'

'Ish,' said Ellie, who'd been a little older than that, though not much. 'I was still working then.'

DI Willis was subduing impatience. It didn't suit her. The tide of red in her face clashed with the badly dyed mahogany hair. Ellie wondered vaguely what the woman's natural hair colour was.

Diana had been caught shoplifting and her excuse had been that, as Frank hadn't given her enough money to buy the outfit she'd set her heart on, he'd forced her to do it. It had taken some fast talking to stop that going to the courts. Luckily Diana had been in awe of her headmistress, and a threat to inform her of what Diana had done had helped keep the girl in check for a while.

'Come on, Ellie! We haven't got all day.'

Ellie stood up, and pushed her chair away from her. 'I've told you all I know. I've not given you permission to call me by my Christian name, and I am rather busy today, so . . .'

The door crashed open and in rushed little Frank, sobbing. Ellie scooped him up and cradled him. 'There, there! What's wrong with my little Frank, then?'

He was clutching an ivory statuette which looked valuable. Rose panted in after him. 'Sorry, but . . . Frank dear! I told you that's not a dolly, and it's not for you to play with. So sorry, Ellie, but he climbed on to the back of a chair and knocked it off the bookcase and Roy's going spare . . . !'

The little boy buried his head into the angle of Ellie's neck and clung to her.

'Let me have that, dear,' said Ellie. She tried to prise Frank's fingers from the statuette, and failed.

The young policeman got up off the floor, and somehow or other managed to lift Frank off Ellie and into his own capable arms. 'Got two of my own, like.'

For a count of three, everyone thought the situation was under control. Then Frank realized he was in the arms of a complete stranger, and threw himself backwards, yelling, his face bright red.

Rose managed to catch the statuette as Frank threw it from him, and Ellie caught Frank as the policeman struggled in vain to hold the little boy.

'Ganny!' cried Frank, burrowing once more into Ellie's arms.

'There, there!' said Ellie, patting him, stroking him. She hooked the chair towards her and sat, rocking Frank backwards and forwards. 'There, there! All gone. Safe and sound.'

The young policeman looked amused. 'I'd forgotten they throw themselves backwards like that. Mine are past that stage.'

Ellie smiled at him. 'Yes, they do grow up fast, don't they?' She banished the thought of Diana's sulky face from her mind. Diana hadn't really intended to steal. Not really. She'd succumbed to a bad impulse, probably egged on by another girl, the one who'd been removed from the school a couple of weeks later. It had just been a bit of fun that had gone wrong. She'd never done it again.

'Well, now,' said DI Willis. 'Perhaps we can get back to . . .'

Rose said, 'Shall I take him, Ellie?'

'No!' yelled Frank and tried to get his head under Ellie's arm.

'It's all right,' Ellie said. 'I'll keep him till he calms down. He probably hasn't had a nap today. He doesn't always need one, but what with all this excitement . . .'

The cheerful policeman nodded. 'Takes some of them like that, doesn't it? Shall I get you a more comfortable chair, Mrs Quicke?'

Ellie shook her head, thinking that this young man was likely to go far. Perhaps even farther than his boss, who had integrity and perseverance but very little in the way of personal skills. 'Thank you, but no. I'll just sit here a while and keep quiet.'

DI Willis cleared her throat. 'Unfortunately, we can't just sit around in a murder enquiry, waiting for a child to drop off to sleep.'

Ellie considered Ms Willis. Had the woman never felt any tenderness towards anyone? Not even towards a child? She wasn't married, of course. She wore no rings on her fingers and her manner was always abrasive. Ellie held back a sigh, fearing to disturb little Frank, who was drowsing in her arms.

'Very well. I'll tell you what I remember.' She kept her voice soft, to avoid disturbing Frank. 'The people before the Chaters were called something very ordinary, like Brown. No, Browning. He was . . .' She concentrated. 'I think he was called Greg. She was Lilian. Yes, that's right. Greg and Lilian. And his friend, the one she married later, he was Ted. I really don't like to think about them.'

Or to think about the way Diana had sworn at the store detective when caught. Diana had said afterwards that it hadn't been the first time she'd pinched stuff from the shops, but really Ellie hadn't been able to believe that. Not Diana!

Ms Willis attempted a smile. 'You do seem to have had some antisocial neighbours. What was the matter with these people, the Brownings?'

'Oh, they were quiet enough. Nice people, we thought. Kept themselves to themselves. They had the house painted up — some very old people had lived there before and had let the place go, you see. He — Greg — he said he fancied a bit of gardening now he was retired.

'They'd come from North London. Possibly Paddington? Not sure. Anyway, it was very built-up where they'd been before, but they'd come into a bit of money — from her father, I think — and wanted to buy somewhere in a nice neighbourhood. Greg fancied seeing a bit of sky, breathing some fresh air, taking on an allotment.

'That was his dream, to have an allotment and grow his own vegetables. He tried to hack down some of the brambles at the back, thought he could grow quite a lot of stuff there. Even started with some Gro-bags on the patio. They were only there . . . what . . . four years? Five?'

'Very quiet, you say. Did they have many visitors?'

'No, not many. He said to me once that his wife had wanted to make a complete break from the past. I got the impression they'd been mixing with rather a rough lot before, and believed they were moving upmarket when they came here. Perhaps they were right.'

She must remember that one mistake didn't mark you for life. Diana had kept her place in the High School and had never stolen from the shops again. It had been just attention-seeking. That's what it had been. She'd learned her lesson. Ellie had never forgotten it, though. Where had she gone wrong, that her only child could have done such a terrible thing? Surely, it must be her fault.

Not Frank's, of course. He'd been livid with Diana. Ellie had even feared that he'd cut off her allowance. Diana had thought so, too. Her face . . . !

'What happened to them?' said Ms Willis.

'Hm? Oh, it was tragic. He'd been a jobbing builder, you know. He was a big, hearty-looking fellow. He used to talk to me when he was clearing stuff from the front garden, asking me what plants he should put in, and that. She didn't have anything to do with the garden. She was a pale, wispy sort of creature. Blonde. A true blonde, almost ash blonde. Nice enough in her way.

'You could hear him coughing through the wall. He smoked, you see. Wouldn't give it up, no matter what the doctor said. She didn't smoke. She worried about him all the time. She couldn't get him to stop. It was cancer, of course. Such a big, strong-looking man, he was. And nice, too. He lost his hair with the chemotherapy and had to wear a wig, which he hated.

She didn't like him going out without his wig, but he said he'd rather wear a cap, and he did, mostly.

'It took him a long time to die. Every time I saw her, she seemed to be weeping. She lost weight. I took her to the doctor's myself once, because she fainted in the Avenue when she was out shopping. It was lucky I saw her. She'd got a raging infection, and it took ages to clear up. Throat, you know. Really, she ought to have been hospitalized but he was still at home then, fighting it, clinging on to life. Shortly after, they took him off to hospital. I offered to go with her to see him, but she said no, she knew Frank liked me to be at home when he got back in from work, and Diana . . .'

Diana had said something awful about the old man taking his time to die, and really Greg hadn't been that old. Diana had been, what — fifteen — when Greg died?

DI Willis said, 'So, this Greg died in hospital. Which hospital? What month?'

Ellie tried to think. 'Ealing Hospital. The month? I seem to remember it was autumn, but I can't get any closer than that.'

'What happened to the widow?'

'I went to the funeral with her because she said she hadn't been inside a church for ages, but he'd wanted a church funeral, so that's what they were going to have. A few of their old friends came to the church, and a few of our neighbours, not that they knew her all that well, but because they'd all seen her around and we were sorry for her. Afterwards, she had a few people round for a cuppa and a sandwich.

'I managed to get Frank to stay with Diana for an hour — she was revising for some exam or other and never liked to be left alone in the house — and I went in to see what I could do to help. I was worried about the poor woman, knowing she was still on antibiotics and had taken Greg's death hard. But she said she was all right, that some old friends were looking after her.

'We thought she might go back North London way, but she didn't. She crept about for a while like a little white mouse. Then one day I heard Frank shouting outside. Someone had parked in front of our house in what Frank considered to be "his" slot. Of course, he had no special right to that piece of road, but . . . anyway, he was shouting at someone who'd parked an old rattletrap of a car there. A big man came out of next door and shouted back at Frank. He wouldn't move. Frank got really angry. Well, you know what men can be like over parking slots.'

'Women, too,' said DI Willis. 'You've no idea.'

'No, I haven't,' said Ellie. 'I don't drive. Anyway, that was the first time we saw the man. Ted, his name was. He was in the building trade, too. He said he'd been a very good friend of Greg's, and I suppose he might have been, but he wasn't at the funeral and he hadn't visited them before Greg died. At least, I hadn't seen him. Certainly that car of his wasn't around before. But he comforted Lilian and I was glad about that. At first we were all pleased that she had someone to look after her. And then we—'

'Who's "we"?'

Ellie reddened. 'Neighbours. People at church. Yes, we did begin to wonder, because he moved in with her. She never went out of the house without him. Didn't want to talk to us anymore. Then the house went up for sale and it sold pretty quickly . . .'

'To the Chaters? The couple who eventually went off to Spain?'

Ellie nodded. 'I caught up with Lilian coming back from the shops one day and she said how excited she was that they were going to get married and go to Australia to live. Or maybe it was New Zealand. What could I say? That it was too soon? That he liked her because she had a house to sell? I said I was pleased for her, and indeed I was in a way, because she did look so much better than she had done. I said she must be sure to send me an invitation to the wedding, but I never got one.

'They got some people who clear houses to take away all the furniture, because they were going to make a fresh start with everything new. Or so she said. We did worry about her for a while. But then . . .' Ellie shrugged. 'Then we had the Chaters and really did have something to worry about. The noise!'

Little Frank was asleep in her arms. He was getting heavy but she didn't want to move, in case he woke up. She looked out of the window. The back garden was quiet and peaceful, dotted with Rose's flowers in tubs. She had even planted some climbing roses against the old walls. The garden was a picture.

DI Willis said, 'You think it's her at the bottom of the garden? You think this man Ted got his hands on her money, killed her, buried her and left the country?'

'I don't know,' said Ellie, feeling wretched.

'How old was she?'

'Again, I don't know. Late fifties, maybe a little younger. She hadn't worn well.'

'Then it's not her. The body in the garden is that of a young female with perfect teeth.'

'Ah. Lilian's teeth were not. I know that because I saw her in the dentist's waiting room once, and she said she'd broken her plate. So, it's not Lilian.'

'So we have to go back even further,' said DI Willis. 'Who was there before Lilian and Greg?'

Ellie's head was aching. Her arms were aching. She said, 'I'm sorry, but can we do this another day? All I can tell you is that there was an elderly couple before the Brownings, so it can't be either of them. And before that . . . when we first came here—' Ellie frowned, not wanting to think about that time — 'there was a family with children still at school. Two boys. It can't be them.'

DI Willis rose to her feet. 'This is . . . disappointing.'

'Baffling,' Ellie agreed. 'What do you do next?'

'We have to check out some of this information you've given us. Then I'll be back to see you. There's a possibility we may have to dig up all the gardens that back on to the church.'

'What? You mean, mine as well?' Ellie couldn't have heard correctly. Frank stirred in her arms.

'It's only logical,' said Ms Willis, doggedly. 'I hope we won't have to. If you could have given us any real help . . .'

'I have tried. You can't dig up my garden!'

'I'll see myself out, shall I?'

The young policeman stood up to go but didn't immediately follow the DI.

He leaned over Ellie. 'Shall I take the little one through for you? He's quite a weight, isn't he?'

'What? Oh. Thank you.' Ellie relinquished her burden with relief. 'Why should they want to dig up my garden? It's ridiculous.'

'I'll see what I can find out for you. They've got to trace the girl somehow. Perhaps there were grandchildren around the old people?'

'I never thought of that.' Ellie rubbed her forehead. 'I can't think straight. Yes, I believe you're right. Oh dear.'

'Don't you worry yourself now. You've been very helpful, given us far more than we expected.' Frank slept on in the policeman's arms.

Ellie opened the door to let them into the front part of the house. 'By the way, I didn't catch your name . . . ?'

'Honeywell. Yes, really. Honeywell. On loan from another force.'

* * *

The businessman settled himself at the computer terminal. The room was crowded with students of all nationalities and all ages, tapping away, sending emails back home to all quarters of the globe. The man was pleased. No one had given him a second glance.

Now for the message. Something short and sharp. It was imperative that the police were distracted from checking up on the families who had once lived in that house.

* * *

DC Honeywell laid Frank down on Roy's settee, and departed with a cheery wave for everyone. Rose said, 'What a nice-mannered young man.'

As she saw the police off, Ellie realized that she would have liked nothing better at that point than to call a minicab, take herself and little Frank home, put him to bed and go to bed herself. All this looking back on the past was churning her up. Exhausting her. But it was only six o'clock and in an hour's time Aunt Drusilla was expecting them at her house for a dinner party.

Roy was gloomy. 'Can't get a television signal. The television engineers won't come out at a weekend, which means I won't have telly over the weekend.'

Rose fluttered away, promising to see if he might borrow the new battery-operated set Miss Quicke had bought for her bedroom, and which she very rarely used.

Ellie began folding up empty cardboard boxes.

Roy wandered around, pushing chairs into a better position, angling a lamp to better effect. He was gradually calming down.

'It won't be too bad, when I've got the pictures up. My mother said I ought to have got all new furniture, gone modern. But I like the mix of old and new. Fancy her wanting me to go modern! She knows all about the latest trends in decor, too. Says I should have had bronzed light switches, instead of stainless steel.' He looked at them, and then shook his head. 'No, I prefer these.'

He hadn't noticed that Ellie was looking jaded. In that moment, she knew she'd never ever marry him. She didn't want another unobservant husband.

The next question was, what were they going to do with little Frank? They couldn't leave him to sleep alone in Roy's place. They decided to take him over to the big house and put him to sleep in his pushchair in the hall there. He'd almost outgrown his chair but it did let down to a horizontal position, so he'd be safe in it and they could hear him if he woke up at any time.

Ellie dashed across to the big house to make sure the caterers had arrived — they had — and that Rose had put on something suitable — she hadn't. Ellie persuaded Rose into a plain grey dress and coaxed her hair to frame her face. Rose grew flustered, wanting to go down to see what people were doing in 'her' kitchen.

Ellie got herself ready. She blocked off all thoughts of police and bodies and how badly Diana had behaved at school, and of the moment when Frank had almost hit his daughter . . .

She made herself think instead about getting in some more bulbs for the spring, and planting them with Tum-Tum and borrowing one of his collection of mystery novels to take her mind off things. Also, she must check with her old friend Bill about going out to the nursery gardens as soon as possible.

CHAPTER EIGHT

When Ellie had got herself ready, she went back downstairs to check on Frank, who was still fast asleep. She found Rose, removed her apron, tidied her hair, and sent her into the drawing room, where a buzz of conversation announced that the other guests had already arrived.

Roy was there, of course, looking suitably suave and urbane. Rose nervously tried to hand round drinks in spite of the fact that the caterers had someone doing just that.

A very large gentleman was standing in front of the fireplace talking to Aunt Drusilla. That elderly dame was wearing a black silk dress which might have been new in the 1930s but which still looked stunningly elegant, especially as she'd set it off with a scintillating diamond brooch and earrings.

Aunt Drusilla held out her hand to Ellie. 'Come and meet my dear friend and solicitor, Gunnar. His mother was Swedish but I don't hold it against him.'

Gunnar had small, brilliant eyes, and a wide smile. He was no youngster, but he still had all his hair, even if it had turned white. He had the sort of bass voice which reminded Ellie of Russian choirs. He held Ellie's hand a fraction too long, trying to assess her even as she tried to assess him. So this was Aunt Drusilla's solicitor, was it? A shrewd choice.

'I thought it was about time you all met Gunnar. Just in case.'

The door opened, and in stepped Bill Weatherspoon, who was Ellie's solicitor and long-time family friend. Bill liked Ellie a lot, and she occasionally went out with him, especially to look at gardens which were open to the public. It was Bill who'd promised to take her out to the nursery gardens to make her final selection of plants for the development on the Green.

Bill's presence annoyed Roy, who scowled at the sight of a man he considered his rival for Ellie's affections.

'Mr Weatherspoon — or Bill, if I may,' said Aunt Drusilla, not bothering to rise from her chair. 'I think you know everyone, except perhaps . . . Gunnar?'

'Of course I know Gunnar,' said Bill, shaking his hand. 'We sit on a couple of committees together.'

'So we do,' said Gunnar, all smiles. 'But I didn't know you were acquainted with Drusilla.'

Bill bowed in Miss Quicke's direction. 'Only by sight. And reputation.'

Miss Quicke produced a laugh which could best be described as a cackle. 'If my reputation goes before me, I have less trouble dealing with people. Ellie, stop gaping and help yourself to a sherry.'

Ellie did as she was bid. Bill moved to stand beside her. 'Ellie, do you know why I'm here?'

She shook her head. 'My aunt moves in mysterious ways.'

'Mm.' Bill had wise eyes in a monkey face. He was tall, thin, ugly and dependable. 'Are we still on for our outing to the nurseries on Monday?'

'Yes, indeed. I'm really glad to see you this evening, by the way.'

'You've been turning up more bodies, I hear. Want some more free advice?'

'Your advice is never free.' They both laughed at that, because any time Bill had to give Ellie advice, he asked her to repay him by accompanying him to a social function.

The door opened again, and in came . . . Stewart and Maria Patel! They both hesitated on the threshold. It was clear neither of them had ever been in the house before. Maria was wearing a three-quarter-length dress in a shimmering dull gold fabric which showed off her warm colouring to perfection. Stewart looked almost handsome, which he often did in company where he was appreciated. Ellie never saw the two of them together without noticing their air of quiet content. Tonight that air of content was tinged with apprehension.

'Welcome,' said Miss Quicke, waving them into the room. 'Stewart, I think you know most people here, don't you? Gunnar, this is my niece Diana's ex-husband to be, and his fiancée Maria — if you can have a fiancée before you've shuffled off your first wife.'

'Delighted,' said Gunnar, inclining his upper torso slightly in their direction. He was too large to bow properly.

Maria smiled and a dimple appeared in her left cheek. Ellie immediately thought that Maria must have put on a little weight, because that dimple was new . . . and then she wondered again if Maria were pregnant, as well as Diana.

Miss Quicke beckoned to the couple, who gave the impression of holding hands, though in fact they were not actually doing so. 'Stewart, we've only met in passing so far, haven't we? You've been doing a good job for me lately . . .'

So, Miss Quicke was aware that Stewart now knew she was his boss?

'And Maria . . . we've often spoken on the phone, but never actually met before, have we?' Maria's cleaning company had been doing their best to fulfil Miss Quicke's demand for the perfect cleaner for years.

Maria didn't quite curtsey to Miss Quicke, though it looked as if she wanted to. Ellie made a point of kissing them both and introducing them formally to Bill, and to Roy.

'So . . . shall we go in to dinner?'

At which point the door opened again, and in stormed Diana, wearing a minimalist black dress, strappy black shoes with heels that looked as if they wanted to throw her forward on to the floor, and a scowl. Diana could scowl for Britain.

'How dare you abandon my son in the hall?'

Miss Quicke got to her feet with the aid of her stick. 'I don't remember inviting you, Diana. I thought it was you who'd abandoned him to us, while you gallivanted off to Town.'

'Well, I would have, but Derek said . . . anyway, the arrangement is that I have him at weekends, and so I cancelled going out with Derek and came back to pick him up, and what do I find? You're all having a cosy party while my son lies neglected, pushed out of sight . . .'

Stewart turned his head away. 'Oh, give it a rest, Diana.'

Rose was indignant. 'Diana, it was you who abandoned him, not us. We took care of him all afternoon, in spite of the police being here and everything. He was as good as gold, too, except when he got hold of that statuette, and say what you like, you can't take your eyes off him for two minutes at once before he's into mischief.'

Roy laughed out loud and the others smiled.

Ellie hastened to pour oil. 'Diana dear, I'm so glad you've come back for little Frank. Now we can sit down to eat without listening out for him to—'

'Oh. Really? A dinner party? Well, since I'm not going up to Town, perhaps I'll join you.'

Everyone blenched except Miss Quicke, who was also accustomed to getting her own way.

'You weren't invited, Diana, so I must ask you to—'

'But these people were? Why, may I ask, have you invited my fool of an ex-husband and his piece of arm candy while I, the mother of your only great-nephew—'

Stewart went pale with anger. Maria, on the other hand, took a hasty step towards Diana.

Ellie stepped between. 'Diana, that was rude and quite unnecessary. Maria dear, let it go.'

There was a wail from the hall. Everyone looked to the door, which a waitress was now holding open, with the intention of ushering them through to the dining room.

Diana stalked out of the room, throwing orders at the waitress as she went. 'Set an extra place for me and bring a high chair for my son.'

The waitress looked to Miss Quicke for instructions. 'I'm afraid we don't have a high chair.'

'No, of course you don't,' said Miss Quicke.

Diana's voice floated back to them. 'Come on, everyone. I'm hungry.'

Maria looked to their hostess for a lead. 'I could have him on my lap at table, if you like. I often do when we go out for a meal.'

Miss Quicke was blinking. Thinking hard. At last she nodded. She took Gunnar's arm and led them through the hall and into the grand dining room. Normally this room was used by Miss Quicke as an office, but tonight the shining length of table had been cleared of paperwork and computer, there were candles in the silver candelabrum, flowers in a centrepiece, shining silverware and a priceless Minton dinner service to eat off. Diana had seated herself at one end of the table already.

Miss Quicke had a lengthy word with the waitress. The place setting in front of Diana was removed and replaced to her right-hand side, while some everyday cutlery and an ordinary glass tumbler was placed in front of her instead.

Miss Quicke indicated where everyone should sit. Luckily there were ten chairs in the dining set, so there was enough for everyone, though Ellie did wonder if Gunnar's chair would bear his weight. Miss Quicke took the chair at the opposite end of the table to Diana, and began to talk to Gunnar about Roy's conversion of the garage. Roy was on her left, and joined in.

Soon everyone was busily talking to their neighbours, leaving Diana in an oasis of silence. Little Frank, roused from his sleep, blinked at the candlelight, sitting on Maria's knee. Ellie kept glancing at Diana. The girl was too thin to be pregnant, surely? Almost haggard, in fact. She seemed obsessed with every move that Maria made.

Ellie had Rose on her right and Stewart on her left.

Stewart was not at ease seated next to Diana. 'Ellie, did you ask Miss Quicke to invite us?'

Ellie shook her head, taking a hot home-made roll from the waitress — who failed to offer one to Diana. How strange . . .

Soup was served, in heavy old plates decorated with flowers, possibly hand-painted? Diana's was served in a plain white bowl.

'Delicious,' said Maria, and laughingly helped little Frank to a mouthful from a small spoon that a waitress had given her.

Miss Quicke gave Maria a glance of approval. 'You'll make a fine mother, my dear.'

Ellie felt as if a cold penny had been dropped down her spine. What had Miss Quicke seen? That Maria was pregnant? Maria was certainly blushing. And then came another thought. Maria was Miss Quicke's natural heir in business terms. Not Roy, who was a good architect but no financier. Not Ellie, who didn't care about money. Not Diana, because she wasn't honest in such matters. But Maria was good with money, she'd worked hard to build up her business, she was honest in all her dealings. And, there was no getting away from it, Maria was pregnant.

Oops!

A light white wine was served to everyone. Diana's was poured into an ordinary tumbler instead of a wine glass.

The soup plates were removed while Ellie talked as sensibly as she could to Stewart. A fish course arrived, beautifully presented and not too much of it. Another light, white wine.

'Why have I been served with a cold plate?' demanded Diana.

Everyone stopped talking to look at her. No one volunteered an explanation, because it was clear what had happened. There hadn't been time to warm a plate for her. Or . . . or was this the caterers getting back at Diana for throwing their numbers out?

Everyone started talking again. Diana was furious, stabbing at the fish with her fork, refusing to acknowledge the presence of her husband sitting next to her. Ellie took a sip of wine, which made her feel braver. She launched into a slightly hysterical but, she hoped, amusing story of the fox that had been seen cavorting on the Green around the church at night recently.

Bill was talking animatedly to Maria about his own very pretty garden, which went down to the river Thames. Soon everyone was talking about gardens, as if it were the only safe subject in the world. Even Stewart was saying how much he looked forward to having a bit of lawn to mow.

Maria was alternately smiling at Stewart and feeding titbits to little Frank, who was slapping the table with glee, enchanted by the flicker of the candles.

The fish course disappeared, to be succeeded by chicken Kiev, which caused everyone — except Diana — some merriment as they reminded one another to cut it open with care to avoid being splashed with garlic butter.

'What's this?' Diana was poking at some slices of cold meat on her plate. Everyone else had beautifully decorated plates, but hers was of the plain white kitchen variety.

'I'm afraid I didn't order enough food for you as well,' said Miss Quicke. 'We're rather short of good plates, too. It's not quite what you'd have got up in Town, I suppose, but needs must . . .'

Diana was furious, but said no more. She drained her glass of wine while sending furious glances in Maria's direction. While Ellie was talking to Rose about the garden, she thought, *If looks could kill! Diana has hardly glanced at Stewart, but I wouldn't put it past her to attack Maria if she came upon her one dark night.*

Poor Stewart became increasingly uneasy as dinner progressed and Diana was so pointedly provided with poor fare on kitchen plates. A nice man, Stewart; he could spare a kind thought for Diana, in spite of the way she'd treated him.

Maria was conscious of Diana's gaze, but bearing up well. Stewart raised his glass in a toast to her. She smiled back at him, and responded. Little Frank wanted some wine but she refused, kind but firm. Yes, she would make an excellent mother.

Everyone was becoming nicely relaxed. Except for Diana. Ellie had been feeling that Diana deserved all she got if she gate-crashed Aunt Drusilla's party, but as the evening wore on, she began to feel sorry for her.

The meat course vanished. A chocolate gateau was served, with a sweet white wine. Diana got a rather tired-looking piece of fruitcake. Rose said, 'Oh dear, I was going to throw that away . . .'

A selection of cheeses. The men made a pretence of taking some, but all the women declined. Frank grew heavy in Maria's arms, and yawned.

Miss Quicke tapped her glass. 'We will have our coffee in the drawing room. I'm sure Diana won't mind having hers in a mug instead of a coffee cup. And then she can take the boy away and put him to bed.'

Little Frank's eyes were closing. He forced them open, forced himself to sit upright and then relaxed, leaning back against Maria.

Diana stalked ahead of them into the drawing room and accepted a mug of black coffee where everyone else had theirs in exquisite fine china. Stewart carried his now sleeping son out to the hall and put him back in his pushchair.

Rose said, 'I'm not letting the caterers wash these cups up. I'll do it myself.'

'Yes, dear,' said Aunt Drusilla. 'But not just yet. Now, everyone . . . I don't like to be up late, particularly as I've lent Roy my portable television set for the weekend. I wanted you all to become acquainted. Gunnar, my long-time friend and solicitor. Roy, my son and partner in developing Endene Close. They're calling it that because it's built on the site of an old house that was called Endene. My dearest niece Ellie and my very dear Rose, who both look after me so well. Bill Weatherspoon, who has been so helpful to Ellie — and to Diana, little though she deserves it. Stewart, who has served me well — and Maria, whom I welcome into the family.'

Diana set her mug down with a smack. Always volatile, she now went stratospheric. 'Am I not your family, too?'

'Perhaps,' rumbled Gunnar, 'the black sheep?'

Ellie tried not to laugh. Roy covered a hiccup with his hand. Maria's eyes lit up and Stewart stifled a guffaw.

Diana went white. 'You'll all be sorry for this!' She turned to stalk out of the room, caught one of her excessively high heels on a rug, and stumbled to her knees.

No one laughed.

Bill helped her to her feet, enquiring if she had hurt herself. She shook him off and limped out of the room. They heard the front door bang.

'Is she safe to drive?' Bill wondered.

Stewart leaped to his feet and charged out to the hall. 'It's all right. She forgot to take Frank with her. We'll get a cab and take him home with us. On Monday I'm going to a solicitor to make sure she never gets to have him at weekends again.'

Bill caught Ellie's eye. 'Yes, I'm his solicitor now, and acting for him in the divorce.'

Gunnar patted his capacious stomach. 'Dear Drusilla. A perfect evening, spiced with your own brand of devilment. Of course, you're right. If it comes to a fight for the boy, I'll back Maria and Stewart.'

'Aunt Drusilla,' said Ellie. 'Is that what this evening's been all about? Diana expected you to side with her if there was a battle for little Frank, and you wanted to make sure that we were all against her?'

Miss Quicke smiled and shook her head. Or did it tremble with age and fatigue? 'Stewart, Maria. Come to see me on Monday. I have a selection of houses and ground-floor flats which might be suitable for you to rent until you're able to buy for yourselves. I'm going up to bed now. Gunnar, will you see everyone gets home safely?'

Roy held the door open for her. She paused, looking up at him. 'Roy, you're a good boy and have behaved well this evening. I'm very glad you're going to be living near me. You may kiss me goodnight.'

Roy put his arm around her shoulder and led her out into the hall.

Rose jumped up. 'The caterers! Have they gone? Have they locked the back door? I must just see . . .' She vanished, still talking.

With the familiarity of an old friend, Gunnar asked if anyone had brought a coat or needed a cab home.

Ellie realized she hadn't thought about murder or police digging up her garden, or poor Armand and Kate, for hours. She hoped they'd be long gone by the time she got back home.

Bill offered her a lift back home and she accepted.

He summed the evening up, 'It looks as though Miss Quicke is setting out her case as matriarch of a dynasty. Roy has failed to give her grandchildren, and you aren't interested in her wealth, so she's going to back Maria and Stewart as parents of the boy, handing the flame on, so to speak.'

Ellie sighed. 'Yes, I suppose that's about it. Maria is a very loving person, and she's done Stewart no end of good.' Also, Diana had behaved very badly.

There were lights on in her hall and sitting room, and the curtains had been drawn, presumably by Armand.

'Till Monday,' she said, taking out her key and wondering if perhaps he would have liked her to kiss him goodnight. But no, he wouldn't rush her. The only thing he'd said on the way home was, 'Diana grows more like her father every day, doesn't she?'

Ellie watched him drive away, wondering if what he'd said about Diana was true. Had Frank been that bad-tempered? No. Of course he hadn't. Not unless something had really gone wrong at work. He'd hated incompetence, couldn't put up with fools . . . but then, wasn't that a natural reaction? He'd been so clear-minded himself, always making decisions quickly, that it wasn't surprising that he grew angry when others 'faffed around', to use his words.

Diana was different. Quick-tempered wasn't in it.

Her behaviour this evening hadn't been typical. Gatecrashing the party like that! Such bad manners. Why hadn't she withdrawn when she realized what was happening? Why subject herself to such humiliation? Of course Aunt Drusilla had given permission for Diana to be treated that way by the caterers. So why hadn't Diana taken her son and departed?

She'd looked ill, too. Far too thin, with shadows under her eyes.

Ellie shrugged. Diana had made her bed by moving in with Derek Jolley, whom anyone could see would always put himself first. It was Diana who had left Stewart, not the other way round. It was Diana who had insisted that little Frank be with her only at weekends. Diana was now finding that arrangement difficult. Well, that was her affair.

Ellie let herself into the hall, thinking longingly of a bath and bed, and wondering if she'd been wise to tell Roy that she'd try to help him get straight on the morrow after church. Unfortunately, Kate and Armand were both waiting up for her, sitting side by side on her settee, looking sombre.

CHAPTER NINE

Armand had done most of his marking, to judge by the pile of papers on the floor beside him. A nearly empty bottle of wine was on the coffee table, with two used glasses.

'I know it's late,' said Kate, 'but we wanted to see you before we went back next door.' Ellie noted that she hadn't said 'back home'.

First things first. 'Have you eaten?' said Ellie.

'We ordered a pizza, but we weren't very hungry.'

Neither Kate nor Armand were meeting her eyes. Why ever not? Had they broken something and didn't want to confess?

Armand spoke to his shoes. 'Believe it or not, that policewoman came round to apologize to us. They've discovered the body's been in the ground for maybe fifteen, maybe twenty years.'

'I know,' said Ellie. 'She came to see me at my aunt's and told me. Wanted me to tell her all about the families who'd lived there long ago. But that's good, isn't it? It means you're completely in the clear.'

'It is, and it isn't,' said Armand, still gloomy. 'They know we changed everything in the house, ripped out the old kitchen and bathroom. They've dug up the garden and found nothing, so now they want to bring in heat-seeking machines, see if there's any more bones under the floorboards in the house.'

Kate threw up her arm to hide her eyes and then laid her arm along Armand's shoulders. It was interesting that Kate, who was such a powerful whizz-kid in the financial world, should lean on Armand, who was just a teacher in High School. And, thought Ellie, very right and proper, too, even if she knew some people thought it old-fashioned for a woman to look up to her husband that way.

Kate spoke to the ceiling. 'It was a girl, they think. Not very tall, and slightly built.'

Ellie ran her fingers through her hair. 'I know. I've been thinking but I can't remember a young girl living in your house. They were on and on at me to remember, but I can't. Unless perhaps it was a granddaughter of the old couple?' She shook her head, bemused.

Armand sighed. 'Digging up our garden can't have done any harm, but if they dig up the extension . . . !'

Ellie nodded. 'They threatened to dig up my garden, too.' She heard her voice shake, and tried to steady it. 'I–I don't think I could cope with that. What I want to know is, why they want to extend the search to your house and my garden?'

'Information received, they said.'

Kate tried to reassure her husband. 'We can make them pay to have everything put back, exactly as it was.'

Ellie knew that her garden couldn't be put back exactly as it was, if they did dig it up. Shrubs took years to settle, and if you moved peonies, they usually died. The thought was horrifying. She couldn't bear it.

She decided it would never happen. 'What information? Do they think Frank and I went around killing young girls and burying them in all the gardens around here?' She heard the hysteria in her voice, and made an effort to laugh. 'How absurd!'

'Yes, isn't it!' said Kate, in a flat voice.

Armand said, 'I don't think I want to go back into that house, ever. I couldn't bear it.'

'Of course we can bear it,' said Kate. But she didn't sound very sure. She stood up, placed her hands on Ellie's shoulders and braced herself. 'There's more. I must warn you. DI Willis was asking questions about your husband, Frank. I couldn't think why at first, but . . .'

'It was rubbish,' said Armand, reddening. 'Told her so, too.'

Ellie blinked. 'Do you mean . . . ? No, you can't mean that . . . ? She thinks that Frank might have . . . ?' She sat down with a bump on the nearest chair. She was breathless with shock. How could they!

Kate sat down beside her and patted her hand. 'Apparently someone who used to live around here has emailed them, pointing the finger at your husband. I told them it was nonsense, but . . .'

Armand said, far too loudly, 'Absolute nonsense!'

'Yes.' Ellie felt faint. Her brain had gone into free fall. She couldn't believe that this was happening. Kate continued to pat her hand, concerned for her. Armand got up, looking at the clock on the mantelpiece, looking at his watch to see if they both said the same thing. He picked up his papers, pushed them into a plastic bag.

Armand wanted out of here.

Kate continued to hold Ellie's hand.

Ellie gave her head a shake to clear it. 'What you're trying to say is—'

'Not us,' said Kate. 'The police got this email and I suppose they have to follow up any leads they get.'

'They think Frank murdered that young girl? But . . . why would he do such a thing?'

Kate didn't say anything. Armand cleared his throat, looked at his watch again.

Ellie said, 'We didn't know any young girls.'

Kate almost smiled at that.

Ellie said, 'Oh, I suppose you mean there was Diana, but . . . you mean they think one of Diana's schoolfriends . . . ?'

Horror. Her brain turned itself upside down. Frank wouldn't have killed anyone, but Diana had been had up for bullying a child at school. Suppose that Diana had caught the girl on the way home from school one dark winter's evening, and . . . and . . . the idea was so appalling that she couldn't take it any further.

She stood up, trying to smile. 'What nonsense! I'll have a word with that inspector in the morning and give her a piece of my mind.'

'You do that, girl!' Kate patted her on the shoulder and looked around for her handbag. 'Now we must leave you in peace, having taken advantage of your kindness for the umpteenth time. Armand, have you got your keys?'

They wafted themselves away and Ellie was left staring into space.

Suppose Diana had gone too far and, not meaning to, had killed someone from school? Diana knew that the garden next door was a sort of No Man's Land, only visited by wild animals and birds. Diana had always been strong, in spite of her slim figure. She could have pushed the girl into a hollow in the sloping garden and . . . and used their own garden tools to cover her with earth? And then brambles and grass would have grown over the girl.

Nonsense!

Someone would have missed a schoolgirl and roused the neighbourhood. They'd have had people round searching the gardens, checking to see if she'd had an accident coming home from school.

No, it couldn't possibly have been one of Diana's school friends.

It was true that Diana was capable of much, but not — thank God — of that.

Of course, if it had been Diana, then it wouldn't have been beyond Frank to help hide the body, to protect his much-loved daughter. But as it wasn't Diana then Ellie needn't worry about that.

The thought of Frank arranging a meeting with an unknown young girl in next door's garden was so funny she laughed out loud. Frank, chasing after a young girl? Her slightly tubby late-fifties husband chasing a young girl? It was ridiculous!

But this would have been fifteen or twenty years ago, when he'd still been fairly lithe but absorbed by work and worry over his senior partner, who was even then making disastrous mistakes. It wasn't till Frank himself became senior partner that he'd been able to relax, they'd got a better car, paid off the mortgage, and she'd been able to stop going out to work.

A treacherous thought: wives often were the last to suspect when their husbands strayed. She could think of at least two wives who'd been horrified when their husbands had walked out on them to live with another woman. But Frank just wasn't the type.

For one thing, he had never been able to hide his emotions. If he was irritable, he expressed his irritation. If he liked the look of a woman — and now and then over the years Ellie had caught him looking with sheep's eyes at some buxom blonde or other — it had gone no further. There'd been no unexplained absences from home, no late-night work hours, no furtive attempts to leave the house 'for a drink with the boys', when wearing his best suit. No committee meetings that she hadn't known about. She'd often acted as secretary on committees where Frank had been treasurer or chairman.

Yes, their original dream of romantic love had faded over time. They'd become used to one another. Comfortable with one another. He hadn't been one to wear his heart on his sleeve as some did, and he'd occasionally been irritated with her inability to cope with modern technology, but he'd always appreciated her cooking and never missed a meal if he could help it. He'd been proud of her in his own way, though he never praised her to her face. What he did was to praise her by inference, saying that he didn't think much of Mrs

So and So neglecting her mother-in-law, or not attending a family funeral, when Ellie had been doing just those things.

He'd expected her to look after his aunt, and Ellie had done so. At a certain cost to herself. But, she had done it. He'd shown his love for Ellie not with gifts or compliments, but with rough anxiety when she'd been ill. With a scolding if she'd overdone things.

He'd adored Diana, of course, and spoiled her right up to the point where she'd got married. After that, his common sense had kicked in and he'd refused to give in to Diana's dream of living a life beyond her means.

She checked her watch against the clock. It was getting late, but how on earth was she to go to sleep with this on her mind?

She locked up and went to bed. She lay in bed, trying not to disturb Midge, who'd decided to sleep beside her. The little grandmother clock in the hall chimed the hours softly. One. Two.

At half past two Ellie slid carefully out of bed so as not to disturb Midge, and went downstairs to make herself a cup of tea. She got the old photograph albums out of the cupboard under Frank's great desk and looked back down the years.

Diana in her first school uniform, looking pleased with herself. Frank standing behind her, his hand on her shoulder. The sleeves of Diana's blazer were too long. Ellie remembered having to turn them in . . . and then let them down again as Diana grew.

Sports day. An outing from the church to Black Park. Tea in Aunt Drusilla's garden, Diana scowling. Frank was in all the photographs, laughing, smiling, very much at ease. She herself wasn't in many of the photos, because she'd been the one to take the photographs with her old box Brownie . . . which she'd lost one summer holiday. Ah me. Modern cameras were far too complicated and didn't give nearly as good a result.

Holidays. Renting a cottage by the sea. She'd wanted to share a large cottage with another family but Frank wouldn't hear of it. 'I need a bit of peace and quiet,' he said. Not much peace and quiet for Ellie, trying to keep Diana amused while shopping and cooking and cleaning for the household just as if she were still back at home.

Ellie shut up the book with a bang. There was something else that had happened all those long years ago, but she didn't want to think about that now. It hadn't been Frank's fault. Nor hers, really.

Down the years she heard Diana's sharp tones, 'Oh, silly Mummy's crying again!'

Ellie sank her head in her hands and prayed for help. And for comfort. Then she went back to bed and, although she'd never thought she'd be able to sleep, the next thing she knew was the alarm ringing in her ear.

* * *

Sunday morning, and for once the sun wasn't shining. In fact, it looked as if it might rain. The garden could do with it, of course . . . if the police didn't dig it up.

Well, she wasn't going to let the police touch her garden. So there! She'd tell Bill about it, and he'd get the police to keep away.

Before that, she had to get ready to sing in the choir for the church service, check if she had something for lunch and be ready to go on to the Gate House to finish helping Roy settle in this afternoon.

One thing: if she were out of the house, the police couldn't start wrecking the place, could they? And they wouldn't do it on a Sunday, anyway. Would they?

Not for a crime committed so long ago.

She allowed herself twenty minutes to go round the back garden, deadheading roses and perennials. She unlocked the garden shed and took out some canes and twine to stake some delphiniums on their second flowering, because otherwise they'd surely be dashed to the ground if it did rain. She also staked some cosmeas which had grown nearly as tall as she was, and pulled up some pansies which were looking the worse for wear after a long period of drought. And yes, she ought to have watered them, she knew that. But they'd been in since the previous autumn, so were entitled to die off now if they felt like it.

Mrs Coppola's boy Tod came to lean over the gate at the bottom of the garden, though he didn't come in as he used to do. 'Want me to mow your lawn, Mrs Quicke? I could do with a bob or two.'

He had mowed her lawn occasionally in the past but not made too good a job of it. His head looked as if it were attached to his body, but not when he had computers or cricket on his mind. She shook her head, smiling . . . and then with a stab of pain remembered that if the police were going to dig up her garden, there wouldn't be any lawn to mow.

'Not this week, Tod. Thanks. Are you off to play cricket somewhere?'

'Nah. It's Sunday, remember. I'm just going up to my friend's. They've got a really cool outing from their church today, and he said I could go, too. But we've got to take a packed lunch, and Mum's not up yet, so I thought I'd get one of those ginormous sausage rolls from the deli first. They're open on Sunday mornings.'

She felt in her pocket and found a two-pound coin. 'Buy yourself some fruit juice as well.'

He hesitated. 'I've got enough. I took some money out of Mum's purse. It's all right, she said to. But if you've got any odd jobs this next week . . . ?'

'I'll remember.'

He went on his way and she got ready for church, remembering at the last minute that she'd promised to do the coffee for Jean, who'd be furious if she weren't there early enough to put all the cups and saucers out and fill up the urn.

* * *

Dressed in choir robes, Ellie processed behind the ample proportions of Mrs Dawes into the choir pew, and checked that she had all the relevant pieces of music. She never felt she could quite relax and enjoy services when she was singing in the choir, but she'd got pushed into doing it after her husband died, and really it was a pleasure to sing praise to God in harmony. Also, she'd made some good friends in the choir. As they belted out the first verse of the first hymn, Ellie began to wonder if she'd remembered to lock up the garden shed. Years ago, a tramp had got in and set the place alight. And hadn't Frank had something to say about that!

She pushed it out of her mind. She couldn't do anything about it now, anyway. Except trust that she'd done it without thinking.

Tum-Tum was on good form today. He told marvellous stories of real life, which he then linked to the Bible reading for the day. She wondered what he'd bring up today. She wondered who had been so stupid as to leave their mobile phone switched on, disturbing the congregation in the middle of the service. The noise stopped. Thank goodness.

In the next hymn, the ringing started again. People started looking at one another, amused or annoyed as the mood took them. Two of the men in the choir surreptitiously dived under their choir robes to check that their mobiles were switched off. And then looked relieved when they found it wasn't their problem.

The ringing was coming from the vestry, where the women had left their handbags. Some stupid person had forgotten to switch their mobile off before coming in to church. What bad manners. No one could concentrate on the service. Even Tum-Tum had lost the thread of what he was saying.

She hoped someone would get out to check. She couldn't, wedged as she was between the altos and the sopranos in the choir pews.

A tenor at the end of the pew slid out, whipped into the vestry and, while everyone pretended to concentrate on the hymn-singing, most eyes switched to the vestry door.

The ringing ceased. The tenor slid back in, red-faced . . . and looked directly across at Ellie.

Oh, horrors! It couldn't really have been her phone ringing, could it? She never left it on. Everyone was looking at her.

She'd never live it down. Already Mrs Dawes was drawing her bulk slightly away from her.

She almost ran into the vestry at the end of the service, gasping out apologies. She couldn't think how it had happened.

The tenor was magnanimous. 'It's easily done. If you leave it in your handbag, something pressing against this key could easily turn it on. Look, there's this key here. If you press that when the phone's turned off, then it locks in position so you can store messages, but it won't ring.'

'Thank you. Oh, I'm so sorry, everyone.'

On the whole, they were forgiving. 'Perhaps it was something important . . .'

Ellie accessed the voice messages. It was Diana. Ah, who else would think of disturbing her at church? But the message *was* disturbing.

'Mum, are you there?' How many years was it since Diana last called her 'Mum'? It was always 'Mother' nowadays. 'Mum, ring me, please. I've been bleeding ever since last night. I'm having a miscarriage, I think.' Something that sounded like a sob. 'Can you come? I'm at the new house, not at Derek's. I need you.'

Ellie played the message back twice.

'Bad news?' Mrs Dawes, with others crowding around.

'Yes. Diana's ill. Needs me. But—' she looked wildly around — 'I'm supposed to be doing coffees.'

They were soothing. 'I'll see to it,' said Mrs Dawes.

'But Jean only rang yesterday to check that I—'

'I'll help you out, Mrs Dawes,' said a youngish woman, fairly new to the choir. 'Don't you fret none, Mrs Quicke.'

The tenor offered her a lift in his car.

'You're all so kind,' said Ellie, trying to remember if she'd brought a jacket to the church or not. 'Do apologize to Jean for me, won't you?'

Rose fluttered into the vestry, with her unpleasant daughter Joyce on her heels. 'Oh, my dear, I've just heard. Somebody's sick or dying, they said?'

Joyce sniffed. 'I expect it was the police, wanting to ask Ellie about her husband! Him with the roving hands.'

Shock, horror. Everyone drew back from Joyce, while Rose went crimson. 'Joyce, how dare you!'

Joyce shrugged. 'Everyone knows . . .'

'No, they don't!' said Mrs Dawes. 'Now, you listen to me, my girl . . .'

Other members of the choir joined in. 'Mr Quicke never, ever—'

'Who did you ever hear complain about—?'

'Well, I never heard anyone say anything against Mr Quicke, so helpful as he was about the finances and everything . . .'

'And as to taking liberties, well! There's some I could point at who would, not mentioning any names, but you all know who . . .'

'There now, Mrs Quicke. Don't you take no notice of what some stupid girl—'

'No, I don't,' said Ellie, struggling to her feet. 'Frank might have looked, now and then . . .'

Several women nodded. They didn't miss anything, did those middle-aged and elderly women. 'He was one who looked, but never touched.'

'That's about it,' said Ellie, grateful for their backing. 'Now I must ring my daughter and find out—'

Rose said, 'I'll tell Miss Quicke and Roy that you won't be making it.'

'I'll ring you later, if I can,' promised Ellie.

'Your carriage awaits, madam,' said the tenor, holding the door open for her.

Once in the open air, Ellie rang Diana, who sounded tearful and weak. The tenor dropped Ellie at the huge old house which Diana had bought on a mortgage, using the money from the sale of the house she'd shared with Stewart in the north.

The front garden had been paved over for car parking, as had most of the rear. The old wooden windows had been replaced with plastic ones. Diana's theory was that upwardly mobile young couples would want a modern environment, and she'd done the house up that way. Everything was sparkling white, stripped floorboards, masses of power points for Internet and other media connections. There were three floors, each divided into two self-contained flats.

Diana staggered to the front door as Ellie rang the bell and beckoned her mother into a room at the back of the house. This had clearly started out as a show room and office, but a clutter of luggage lay around and someone had been making coffee in the streamlined kitchenette at the back of the living room. The furniture was minimalist and there were a couple of striking modern prints on the wall.

'Yes, I'm still bleeding,' Diana said, collapsing into a large chair and clutching her stomach. 'And yes, it was a miscarriage. It started on my way back home last night. Tripping over my heels did it.' Her face contorted and she bit her lip.

'I'll make you some tea. A hot-water bottle might help.'

'I'm all right,' said Diana, through clenched teeth. 'What I want is for you to show these people round at one o'clock. They're coming to see the flats upstairs, and at the moment I just can't . . .' She stopped, squeezing her eyes shut.

Ellie counted to ten and took a chair opposite Diana. It was the only other chair in that big room. It was a pleasant room, looking out on to what remained of the back garden. What wasn't so pleasant was that Diana wanted Ellie to help her out . . . again. Ellie had refused to help Diana buy this monstrosity of a house and do it up. Ellie had agreed with Miss Quicke that Diana was asking for trouble ripping all the traditional features out of an old house and creating minimalist settings for young professionals. There wasn't a cornice, or a rose for a ceiling light, or a fireplace left. The room was stark, bare, functional.

Ellie was furious. She felt she'd been tricked into going to Diana's rescue. She'd always made it clear she wouldn't have anything to do with this place, and now . . . look at her! Even in her agony, white-faced and shivering, Diana had got Ellie exactly where she wanted her.

Diana said, 'You will help me out, won't you? Just let them in, show them around. The keys are on that chest over there, and a list of who's coming to see the flats. I sold the other one on the ground floor yesterday, but there's four more to go. Only one of them's got any furniture in it, but people can get an idea what they're like. You'd better have a look around, see where everything is before they come.'

'Diana, if you weren't ill, I'd walk straight out of that door.'

'I know.' Diana flickered a smile. 'I'm desperate. I've left Derek. Will you help me?'

* * *

If you want to hide, go where you won't be noticed. And the murderer had never been noticed in Ealing.

He and his family piled into their cars and drove to Southall to visit a cousin. Only Grandpa stayed behind, with one of his daughters-in-law to look after him. The house was very quiet, with only the two of them there. The old man sat propped up in his chair, hooked up to the oxygen cylinder, his eyes half closed, thinking . . . dreaming . . . of the past? Or of the next meal?

CHAPTER TEN

It was after eight on that exhausting day. The last of the viewers had left the house and no more were expected that evening. Ellie was worn out, not only from tramping up and down the stairs so many times, but also from the major shift she'd had to make in her ideas.

Little though Ellie wanted to live in what — to her mind — were soulless apartments, it appeared that others did. Almost everyone had praised the spacious layouts, the futuristic bathrooms and clever kitchens. They'd exclaimed over the modern lighting, the multiple power points, the fact that, as they were all two-bedroomed flats, one room could always be let out to help with the costs.

The only people who hadn't been impressed were those with children, and they'd wanted access to a garden. There was plenty of parking space; enough to accommodate two cars for every flat, but the only flat which had access to the garden was the one in which Diana was asleep and which could therefore not be shown.

Ellie told herself that not everyone who said they'd make an offer for a flat would actually carry their interest through to completion, but when she added up the pluses, she realized that if even half of the prospective buyers were serious, the apartments — except for the garden flat — could all be considered sold. Ellie had to acknowledge that Diana had been right in wanting to cater for young professionals, even though her hectoring tactics had alienated both Aunt Drusilla and Ellie herself.

Ellie phoned Roy and got his answerphone. It was Sunday evening, and no doubt he'd be out at the golf club. She phoned Rose and made her excuses, explaining what had happened and saying she'd not be able to get round there that evening.

Diana had slept uneasily throughout most of the afternoon, but was now struggling to get back to normal. She stripped off, showered and dressed in clean clothes. Then she picked up the list, with Ellie's comments in the margin, of people who'd been round to view the flats.

Ellie said, 'They all wanted to look at this garden flat. I didn't know what to say. I told them someone had made an offer for it but it might fall through, so they should ask again later.'

Diana dropped the list, and yawned. 'Now I've left Derek, I think I'd better keep it, don't you?'

'For yourself?' Ellie knew the asking price for these flats now. If Diana kept this flat, she'd lose out on a big sale. Ellie felt she ought to offer Diana a home, but no; she really did not want to do so. Diana living back with her? Ellie wouldn't have a minute's peace.

She was shocked at herself. How could she consider her own comfort when Diana had nowhere to live? Granted, Diana had made herself homeless, but still . . . Ellie steeled herself to offer, sending up an arrow for help. Please, Lord, make me strong enough to cope.

'Why don't you move back in with me?'

Diana grimaced. 'I give you full marks for offering, mother, but you don't really mean it and I've grown out of all that. No, this will do me nicely. Besides, I've stained the mattress on the bed here, so will have to buy it. The furniture's all rented at the moment. Some of the punters will want to buy—'

'Yes, some of them did enquire about that.'

'Thanks for showing them round. I'm sure you added the right touch of respectability.'

Ellie had already realized that. Had Diana been using her again? Was her present weakness faked? On the whole, Ellie thought it was genuine.

Diana sank back into her chair and closed her eyes. Her colour was better than it had been, but still not good.

'Food?' asked Ellie.

Diana didn't bother to open her eyes. 'Dad always said that you could magic a meal out of nothing, but I'm afraid these cupboards are bare.'

'I'll send out for something. Chinese?' Chinese food would be lighter than pizza and easier for Diana to digest.

'I'm skint. Every penny I've got or could raise has gone into finishing these flats. My overdraft is horrendous.'

'I'll pay for the meal.'

They ate in what for them was almost a state of harmony. Ellie was determined not to ask Diana whether the lost baby had been Derek's, but Diana eventually told her.

'I know people couldn't understand what I saw in Derek. Sometimes I couldn't understand it myself. I know you didn't like him, but I don't suppose you ever felt about a man the way that I did about him . . .'

Ellie let that pass. Perhaps — a sigh — perhaps she hadn't. Sex with Frank had been fine; at the very beginning it had been awkward, then good, and after that more than just fine. She'd heard that men thought about nothing but sex all day long, and yes, she'd had times when it had obsessed her . . . but that had faded with the routine of years.

'. . . because Derek could make me want to do things I'd never even thought of, certainly not with poor Stewart, though perhaps with . . .' She touched her lips with the tip of her tongue and smiled. 'Yes, once or twice, I've had an inkling of what it could be like with the right partner. But then . . .'

She threw her head against the high back of her chair. 'Derek didn't like having little Frank around. He made excuses not to pick him up. Argued with me. What did we want with children coming between us? He said that Stewart and Maria wanted the boy, so I should let them have him. Then we could go away together whenever we wanted, the West Indies, a cruise, anything. He said we could have a child of our own later on, that he'd feel different about his own child. I know you think I'm a bad mother, that I always put Derek first . . .'

What Ellie had thought was that Diana always put Diana first.

'. . . but I love my son. You won't understand, but the bond between mother and son is so strong . . .'

Stronger than that between mother and daughter? Ellie raised her eyebrows but didn't interrupt.

'. . . that I'd have done anything to keep him. I thought you and Great-Aunt would back me up and that Derek would come round eventually. Then I found out I was pregnant. I didn't mean to get pregnant so soon. It was a mistake. I thought perhaps I'd just missed a period because of all the stress in my life, getting this place ready, keeping Frank away from Derek. Luckily I had this flat fixed up as an office, and could bring Frank here to play. He loves this garden.'

Ellie looked around but couldn't see any evidence of a child playing in this flat.

Diana gestured towards a cupboard. 'I keep his things in there, and there's a shed outside for his toys on wheels. Things were coming to a climax. These flats were ready to go on sale and I asked Derek if he'd sell them at a reduced commission, but he said he couldn't do that. So, I told him I'd sell them on the Internet rather than through him, to save money. He didn't like that. But I needed the money and he hadn't helped me out here at all, so it was only fair.

'Yesterday was agony. Knowing I was over three months pregnant with Derek's child and that Stewart and Maria wanted Frank so badly, I convinced myself that I must make the final sacrifice. I must give little Frank up, though it almost tore me in two even to think about it. I told myself that if I did that, everyone would be happy. Frank would miss me for a while and I knew I'd miss him, but he'd be safe with Stewart and Maria. And then everything would be all right with Derek. You were already looking after him yesterday, and I wanted to tell you what was going to happen so I drove over to Great-Aunt's — and walked into the dinner party from hell.'

Ellie nodded. Now she knew why Diana had put up with all that rudeness.

'I sat there watching that cow Maria cuddling my son and I told myself that this was what I wanted, that Derek would be pleased that I'd given Frank up, and thrilled when I told him about our own baby. I don't know how I sat through dinner, with everyone shutting me out . . .'

'You weren't invited. It was a difficult situation.'

'So what? They could have tried to see it from my point of view. It was the hardest thing I've ever done, to leave Frank there . . .'

Ellie reflected that Diana had left her son with other people before, whenever it had suited her, though not of course, for good.

'. . . and I didn't think anything of it when I tripped and fell over, but I did have one awful pain in my guts on the way home. Derek was there, and he said how pleased he was that I'd got rid of Frank, so I told him about our baby . . .' Diana drew in her breath.

Ellie felt sorry for her, almost. 'He wasn't best pleased?'

'He told me to get rid of it. That's when I saw him for the monster he was. I'd given my son away to please him and he'd obviously lied to me about us having a child of our own. So I began to pack. I was sure he'd stop me. But he didn't. He started drinking instead. So I got out of there with what I could put in the car and came here because I knew it would be quiet and I wouldn't have to answer any questions. I found I was bleeding and I began to get these pains. I thought if I lay down quietly it would stop. Then I thought why make it stop? If Derek wasn't bothered, why should I try to keep the child?

'So, I started moving furniture around. I'd only rented enough furniture to dress two of the flats. I knew there were more people coming round today, so I had to move furniture from the ground-floor flat, which had been sold, to one of the upstairs ones. I couldn't move the heavier pieces, but I got the double bed up — it takes to pieces — and some of the chairs and the candles and flowers and cushions and stuff. I kept at it till . . . oh, about three o'clock this morning, I suppose. Then I lay down for a bit, but the pains didn't stop. I showed a couple of prospective buyers round at half past ten, but I'm not sure how I managed that. So I phoned you and then . . . well, I just sat on the loo and everything came away.'

'Will you go back to Derek, now you've lost both your children?'

'Don't say that! As if I were careless!'

Ellie didn't know how else to put it. She realized Diana had used her — again. But looking back, how could Ellie have refused to help Diana out? She stood up. 'Shall I help you make up the bed with fresh sheets?'

'What, no more offers to take me back home? Which will be half mine when you die, anyway.'

Ellie held on to her temper. 'No, you've made your point.'

'I've proved I was right about doing up a house with young professionals in mind, too. So, snubs to you and to Great-Aunt, who said I couldn't!'

'Yes, you've proved you can do that. I only hope you're going to play fair with your buyers, Diana. Your reputation in the past has—'

'This is real life, mother. Not a Disney film.'

'If you've used me to cover up something crooked, then—'

'I know better than that,' said Diana, sullenly. 'This venture has to be on the up and up. Your saintly reputation is safe.'

'Thank you, dear.' Ellie kissed the air near Diana's ear. 'Now I'll be off home if you don't mind, but I suggest you get yourself checked out at the doctor's tomorrow.'

Diana shrugged and let her mother out, not offering to drive her home even though it was now getting dark and Ellie's house was a good twenty-minute walk away. Ellie thought about walking down the Avenue past the burger bar where the men hung around after the pubs closed, and decided to phone for a minicab. Better be safe than sorry.

* * *

Consternation. The businessman and the surgeon were furious! While they were out, that stupid woman had gossiped the local news to her father-in-law, and now he was in a bad way. Should they call the doctor? His breathing was laboured, despite the oxygen.

They walked up and down the back garden, faces tight.

'I thought you warned her not to . . .'

'I did. But women are so stupid! She said it soothed him when she chattered away to him . . .'

'But not about that!'

'She had no idea. She still has no idea!'

'That's no excuse.' They halted, listening. One of the businessman's daughters, who was a trained nurse, was tending to her grandfather. It ought to have been her who'd been left behind to look after her grandfather, but she'd wanted to be included in the party, and the men had encouraged her to go, because there was a cousin of a suitable age going to be there. It wouldn't be a particularly good match for her, since the lad had nothing much in the way of education, but the boy's father would pay well for a bride with a British passport.

The businessman's wife was locked in their bedroom, weeping.

'What do we do now?' asked the businessman. 'You're due back at work tomorrow, aren't you?'

The surgeon looked at his watch. 'I should be on the road now. I'll have to leave it to you to follow up with the police. If they know their business, we should hear news of an arrest any minute now.'

'I'll check it out locally tomorrow.'

'I'll ring you on your mobile at noon.'

* * *

Monday morning. Ellie turned over in bed and thought about staying there. Why did life have to be so complicated?

Yesterday . . .

She didn't want to think about yesterday. Diana's miscarriage. Would Diana now fight to get little Frank back? It was good that she seemed to be making such a success of the house conversion, but her costs must have been horrendous.

Next Ellie remembered the rumours about her husband chasing a young girl . . . and the police threatening to dig up her garden.

She nearly screamed the word 'Nonsense!'

Dear Lord, it is not possible, no, it's not! I can't bear it. Any of it.

She sat upright. Bill was taking her out for the day, so she could talk to him about it. He'd know what to do.

Dear Bill hadn't had a proper holiday in ages, but he was taking a day off work so they could go out into the country together to visit a nursery garden and look at plants. He wanted some for his garden and she needed to check the plants she'd ordered for the grounds of Roy's development at Endene Close. She must get dressed, have some breakfast and be ready for half past ten. Look at the time! She dislodged Midge from the bed and leaped out.

Bill was on time, as always. Car gleaming, newly washed. Clothes casual but good. Shoes shining. Glasses glinting. Smiling in anticipation of his day off work in Ellie's company.

Ellie had got up feeling disagreeable, but she made an effort to be pleasant. 'Coffee before we start?'

Bill had known her for years. 'Now what are you up to, Ellie? I thought we'd stop for coffee in that old inn in Cookham.'

'I need to ask your advice before we leave the house . . .' She poured out some good coffee for him, and told him about the threat to her garden. As she did so, she realized she cared more about her garden being disturbed than about the rumour concerning her dead husband.

This annoyed her. Surely she ought to care more about what people said about Frank than about a garden? Well . . .

the garden was still with her, while Frank wasn't. This reasoning didn't satisfy her sense of what was appropriate either.

She concluded, '. . . so is it safe for me to go out for the day, or will I find the garden all torn up when we get back? Can they do it without my permission?'

Bill massaged his chin. They could, if they got a warrant. But they'd need good evidence to get a warrant, and from what you say there's nothing except an unsubstantiated rumour. Possibly a spiteful phone call from a neighbour?'

Ellie thought of Mrs Coppola. Would she go to such lengths? She'd always been jealous of Ellie, resenting her son's affection for the older woman.

Ellie threw up her hands. 'I can't think straight on this one, Bill. What they've been saying about Frank, and having to look back on the past, has got me all mixed up.'

'Brought it all back, has it?' He didn't specify what 'it' was. He didn't have to. He said, 'I'll have a quick word with this Inspector Willis if you like, and then we'll be off out of it. Do you good to get out into the country for the day.'

'You, too,' said Ellie, dumped the coffee cups in the sink, made sure the shed at the bottom of the garden was locked up — it was — and that the top windows in the conservatory were open, because it looked like being another warm day. If Bill said he could fix it, then fix it he could. She could always rely on Bill.

He wound up his conversation on the phone as she picked up her handbag and made sure her mobile phone was turned off.

He said, 'Inspector Willis is off today, but I spoke to some sergeant or other and he said their enquiries were continuing but that they wouldn't be digging up any more gardens today. I think it's safe for us to go out.'

They took their time driving out of London on the A40 and then turned off through narrow lanes between hawthorn hedges, through tiny picture-book villages and common land with road signs saying *Gypsy Lane* . . . and then not giving any road signs at all.

There were wild roses in the hedges, and some honeysuckle still. The sights rested Ellie's mind. Bill was a cautious driver, but a safe one.

They didn't talk much. Arrived at the garden centre, he wandered off with his list to search for some special plant or other that he fancied, while she checked on the plants she'd ordered for the beds at Endene Close, and arranged for them not only to be delivered, but also planted up.

'There's a special senior-citizen's lunch on today,' said Bill, trundling along a trolley laden with various plants. 'I've just qualified for it, but I'm afraid they won't give it to you.'

'Are you really sixty? You don't look it.'

'And you still look as young as when I was first introduced to you, all those years ago. If only Frank hadn't got to you first!'

This mild flirting amused her. 'And you already happily married to your dear wife, whom I still miss so much.'

'Ah, well. Life sometimes gives us second chances.'

Ellie rather hoped he didn't mean that she was his second chance for marriage. She liked him enormously, but not that much. Come to think of it, she couldn't think of a man she'd want to marry right at this minute.

They had a good, solid cooked lunch in the restaurant at the garden centre, and only then did Ellie tell him what had been happening with Diana. He heard her out, stirred sugar into his coffee and drank it before speaking.

'Do you think she'll make it up with Jolley?'

Ellie shrugged. 'He's very sexy, apparently. She's been torn in two.'

'Are you defending her after the way she's treated you?'

Ellie didn't reply.

Bill tapped his empty cup with a teaspoon, an irritating habit of his when thinking. 'I can't act for her if there's a tug-of-love with Stewart over the boy. I'm already acting for him in the divorce case. Would she consider going back to Stewart?'

Ellie shrugged. Shook her head. She didn't know, didn't think so.

Bill laid the spoon down. 'Well, we'll give it some time to settle down, shall we?'

That was the worst of men. They always thought things would get better if you 'gave it time'. In Ellie's experience, things usually went from bad to worse before they got better. But who was she to talk?

Bill said, 'How does all this leave you, Ellie?'

'Confused. The police keep on at me to look back and remember how things were in the past.' She tried to laugh. 'We've had a fine lot of neighbours over the years, haven't we? I never got to know any of them properly. I see now why Frank always told me not to get involved with them. That really would have been the most sensible thing for me to do. But I did feel so sorry for them, some of them. Poor things, they never had a chance, probably born into the hands of social services and never out of it . . . or sad immigrants . . . or just . . .' She shrugged again.

She moved her chair to face him more directly. 'What did you think of Frank? You knew him longer than I did.'

'Why, yes. We met at the tennis club — which was where you met Frank, wasn't it, all those years ago? You had a wicked forehand, I seem to remember.'

'I asked about Frank.'

He lifted the spoon and tapped his coffee cup again. He smiled. 'What I remember was how pretty you were. "My pocket Venus", Frank said, when he brought you over to meet us. And you looked up at him as if he'd just stepped out of a story book.'

'I was very young. My mother had just died and I hadn't had much of a social life before that, because she'd been so poorly for so long. I was working at an accountant's in the Avenue. Someone there said I should try to get out more and suggested I joined the tennis club. I was very shy that first day, but Frank rescued me and was so kind.'

'He knew when he was on to a good thing.'

Yes, thought Ellie. Perhaps he did. Perhaps it wasn't all one-sided, as I've always thought. I was so grateful to him for loving me and making me his wife, even giving me a brand-new family to look after — though Aunt Drusilla was not exactly the most loving aunt you could have, and Diana never did respond to the love I gave her.

Bill was looking at her with . . . compassion?

She said, 'What I need to know is, did Frank ever chase after other women? I mean, wives are often the last to know. I really do need the truth, Bill. Don't try to fob me off with lies.'

'No, I wouldn't do that, Ellie. Frank never chased after any other woman but you, all the time I knew him. Yes, he looked at one or two other women over the years, in the way one does. All small and fragile, all blondes. Your type.'

She laughed. 'I've put on too much weight to be considered fragile nowadays. And my hair turned silver when I was only forty.'

'You still look good to me.'

'We're talking about Frank.'

'He looked. No more. A good pair of legs, a pretty bust. All men look. I never heard of Frank doing any more than look, and I would have heard, Ellie, if he had. Believe me.'

She let out a long sigh. 'Thank you, Bill. I needed to hear that. I began to worry that I'd got him wrong, all these years. He could be sharp, I know that. And sometimes he wasn't as sympathetic to other people's troubles as he might have been, especially when I was ill.'

'All those miscarriages you had. Five, was it?'

'They took it out of me rather. I don't blame him for getting impatient once or twice, I was such a weepy little creature, dragging myself around . . . oh, I don't want to think about those days. Thank you, Bill. I feel so much better. Now, will you show me what plants you're buying for yourself?'

He wanted to buy a young monkey-puzzle tree. How could he! Ellie had always considered monkey-puzzle trees the most useless trees in creation, and Bill wanted to buy one? He'd also hovered over a mahonia, which did at least produce flowers, but whose leaves had the cutting edge of a sharp kitchen knife. She'd found one in her garden when they moved in and given herself a nasty gash on it. Somehow the fact that he liked those plants lowered him in her estimation.

On the drive back, she worked it out that if she'd loved Bill, she'd have felt indulgent towards his choice of plants. It was comforting in a way to realize that she didn't love him that much. She really did not want to be as dependent upon a man again as she had been with Frank.

CHAPTER ELEVEN

Ellie asked Bill to drop her off at the church and thanked him for taking her out. He was anxious to get back home to put his new plants in, so didn't make a fuss. They'd go out for a meal later that week, he said.

The Endene Close development was coming along. Roy was there, checking that the plasterers had finished, and chivvying the kitchen fitments into place. He was talking on his mobile, jotting down notes on a clipboard. Busy, busy. He waved at Ellie but went on talking on the phone, so she stood back to imagine how the planting would look when completed in a few days' time, and then went on her way to Aunt Drusilla's.

Rose was out shopping but Aunt Drusilla was very much in evidence, sitting in the best chair in Roy's new living room and scolding a television man for not having arrived when he'd said he would.

Ellie kissed Aunt Drusilla and obediently supplied her with a nice cup of tea, while wondering how soon Roy would find it irksome to live under his mother's eye.

'You're hovering, dear,' said Miss Quicke. 'Sit down where I can see you and tell me what you've been up to. Rose tried to ring you this morning but got no reply. Little though she deserves it, I would like to be kept informed if my great-niece has been taken ill.'

Aunt Drusilla ignored the television man, who was working frantically to adjust the set.

Ellie decided to ignore him, too. 'She had a miscarriage. Just over three months.'

The television man hunched himself over, applying himself to his controls. Embarrassed.

Miss Quicke frowned slightly. 'Not Stewart's, I assume?'

Ellie shook her head. 'A lot's been happening. Do you want a report now?'

She glanced meaningfully at the television man, whose ears had turned scarlet.

'If you please,' said Miss Quicke.

Ellie reported. In detail. Miss Quicke listened. So did the television man.

At the end, Miss Quicke enquired whether Diana would now get back with Derek. Ellie shrugged. She didn't know.

'Or with Stewart?'

'I doubt if he'd want to. And then, there's Maria.'

'Hmm. I believe it would be better for the child to stay with his father.'

The television man made an inarticulate sound, and gathered his tools together. Miss Quicke ignored him.

Ellie said, 'Suppose Maria's pregnant . . . ?'

The television man scrambled to his feet, presented Miss Quicke with a chit to sign, said everything was in order now and that it had been as good as a soap opera. And fled.

Ellie waited on the older woman's reactions, but Miss Quicke was in no hurry to reveal her thoughts. Ellie washed up the cups they'd used and wiped off the dirty marks the television man had left on the wall and the control knobs.

Miss Quicke asked, 'What did you think of the way Diana's got the flats done up?'

'Not my taste, but the young professionals seemed to like it. I don't think she'll have any difficulty selling them.'

'So I was wrong about that.'

'No,' said Ellie. 'You were right. You aren't in that market.'

'Perhaps I ought to be. I don't like missing out . . . but I don't like dealing with rude children who try to cheat me, either.'

'Neither do I,' said Ellie. 'I don't think she's really aware of how awful she sounds, or that cheating rebounds on you. It's as if her ability to assess what impact she has on other people never really developed.'

Miss Quicke spurted into a coarse laugh. 'Except with men of a certain type.'

She got to her feet, leaning on her stick. 'Well, it's all in the genes. I was just like her at her age. Which doesn't mean I'm going to put up with the way she carries on now. I'm still backing Stewart and Maria to keep little Frank.'

Ellie held the door open for her aunt. 'I'm not sure how I'm going to act. I suppose it depends on whether or not Diana gets back together with Derek.'

They walked across the courtyard but instead of going into the big house, Miss Quicke led the way round to the back garden, and seated herself on a bench in the sun. 'I never sat out here till Rose showed me how pleasant it could be.'

She patted the seat at her side. 'Sit down, Ellie. Rose tells me there were all sorts of rumours going round at church yesterday, about my nephew Frank. I shouldn't be the last to hear about this from you.'

Ellie shook her head in frustration. 'It's a something and a nothing. Nothing you can get hold of. No one really believes it, but it's something for everyone to talk about. I don't know how the rumour started, and the police haven't been to see me about it so presumably they don't think it's important, either.'

'It's a nonsense,' said Miss Quicke. 'Having it off with someone of the opposite sex outside marriage may be in the genes, but it seemed to have missed my nephew completely. Our own father had it, more's the pity, for it caused my poor mother no end of worry. I had it. Diana obviously has it. But

I often wondered if Frank was undersexed. He never took any interest in girls while he was growing up, though I was on the lookout for it, be sure of that. He took after my brother in that. Only ever looked at you, married you and was faithful. I used to think he missed out on a lot of fun that way, but there . . . it takes all sorts.'

'Er, yes. Bill said that, too. I never gave it a thought till the rumour started and then I did get worried for a bit, wondering if I simply hadn't noticed him straying, perhaps when I was off-colour for so long.'

'His fault. He should have let you recover from having Diana before he started in on you again.'

'The doctor said it was all right to—'

'Doctors! I said you were anaemic at the time, didn't I? But no one listens to me. You needed an iron tonic and separate beds for a few months.'

'Yes. Well. It was all a long time ago.'

'You let him have his own way too much.'

Ellie closed her eyes and leaned back, allowing the sunshine to relax her. Beside her, Aunt Drusilla sat upright, hands folded on her stick, feet planted firmly on the ground.

At the back of Ellie's mind she heard Frank's voice, urging her to be co-operative, saying didn't she love him anymore, couldn't she see what it was doing to him when she just lay there like a sack, come on, girl! Come on!

Aunt Drusilla had been wrong about Frank being undersexed. He hadn't been lacking in that direction with her. If he'd been a little less keen on it, perhaps she wouldn't have found sex a burden after Diana was born, instead of a pleasure.

If he'd not been so insistent, she might have been better able to cope with all those pregnancies, all ending in disaster. Although things had been better for her and for him after the hysterectomy.

Looking back on those years hurt. She could hardly remember any significant events, any detail from those years. She'd gone from being a cheerful little thing, ready for love, to an anxious thirty-year-old, desperately trying to please her husband and daughter and keep her job . . . because they'd needed her salary in those days.

Anxiety. Yes, that was the right word for those years. Hoping against hope each month that this time she'd be able to carry the baby to term.

'Silly Mummy's crying again!' Diana, in a strop because her mother couldn't drag herself off her bed to take her to some party or other.

Perhaps Diana would realize now what it meant to have a miscarriage. Or two. Or five. And perhaps not. Diana was too self-centred to learn from other people's mistakes.

She slipped into prayer. 'What a beautiful day, Lord. Thank you for it. For the sunshine which warms me and banishes unpleasant thoughts. For the flowers. For Rose's gifts of homemaking and love. For Aunt Drusilla's robust attitude to life. I ought to be grateful for all the blessings you have given me. I am grateful. Really I am. Please remind me to be grateful, when little things go wrong. And please help me to say the right thing to Diana, and Stewart and Maria. I don't know what's best for little Frank, but you do.'

* * *

The surgeon rang on time. The news was bad. 'You say the man's dead? He can't be! Who told you?'

The businessman said, 'They were all talking about it in the paper shop in the Avenue. There was this big woman, something to do with the church, said she was a great friend of the widow's and how shocked they'd all been to hear he'd been accused of murder. Someone said something about there being no smoke without a fire, but no one else would have it. They said it was just like the police to get the wrong end of the stick. They seem to like the little widow. They called her "a nice little thing".'

'The man can't be dead. He wasn't that old!'

'Cancer, last year, they said. Very sudden.'

'You should have known!'

The businessman defended himself. 'Easy for you to say. Listen, it doesn't matter, does it? If he's dead and the police blame him for it, then that's all right, isn't it? No one will look at us. No one knows about us. We took a risk sending that email, but it's paid off, hasn't it? The case is closed and we're in the clear.'

'We don't know that the case is closed. We can't risk it. You'd better keep watch, see if the police take any further action. Suppose . . . suppose we put it on the widow, say she was jealous of her husband's interest in the girl, and that's why she killed her?'

'That's ridiculous!'

'It might work. It just might. Use a computer at a different library this time. Somewhere so large and busy no one will notice you. Send an email accusing her this time. We can't risk them looking for us. For Father. How is he, anyway?'

'He had a bad night, but seems easier this morning. I told him there was nothing to worry about.'

'You do as I say, and there won't be.'

* * *

Ellie walked back home through the late afternoon's sunshine. Really it was warm enough to avoid the sunny side of the road and walk in the shadows. She bought some fish for her supper and some French beans to go with it. She also bought some more freshly ground coffee for those who would be working in the church garden the following morning. She decided she wouldn't think about anything worrying, but concentrate on the beauty of the tobacco plants in a neighbour's garden, and how sweetly they scented the air as she passed.

There was an old-fashioned double rose in a garden on the corner of her road. She paused to sniff at one of the blooms, as she did every time she passed that way.

And there outside her house was DI Willis, sitting alone in an unmarked car, waiting for her. The policewoman got out, and stood waiting for Ellie to arrive. Both women stiffened in readiness for the encounter.

Ellie thought of asking what the woman wanted, but really she knew so she said nothing but gestured her inside.

DI Willis followed Ellie as she picked up the post — mostly bills — and went into the kitchen. Ellie fed Midge and stowed her purchases in the fridge.

Ellie put the kettle on. 'Tea or coffee?'

'Either. Whichever you're having.' The woman seemed distracted, the side of her face swollen. Toothache?

Ellie made a pot of tea, investigated the biscuit tin, which contained more than it had done when Tod had been a frequent visitor. She poured tea out into a couple of mugs and took them through into the sitting room. She eased off her shoes and leaned back.

DI Willis couldn't relax that much. 'I expect you know why I've come.' She sipped her tea, and put it down. If she did have toothache, the tea was probably too hot for her.

Ellie shrugged. 'I heard a rumour at church. I don't suppose you took it any more seriously than I did.'

'Depends what you heard.'

'What I'd like to know is who started the rumour?'

'If we knew that . . . ! It was on an email sent to the station. You must see that we had to follow it up.' She scrabbled in her handbag for painkillers and took two, grimacing. Definitely, she'd got toothache.

'So did I,' said Ellie. 'I enquired within myself and I asked other people who'd known my husband longer than me. Result: no, he didn't play around.'

'We did check, and that's the conclusion we came to, as well.'

Ellie raised her eyebrows. 'As I've now destroyed his reputation by asking all his friends, everyone will say the wife's the last to know, and that he must have been playing around for the rumour to have started.'

'I know,' said DI Willis, apologetically. 'But you must see we had to check.'

'I suppose so. And you're here now because . . . ?'

'You and I've never really hit it off, have we? Which is a pity, because I'm convinced that you're the key to this mystery. Or rather, that your memory contains the key.'

'I've told you all I know.'

'So you say. For your information, we've checked out your story about the Chaters, the people who went to Spain. You were right. He did die out there, and his widow married again. Dead end.'

'And the Shrieker with her noisy kids?'

'Social services took the children into care. She gets reasonable access and there is some hope they will be reunited as a family in the near future. I went to see her today, and she's certainly still alive and kicking. She blames you for setting the police on to her, by the way.'

'She would. In any case, the body had been in the ground far too long to belong to any of the families who lived here recently. So what's left? The woman who went to Australia or New Zealand?'

'We've traced her, too. You were right to be concerned. She never left England. The man took the money from the sale of the house and disappeared on the eve of their departure. She's now living in digs in Brighton and working in a restaurant. Someone's going down to see her tomorrow. You're quite right. She's not the one. So we do have to go further back.'

'The Bosnians?'

'Too recent, and you know it. Ellie, we've got the names of those who lived here before the Brownings. You talked about an elderly couple. You said first he died, and then she did. Did they have any family? Children? Grandchildren?'

Ellie's mind swam back through the years to that time. Frank shouting at her, Diana shouting at her. Constant tiredness. Work, work, work. Diana wanting this and that . . . Frank wanting sex, which she couldn't have cared less about at that time. No more miscarriages, though. At least the hysterectomy had put an end to that, although she had always regretted it, wondered if the doctors couldn't have found some way to let her carry her babies to term.

The DI tapped on the table. 'Come on, Ellie!'

Ellie had had enough. She slipped her shoes back on and, plucking the mug out of the DI's grasp, took it out to the kitchen and tipped it down the sink. She then went to the hall and opened the front door.

'I think you'd better leave.'

'What?' The DI was first amazed, then annoyed. And finally, she turned conciliatory.

'Look, I wanted to do this quietly, but I could ask you to come down to the station . . .'

'On what grounds? Just go.'

The DI flushed an unbecoming red, then went pale. The effect against her dyed hair was not pleasant. 'Look, I'm sorry if I . . . you must see that . . .' She started again. 'All right. Let's start again. I know you think this is an imposition, but this is what police work is all about. I have to ask questions. A young girl was murdered out there. We don't know who she was or where she came from. Some mother is probably still waiting for her daughter to return. Grieving for her. Hundreds of young girls go missing every year and some of them turn up in worse condition than that poor girl out there. I want to know — I need to know who that girl was. It's not only my job, you understand. It's a compulsion.'

Ellie thought about a mother waiting to hear from a lost daughter. She wondered how she'd have felt if it had been Diana who'd gone missing. Yes, she'd have grieved. Every knock on the door might bring news. Every letter that dropped into the letterbox. Would that grieving have faded over this length of time? Perhaps. Perhaps not. Particularly if the girl had been an only child.

'Do you know yet how she died?'

'We can't be sure, but . . . some kind of garrotte, they think. That's an educated guess. The skull wasn't fractured. There was no knife left in the body. The bones of the neck might have been disarranged when it was unearthed. We really don't know, and that's the truth. So, please will you do what you can to help us?' The woman found it hard to plead.

Ellie gave her credit for the effort. She forced her mind to go back in time. Certain images popped up: Diana screaming for attention, the shoplifting, Frank's fury, the consternation in the office when she'd had to take time off yet again, the doctor saying, 'I'm so sorry, Mrs Quicke, but . . .'

She pushed those memories aside. The DI was right. They had to trace the girl and if she, Ellie Quicke, could help, then she must do so.

She could do it, if she put her mind to it.

Right, the elderly couple. Good neighbours, except that they hadn't had the time to deal with a garden running to ruin. Quietly spoken, gently fading like sepia photographs. She led the way back to the sitting room. 'Ten minutes, then. And you will not call me by my Christian name again. Understood?'

She resumed her seat, trying to remember.

'Did the old people have children? Yes, I think so. A son, definitely. I think he went to live in Scotland. A daughter . . . ? A daughter and son-in-law, who lived . . . not that far away. The old people's name was . . . ?'

'Cullen,' said the DI.

'Ah, yes. I'd forgotten. I can't remember their daughter's married name. The old folk had been living in a much bigger house in the Acton area, but when he retired — no, I don't think I ever knew what he did — they downsized and moved here.

'She was younger, still working in the pharmacy in the Avenue then, an old-fashioned shop with old-fashioned remedies. The sort of place where you go in and say you think you've got a cold coming and what would they recommend? I think it even still had those pretty jars with coloured liquids in them in the window. They sold herbal remedies and corn plasters and knew everyone. It was old-fashioned, even then. The place was a hairdresser's after that, and now it's the Sunflower Café, where I often go for a mid-morning cuppa or a meal with a friend.

'Mr Cullen was always frail, looked as if he'd go down with something in the next cold snap. She was a bustler. Always busy. Doted on her grandchildren, spoiled them, talked a lot about the son who rarely came to visit. She couldn't abide her daughter. Was always criticizing her.'

'Go on,' said DI Willis, making notes. 'This is just what we need to know.'

'There'd never been much of Mr Cullen to start with, but after he moved here he seemed not to know what to do with himself. He joined the bowls club in the park. I think he was secretary for a time. I used to see him going out all dressed in his whites, carrying his bag of bowls. But he gradually faded away, and died a couple of winters after they came. Pneumonia, heart? Something like that.

'She went on bustling about. I thought she'd go on for ever, but she slipped on a patch of ice in the road one morning about a year later, and broke her leg. She was in hospital for a long time and when she came out, I hardly recognized her. She'd shrunk, you know? And walked carefully, with a Zimmer frame.

'Her daughter lived not far away. I know that, because she used to walk over to see her mother. The daughter worked full-time. Now, where . . . ?' She pondered, shook her head. 'No, I don't know where she worked. Maybe I never heard. There were grandchildren, two girls, both great big lumps, neither of them very kind to their poor old gran. That's what old Mrs Cullen used to call herself. "Poor old Gran".

'Her daughter forbade her to go out of the house in the winter, in case she fell again. Either the daughter or one of the grandchildren used to come round every day to see if the old dear were all right, bring her food, that sort of thing. But there was nothing for the old lady to live for really. I mean, she'd worked all her life, and had had other people depending on her. And then . . . woof! She was the dependent one. She didn't like it one little bit. She lasted maybe one year, maybe eighteen months after her husband. Then she went the same way. Not pneumonia, no. She wasn't hospitalized. I think she just died in her sleep.'

'Which is when Greg and Lilian Browning came in — the man who got cancer and had to wear a wig and died?'

'That's right. I really don't think either of the grandchildren can be your corpse in the garden. Big, strapping girls. Besides, if one of them had gone missing, there'd have been a manhunt to end all manhunts.'

'I agree. So before the Cullens . . . ?'

Ellie sighed. 'A couple with two children, both boys. It can't be them.'

DI Willis stopped making notes, leaned back and looked at Ellie. 'Tell us about them. Come on, Ellie, you can do it, I know you can!'

'You call me "Ellie" again and I won't be answerable for the consequences. Your ten minutes are up and I've had enough. So if you don't mind . . . ?'

'We'll need more.' But the woman did rise to her feet. 'I'll have to come back again.'

Ellie said, 'Is that a threat?'

DI Willis didn't answer.

CHAPTER TWELVE

It was getting late. Ellie listened to the messages which had been left on the answerphone. Two were from Diana, asking plaintively where her mother was. One from dear Tum-Tum at the church, asking if Ellie were all right, and did she want to cancel giving everyone coffee after their gardening at church tomorrow?

One message was from Stewart, asking if Ellie would like to babysit on Thursday, as he and Maria had to go out. One from Roy, wondering if she'd like supper with him on Thursday, and asking when the plants for the gardens at the new development would be put in. Everything was for Thursday evening, when the Women's Guild had an invited speaker at the church. Ellie had been looking forward to that.

It annoyed her that she'd nothing else in her diary all week, and now there were three things on the Thursday. Oh, and she supposed she'd have to make time to go out with Bill, too.

She scolded herself. How come she'd got so spoiled that she resented being asked out by two pleasant men? She decided it was she herself who was at fault, rather than them. All this looking back over her own marriage had made her wary of any more involvement with the opposite sex.

She rang Diana, and got an earful of complaints. Why hadn't Ellie been round to see her that day? Ellie could at least have rung to see if her only daughter were all right, and not fainting away on the floor. Ellie could have helped by taking Diana to the doctor's, though, as it happened, they hadn't got a slot for her and she'd had to go down to Accident and Emergency at Ealing Hospital, and they'd wanted to keep her in, but of course Diana hadn't agreed to that. And the least Ellie could do was to bring her round some nicely cooked supper. Oh, and while she was at it, Diana was out of butter and . . . oh, yes, some bread. And perhaps some of that thinly sliced ham from the deli . . .

Ellie listened with part of her mind on the mystery of the girl in the garden. Now that DI Willis had pointed out the agony of a mother not knowing what had happened to her daughter, Ellie found it hard to put it out of her mind.

She pulled herself back to the present. There would be no fresh bread left in the bakery at this time of day, but she promised Diana she would do what she could. She reminded Diana that Monday evening was choir practice but she'd pop in to see her after that. Predictably, Diana exploded. Couldn't her mother cancel choir practice for once?

'No, I couldn't. I'll be round after that.' She put the phone down. Midge was sitting on the hall chair. Her hand found his head and stroked it. He liked that. Within reason. Presently he nudged her hand away and leaped down to make for the kitchen. She fed him and then went out into the garden, secateurs and trug in hand, for half an hour of self-indulgence.

The early evening was a wonderful time in the garden. She deadheaded a prolific Compassion rose near the house, and went down the herbaceous border, tidying up, snipping deadheads here and there, filling the trug and emptying it into the big compost bin by the shed at the bottom of the garden.

Tod and his friend went past, and waved to her. She watched them out of sight, wondering what her life would have been like if just one of those miscarriages had failed to happen, wondering if she'd have produced another child as demanding as Diana, or whether he or she would have been as lively and good-tempered as Tod.

Not that Tod was perfect, of course. He'd taken advantage of her just as much, at times, as Diana had done. The difference was that Tod had been generous in his affection in return for the little she'd been able to do for him.

A bleak thought: was little Frank going to be as self-centred as his mother, demanding everything and returning nothing?

Had it been her fault that Diana had turned out this way?

Or indeed that Frank had become a bit of a domestic tyrant?

She went down into the alley and turned left to stand at the bottom of Kate's garden. The tape was still there but there was no policeman on duty and no tent. The skip had been removed, as had the earthmover. The earth had been scraped bare of vegetation and reminded her unpleasantly of pictures she'd seen of no-man's-land in Flanders during the First World War. All bumps and craters and nothing green in sight.

Ah, a couple of nettles had survived over there, and at her feet was a root of creeping buttercup, dratted thing. But it was good to see that life survived, somehow, even in that desolation. Her plans for the garden makeover lay in a drawer in the study, and there, presumably, they'd stay. If she were Kate and Armand, she wouldn't want to stay in that house, knowing what had happened here.

She shook these thoughts away and took off for the Avenue with a list of things Diana wanted. The baker had a couple of rather tired-looking loaves left. She bought one. Some flowers for the flat to cheer Diana up. Ham and a selection of the salads Diana liked from the deli. A selection of frozen meals from the old-fashioned grocery, and some milk, of course.

This was the place where she'd once seen the assistant chatting in a foreign language to one of the Bosnians. For once the shop was empty, and Ellie took advantage of the fact to talk to the assistant. 'Another For Sale sign going up in our road. People never seem to stay long nowadays, do they?'

The assistant shook her head. 'Some do. Some don't. It's sad to see the old people losing their grip, going into a home.'

'Yes, but they're still in the community. We can still go to visit them. I worry sometimes about the refugees. They seem to get moved around so much. There were some living next to me for a while.'

The assistant nodded. 'From my country, yes. They had relatives in my home town. I'd almost forgotten my own language, think of it! But they were happy to move to a bigger house, which allowed them to take in the old people. At least they do look after their old folk, not like us, shoving them into homes all the time.' She rang up the total.

Ellie fumbled in her purse. 'Was that why they moved? I did wonder. Only, not being able to talk to them . . .'

'The children learn quickly and translate for them. The men find it more difficult, they are professional men in their own country, and now . . .' She shrugged. 'But the old people are happier, sitting in their little huts on the allotment . . .'

'Allotment?' There were some allotments on the other side of the park, but Ellie hadn't been that way for ages.

'There is this woman, very nice, helps those who want to, to get an allotment. The grandparents were usually farmers. So the whole family, or maybe two families together, go down to clear an allotment, all working together. They build a little hut, and the grandparents can sit outside in the sun and cook their meals, just as if they were back in the old country. Then they can grow the things they like to eat. It is a good way, yes?'

Ellie handed over a couple of notes. 'So they are all happy and well? I'm glad. However many of them were there in that house next to us? I was never quite sure.'

The assistant smiled. 'Plenty. All healthy except for one grandma who has bad eyesight, but they look after her well.'

'Do you think they'll ever go back to their own country?'

'This is their country now. I never think of going back, not since my parents died and my sister came over here too.'

Another customer was now waiting to be served, so Ellie had to move on.

At least she'd cleared that point up. None of the Bosnians had gone missing. Not that she'd really thought it had been one of them.

* * *

The man knew exactly what to do this time. He chose a different library, one even further away from his home. He gave a different false name and address, and took his place at one of a row of identical computers. Because of the nature of his business interests, he'd the email addresses of many people in his notepad. It was even easier to send a message to the police a second time.

He'd thought about the words to use already. He tapped them in, sent the email and surrendered his seat within ten minutes of entering the library.

No one took the slightest notice of him.

Why should they?

He walked back to the side street where he'd left the Mercedes, and used his mobile to ring his wife. He was anxious, very anxious about his father, but what he'd just done would point the police in a new direction. His brother had been right. They couldn't risk anyone connecting them with the girl.

On the way home, he'd stop at the new development on the Green, to monitor the comings and goings at the place where they'd buried her.

* * *

Monday evening was choir practice, and Ellie had to face the members of the Inquisition — otherwise known as the choir — at church before she could go to Diana's. Naturally they all wanted to know how Diana was, and avoided the subject of the police enquiries about Ellie's husband. Though that leaked out around the corners of their speech, so to speak.

Had Diana really had a miscarriage, had she had to go to hospital? What a terrible thing. And of course they didn't believe that stupid rumour about dear Frank; really, what the police were coming to, they didn't know! They'd called just at the most inconvenient moment, just as she was turning out the sitting room . . . when she'd just sat down for coffee . . . just as she was about to go out to collect her daughter from school . . . and so on.

The kinder members of the choir expressed their condolences that Ellie had lost another grandchild, and assured her they'd told the police there was nothing in the stories about Frank.

The less kind exchanged catty remarks about Diana to one another, reported what they'd said to the police about Frank, and avoided eye contact with Ellie.

In some ways, Ellie agreed with the catty ones. About Diana, anyway. On the whole, the choir was composed of people who valued children and stable family relationships. Even the young ones did. They knew that Diana had broken her marriage vows — vows made in that very church not so many years ago. Some of the older ones even used the word 'adultery', which was not a word that tripped off people's lips easily today.

There was a slight air of *Well, it's better she lost the baby than had an abortion.* And an almost equally strong, *Ellie ought to have made sure her mobile was switched off and didn't disrupt the service.* With both of which sentiments Ellie agreed.

There was also an undercurrent of, *Well, I never actually caught her husband doing anything he shouldn't, but he did used to look at my legs in a way that made me most uncomfortable!* Ellie set her jaw and said to herself, *He looked but didn't touch.* Several times.

She thanked Mrs Dawes and the alto who'd volunteered to take on Ellie's duties making coffee the previous day, and they both said, 'Think nothing of it.'

It was coming up to Harvest Festival time, so there were some new hymns to learn and some old ones to resurrect. When the rehearsal was over — and Ellie was hard put to it to concentrate, with everything that was going on — Mrs Dawes suggested she see Ellie back home. It was clear to Ellie that this meant Mrs Dawes needed paying in information for her kindness to Ellie. But Ellie had promised Diana she would deliver her some groceries, so she made her excuses, suggesting that Mrs Dawes call in after the gardening session in the church grounds tomorrow, and perhaps have a sandwich lunch with her?

To which Mrs Dawes agreed, while leaving Ellie with the impression that she'd somehow not played fair.

* * *

After an evening spent administering to Diana and listening patiently to her grumbles, Tuesday morning was bound to be a breath of fresh air in every sense of the word. Tuesday morning was gardening-at-the-church time, when whoever happened to be available would turn up to mow the grass, tend the herbaceous borders which Turn-Turn had created, and gently chatter the morning away.

At twelve, everyone would down tools and make their way to Ellie's for some good coffee and biscuits. This kept the area around the church looking good, kept neighbours in touch with one another — finding out who was poorly, who needed a visit, who needed cheering up — and it gave people a chance to chat to Tum-Tum about their problems if they wished to do so.

Mrs Dawes usually brought her collapsible stool and sat, directing operations. She was always the first to come and the last to leave.

Ellie's speciality was deadheading and light pruning, so she'd brought her secateurs and trug. The morning was overcast and rather humid for the time of the year, so she wasn't surprised to find more people standing and chatting to one another than actually getting down to the job in hand. That didn't matter. If one person had to leave after half an hour, someone else would probably finish their weeding or whatever.

It was unusual to have someone from outside the area join them. Even more unusual when he started working next to Ellie.

'Constable Honey? Is that right?' Ellie was surprised. He was in casual gear, looking quite at home as he dealt with a nasty piece of couch grass which had got itself tangled up with a potentilla. 'What are you doing here?'

He grinned. 'Honeywell's the name, actually. Day off. Well, actually, the boss has got an abscess and is spending the morning at the dentist's, waiting for a cancellation, and she asked me to keep an eye on you. Said you needed to be addressed as Madam, and if I had ever learned any Ps and Qs from my granny, I should brush them up before I saw you.'

Ellie laughed. He really was a most engaging young man. 'I suppose I was a bit sharp with her, but sometimes . . . no, I won't say it.'

Now it was his turn to laugh. It seemed they shared a similar opinion of DI Willis.

'I think you're something of a rogue,' said Ellie, amused. Also thinking that this was a very clever young man, who could probably wheedle his way into the graces of anyone foolish enough to take him at face value.

He stood, stretching. 'Aaaah. My back's not what it was. The wife's always telling me to bend my knees, rather than bend right over. She's a physio.'

Ellie guessed he'd now tell her all about his family in order to put her at her ease and convince her she could trust him.

'Shall I dump those for you?' he asked, taking her trug. 'My youngest daughter can't be doing with gardening. All for football. But the eldest wants to know all about it. Gone Green, she has.'

Ellie awarded herself a bonus point. 'I've got the picture. You're a settled family man and understand how an ancient woman like myself likes to be treated.'

He flicked her a conspiratorial smile. 'Not so ancient. And still plucking heart strings, or so I've heard.'

She revised her opinion yet again. This was an *extremely* clever young man. 'Did DI Willis send you to mend fences with me?'

'Partly. May I treat you to a coffee in the Avenue?'

'Unfortunately, no. I hold open house for the gardeners on Tuesday mornings. But if you like to come across with me now, I can get the kettle on and we can have a chat before the others join us.'

As soon as he'd got himself seated in the big armchair — the one that had once been her husband's favourite — Midge leaped on to his lap. Midge was supposed to be a good judge of character. Hmmm.

He'd taken the room in at a glance. 'Nice,' he said. 'A proper home. Kids' toys, library books, daily papers, telly and radio . . . but you prefer plants to people, I think.'

She blinked. She'd never thought of comparing them. Surely she didn't, did she? Though it was true that she often sought consolation by working in the garden, rather than ringing up a friend for a chat. What a very acute young man this young man was turning out to be.

She handed him a mug of coffee. 'Flattery will get you some of the way. Truth might get you what you want.'

'Right. Yes.' He put his cup down. His face sharpened, letting his keen intelligence show. 'I'm going to tell you a couple of things we haven't released to the press, for obvious reasons. You can keep your mouth shut, can't you? Yes. Now, this body. Very odd. No clothing at all. Might have decomposed, but no jewellery, no purse, no belt, no handbag, no shoes. There's always something to be found, no matter how far decomposition has advanced. Some fragments of metal from a belt or a purse, usually. Nothing. So, the body had been stripped. That's the first odd thing.'

He held up two fingers. 'Second odd thing. You've been most helpful with your thumbnail sketches of all the people who've lived next door. We've been checking them all out and everybody's accounted for. Which means that the girl didn't live next door but was dumped there after she was killed.

'Three. We widened the search to look through the files of all the teenage girls who went missing about that time. No one of her description was ever reported missing. We've looked at hundreds of photos, descriptions, addresses, and though there's plenty of teenage girls go missing every year, we haven't been able to match this one up with a name . . . and no, I won't tell you why we're so sure about that, but take it from me, this girl's not been reported missing. She's not only a Jane Doe; she's dropped from another planet.'

'A student from abroad?'

'There weren't so many twenty years ago, but yes, we're working on that line too. In fact, if we can't get an ID soon, that's the way her file will be shelved.'

'Which means her mother will never know what happened to her.'

'True. So I suggested tackling it from a different angle. Why was the girl dumped in the garden next door? What made it so attractive to the murderer?'

Ellie nodded. 'The garden was neglected. They thought no one would notice if they put the body there.'

'Right. It's not far off a main road. It's secluded. Someone could have parked their car by the church or even taken it into the alley, with a bit of a squeeze, and left the body in the first neglected garden they came to.'

She shivered. 'That's horrible, but yes, it makes sense. The next rainfall washed earth down the slope over her, and gradually over the years she got buried deeper and deeper? Oh. No. That can't be how it happened. She'd been properly buried, hadn't she?'

He held up his fourth finger. 'As you say, she'd been properly buried. So where did the tools come from to bury her, eh?'

Ellie's head turned to the garden. 'From our garden shed?' They went to look out of the conservatory, down the garden to where the shed stood, tucked into the corner by the gate to the alley.

He leaned against the window. 'I've been walking up and down that alley and time and again I've stopped by your garden, admired the flowers and looked at the shed. It's within touching distance from the alley. I tested your garden gate. It isn't locked.'

'No. We put a padlock on it when we first came, to stop Diana straying out into the alley when she was a toddler, but once she could climb over . . .' Ellie shrugged. 'I suppose I ought to get a padlock put on it now for security reasons, but it's convenient for neighbours to drop in that way.'

'There's a padlock on the door of the shed now. Quite a new one. Solid. Do you always lock up?'

'Mostly, yes. I don't always remember, but I do try to lock it at night.'

'And in the past?'

'In the past. No. That shed's newish. When we first came, there was a ramshackle old box of a shed there, falling apart. We didn't bother to lock it, because the door wouldn't close properly and there wasn't really anything to steal. A push mower, a spade and fork, lots of old pots, cobwebs.'

'Can you remember when you replaced the shed?' He was carefully not looking at her, but she could feel the tension in him.

She could see the significance of his question, and where it might be leading her. 'The old shed burned down while we were at the seaside one summer holiday. We assumed it was a tramp, taking shelter. You're saying that . . .'

'Someone might have used your tools to bury the girl and then set light to the shed to hide any traces.'

'A tramp?' she said, sitting down rather suddenly. 'I thought the girl might have been on the streets, right at the beginning. Someone who'd run away from home and was living rough.'

'In which case, she'd have been burned to death in the shed, not buried in next door's garden. She wasn't buried in your garden, because it's open to the skies, carefully tended and full of flowers. Nobody could dig a grave in your garden without it being spotted straight away. She was buried next door, where she wouldn't easily be found, which means someone didn't want her body found.'

Oh. This boy was really very bright.

He said, 'Now, can you remember which year the shed burned down?'

She looked away from him. She could and she couldn't. She didn't want to think about that time . . . that terrible time, the worst time of her life . . . the doctor saying, 'I'm so sorry.' And Diana . . . well, the police hadn't been called in, although the other parents had wanted to . . .

She switched her mind away. 'I'm not sure. The years run into one another after a while. It may have been Diana's last year at primary school.'

'We can probably get the dates from your insurance company. You were insured, weren't you? You did claim for the loss of the hut?'

'I'm not sure. We probably didn't bother. I mean, it was such an old wreck. Anyway, Frank, my husband, would have seen to all that.'

He said, 'What are you hiding?'

She jumped. 'Nothing!' He was altogether too bright, this lad. 'Look,' she said, turning into the kitchen. 'They're coming back up from the church. Do you want to stay, or have you something better to do?'

'I'll go now. Come back later. Because, you see, Mrs Quicke, there's one more odd thing about this case. How did the killer know about that neglected garden? How did he know where to leave the body and where to find the tools to bury it? How does the killer know your name?'

'He doesn't. He can't. You said yourself the girl had nothing to do with this area.'

'No, that's not what I said, and you know it. I'll come back later, shall I?'

He went out of the front door as the others piled in through the back. Then it was all hustle and bustle and overloud voices as the gardening party arrived for their coffee and chat.

Mrs Dawes seated herself in the big armchair while Tum-Tum made himself useful pouring out coffee and handing biscuits. Ellie dropped a spoon on the floor, picked it up and dropped it again.

'Not like you, Ellie,' said Tum-Tum. He followed her out to the kitchen. 'Are you all right? Shall I pop back for a bit this afternoon?'

'Mrs Dawes is staying on to hear all about the body in the garden. Payment for doing coffee on Sunday for me.'

He nodded and didn't press the point. She wanted to burst into tears and throw herself on his manly chest. She was surprised how much she wanted it. Ridiculous! She was acting like any woman in trouble, flinging herself at the nearest man. She despised such women even though she understood them. She'd been one of them herself before Frank died. The number of times she'd said, 'I'll have to ask my husband about that!' It made her cringe to think of it.

She didn't feel like that with Roy or with Bill. She only felt like that with Tum-Tum because he was a man of the cloth and had a warm, soothing presence and broad shoulders and didn't want either to take advantage of her or marry her.

She found her handkerchief, blew her nose and attended to her guest's wants.

They were arguing, of course, about whether they should cut the flowers in the herbaceous border to decorate the church for Harvest Festival, or whether they should leave them there, to add to the beauty of the church on the day.

Mrs Dawes was all in favour of cutting them. Ellie wasn't. Amiable argument followed, with Tum-Tum taking no part in it, but laughing when anyone made a particularly telling point.

Ellie was very fond of Tum-Tum, but looking at his rounded body across the room, she wondered at her momentary desire to feel his arms go around her. He was — sigh — no one's idea of a perfect partner.

Mrs Dawes stayed on after the others made their excuses and left. Ellie brought out the sherry bottle, Mrs Dawes' usual tipple.

'Now, tell me All!'

Ellie mentally expunged various aspects of the situation from her mind. The policeman would know who'd talked within hours if Mrs Dawes got hold of one or two juicy items. But there was still enough for Mrs Dawes to say, 'Gracious me!' several times. She wondered aloud when they'd all be able to leave the house again without worrying about being mugged. Though what the murder had to do with Mrs Dawes' chances of being mugged, Ellie really didn't know.

Mrs Dawes was a shrewd lady, even if her tongue was sometimes hinged in the middle. When Ellie had finished, she said, 'I've been wondering who it might be, too. Like you, I couldn't think of any young or even youngish girl living in that house. I was saying to my friends . . .'

Ellie had a mental image of Mrs Dawes and her two friends with their heads close together, exchanging gossip.

'. . . that between us we should be able to remember who lived there. Two of us were born here I won't say how many years ago, and my friend from the next road came here in '65. We've seen some changes, I can tell you. Years ago the school here wasn't very good and you hardly saw any young families around. Nowadays the school's top of all these league tables they keep talking about in the papers, and there's nothing but young families coming in to buy our houses and put up loft extensions and build out their kitchens at the back.'

Ellie smiled, and nodded. She'd noticed the change herself. If ever Kate and Armand got down to having a family, they'd be typical of the people who'd bought into the neighbourhood.

Mrs Dawes leaned across to test the soil in a pot in the conservatory. The day had clouded over and, with the sun veiled, it wasn't too hot to sit there, as it usually was in the afternoons. 'That's a pretty geranium, Ellie. You must give me a cutting. And of the tibouchina, too. I've got a sheltered spot where it could stay through the winter, and it does give colour in late autumn when everything else is dying down.'

Ellie nodded.

Mrs Dawes patted her improbably jet-black hair. 'We came to the conclusion that the girl was a visitor to the Cullens'. You remember? The old couple who retired here, she worked in the pharmacy in the Avenue, nice enough woman. Their grandchildren were over here a lot after school, because their mother worked up at the Town Hall, didn't she? My friend remembers seeing her there one day and it gave her quite a start, because when you don't expect to see people you don't recognize them, do you?'

'I'd forgotten that. I remembered there were two grandchildren, both girls, and they used to come over . . .'

'To keep tabs on the old biddy, we reckoned. Couldn't wait to get her into a home so they could sell the house. But she clung on, didn't she? Used to come to Women's Guild sometimes, moaning, always moaning about her greedy daughter, and how she wanted to sell up and move down to a nice little flat on the front at Eastbourne . . .'

Ellie winced, remembering how Diana had always had greedy eyes on her mother's house.

'. . . but then she fell, and that was the beginning of the end. My friend used to visit her and Mrs Cullen was ever so grateful. But after a while those pesky grandchildren were always there, saying Gran didn't need anything and was too tired to see visitors. They used to boss her around, speak to her loudly as if she were deaf and dumb, you know. Needed their backsides tanning, if you ask me.'

'I'd forgotten that, too. I did go round there myself a couple of times, but . . . yes, you're quite right. I never got further than the front door.'

Mrs Dawes shook her head. 'You never know what goes on behind people's front doors, do you?'

'True.'

'And they — the grandchildren — they had friends staying over. I know because my friend called one time and there were three of them giggling in the hall, in their school uniforms, but with overnight bags. Sleeping over, they call it.'

'I didn't know about that. Although . . .' Ellie thought back. 'Come to think of it, we did used to hear a lot of pop music through the party wall. I said it was odd at the time, because you wouldn't have thought Mrs Cullen would want to have pop music on. And so loudly, too.'

'I don't say there was anything really wrong in the girls stopping over,' said Mrs Dawes, doing her best to be fair-minded. 'But what I do say is, they were taking advantage, out from under their parents' eyes. Old Mrs Cullen ought to have sold up and gone down south, spent the money on a nice nursing home place, ended her days in peace.'

Ellie sat very still. Did Mrs Dawes mean . . . ?

'I'm not hinting they did for her,' said Mrs Dawes. 'No. Maybe a sleeping tablet too many? But she did go quickly at the end, didn't she?'

'She was worn out,' said Ellie, hoping it had been true.

'Maybe so. But we talked it over, and my friend said she still got a Christmas card every year from the daughter. There was a husband once, but he disappeared when the girls were little, and she went back to calling herself Cullen, for which I can't blame her. Anyway, my friend found her last card, where she said she was selling the house and moving to sheltered accommodation, a one-bedroom flat at the back of the Avenue. She's not that old but she's had breast cancer and it's taken it out of her. So my friend gave her a ring and arranged for us to go over there this afternoon.'

CHAPTER THIRTEEN

Ellie was amused. Was Mrs Dawes fancying herself as a private detective?

Yes, Mrs Dawes was definitely enjoying herself. She was in the happy position of being able to poke and pry without being in any way emotionally involved. Ellie, however, was beginning to feel that she'd been partly to blame for all the misery that the next-door house had seen.

She ought to have realized that old Mrs Cullen was being treated unkindly — if that is what had happened. She ought to have made a greater effort to see her. She ought not to have let Frank dissuade her from making neighbourly gestures.

At that moment she almost hated her husband. Then she sighed, because, after all, that was the way he'd been brought up, to keep himself to himself, never to go into debt with money or people. Who was to say he was wrong? He hadn't actually seen anything untoward happening.

Ellie offered Mrs Dawes another drop of sherry. 'You know, Mrs Dawes, I really don't think we can interfere in a police investigation.'

'It's not interfering to visit an old friend who's asked to keep in touch, poor thing. She must be lonely nowadays, with both girls grown up and settled. Knowing them, they'll hardly bother to visit their mother. Think of this visit as an act of charity.'

'If you put it like that . . .'

Mrs Dawes drained her glass, gathered herself together, checked that her hair was smooth, that both her dangling earrings were in place, and stood up. 'I think we'd better get a cab to take us there, though. I'm not sure my legs are up to a walk.'

Ellie meekly phoned for a cab while Mrs Dawes tested the earth in every container in the conservatory and peered at the fish swimming in the lead tank. 'That plumbago needs a drop more water, dear. Don't forget to do it when you get back.'

* * *

Ms Cullen's new address was in a quiet, tree-lined road on the far side of the shops, not too far from Miss Quicke's house. It was a purpose-built block of one-bedroom and studio flats with warden accommodation attached. There was limited car parking.

Ms Cullen was a faded blonde with a deeply lined face. She recognized Ellie and Mrs Dawes at once and said how little they'd changed over the years, but they could hardly say the same of her. She had shrunk into herself, and her voice was querulous. Ellie was rather unpleasantly reminded of how old Mrs Cullen had looked in the last few months of her life.

Her daughter was not that old. Possibly sixty? But looking seventy.

Ms Cullen was a complainer. She moaned happily about her new flat — always either too hot or too cold and one of the windows wouldn't open, and she didn't know how many times she'd told them about it. She criticized the meals on wheels, which wouldn't deliver daily any more, but you had to have a freezer and a microwave and prepare them yourself, and of course nobody but nobody ever came near you at weekends. She complained about the hospital cancelling one of her appointments, and the new district nurse who came to see to the ulcer on her leg, which wouldn't heal properly, no matter what.

Mrs Dawes and Ellie had nothing to do but listen and say, 'Oh dear,' now and then. The living room was overcrowded with furniture and smelled of medication. There were no plants in evidence, but a great many souvenirs from long ago trips to Ireland and Spain.

'The girls bring them back for me, you know,' said Ms Cullen, seeing Ellie look at a Spanish flamenco dancer doll.

'How are they keeping?' asked Ellie, wondering if they'd be offered a cup of tea, and deciding that she wouldn't much want to accept, even if it were offered.

'Both married, I'm thankful to say. Well, one of them's with a partner, if you know what I mean, but they're all the same nowadays, aren't they? Need their space, as they call it. Neither of them do I see from one week's end to the other, especially since I moved here, which the doctor said I should, and it's not that far for them to come, especially as they've both got cars of their own.'

'No grandchildren yet, then?' said Mrs Dawes, bright eyes taking everything in. There were photographs in silver frames — rather tarnished silver frames — on a side table. One girl in a wedding dress with a toothy groom behind her. Another of a girl in a very low-cut dress, holding a balloon and looking rather the worse for wear. Two other photographs were of Ms Cullen's elderly parents, probably taken before he retired. Ellie leaned forward to have a closer look. Had the photograph been taken next door to her? No, probably not. The house — what she could see of it behind the couple — looked stockbrokerish.

'Too selfish to have children,' pronounced Ms Cullen. 'I've said to them, time and again, what will you do when you're old like me and have no one to look after you? But they don't listen.'

Mrs Dawes agreed. 'No, the young ones don't listen.'

Ellie hated being in this flat. There was something cloying in the air, almost stifling. All the windows were fast shut, yet it was a beautiful afternoon outside. 'It must be nice for you to know they're not far away, though. It means they can keep up with their old friends from school, people they grew up with.'

'Yes, indeed,' said Mrs Dawes, picking up the reference to the girls' old friends. 'Now, who was that girl your eldest was so friendly with? It's on the tip of my tongue, it will come to me in a minute . . .'

'I know the one you mean,' said Ms Cullen, her mouth turning down even further. 'They were great friends right up to the time my Lana settled into her job in the travel agency in the Avenue, but she doesn't give my Lana the time of day nowadays. Gone up in the world, you see. Got herself a nice little job at the BBC at White City, married a producer, no less. She invited my girl to her wedding but didn't include her husband, so naturally they didn't go. The wedding was in some posh hotel up in Town. My Lana said that it was in one of those magazines, *Hello* or *OK* or something. She promised to bring me a copy but she never did.' And her mouth turned down even more.

Mrs Dawes was enjoying herself. 'And what about that dark girl that used to hang around with your younger daughter, Trudy? Trudy went to train for something, I can't remember what . . .'

'She got her degree, the first in our family. She's at the High School now. As for that girl you mentioned, she was a wild little thing, got into bad company . . .'

Ellie and Mrs Dawes both leaned forward, thinking that this was the girl they were looking for.

'. . . had up for shoplifting . . .'

So Diana wasn't the only one, thought Ellie.

'. . . but when she got pregnant, her boyfriend did marry her, which none of us expected, I can tell you. Trudy was bridesmaid at her wedding, would you believe! My girl, that's never been in trouble, acting bridesmaid to that little trollop!

They see one another now and then, but it's different when you've got children, isn't it? You move with a different set. She's settled down now, they say. Why, her little boy must be about ready for school this September. How time flies.'

'Yes, indeed,' said Ellie, looking at her watch. 'Which reminds me . . .'

'You're not going so soon, are you?' Ms Cullen had no intention of letting her visitors escape so quickly.

'I'm afraid I have to visit my daughter this afternoon, too,' said Ellie, being truthful but thankful that she did have a perfect excuse to leave.

Ms Cullen cackled. 'Is she still as wild as ever, that daughter of yours? My Lana used to tell tales of meeting your Diana at night in the town centre when she was supposed to be tucked up safely in bed. Trudy says Diana went with boys long before she did!'

Ellie sat down again with a bump. At fourteen, Diana had been going with boys? And parading round the town centre when she was supposed to be tucked up in bed? No! Surely not!

Ms Cullen was happy, now she could pull someone else's daughter to pieces.

'Yes, I remember her all right. Tarty piece, your Diana. Swore my girls to secrecy, taught them how to get drinks in pubs under age and how to buy cigarettes! Dear me, yes. Up to all the tricks. I heard she tried to diddle you out of the house when your husband passed on, is that right?'

Ellie forced herself to be pleasant while wanting to hit their hostess with something hard. 'Diana married the nicest of men and has a little boy now. She's setting up in the housing line herself, now. She has quite a talent for it.'

'And for other things, too, I heard,' said Ms Cullen, grinning. 'I told my girls, "Don't you think you can cheat me out of my house. Not me." I've got an arrangement with one of those pension companies that I get an annuity from them and after my death the girls get nothing. You should do the same.'

'Yes, thank you. I must think about it,' said Ellie, hardly knowing what she was saying, she was so anxious to get away. 'But I'm afraid we really must be on our way.'

'Wait a minute,' said Mrs Dawes, heaving herself to her feet with an effort. 'Ellie, didn't you say you had some old photos of the girls which you found the other day in a box in the attic? You said you'd contact them, see if they'd like to have them now.'

Ellie understood at once that this was a way to get the girls' current addresses. She admired Mrs Dawes' invention, as she'd said nothing of the sort.

Ms Cullen said, 'Don't you bother none about them. You let me have the photos and I'll ring the girls and tell them they'll have to come round to see me if they want them. Right?'

'Right,' said Ellie, feeling limp. 'Well, we really must go.'

'You'll come again.' It was a challenge.

Ellie braced herself. 'Yes, of course.'

They got out into the open air somehow and Ellie scrabbled in her bag for her mobile. If she'd been by herself she would have walked home, but Mrs Dawes wouldn't be able to manage it. 'Let's just go round the corner. She may be watching us from the window.'

She phoned the cab people, who said they'd pick them up in five minutes.

Mrs Dawes said, 'You needn't have promised to go again.'

'She's lonely. And sad. You were brilliant. You'd make a better detective than me, any day.'

'Hah! I enjoyed that.'

Ellie took Mrs Dawes' arm. 'Was Diana really like that? I'd no idea.'

Mrs Dawes patted Ellie's hand. 'Yes, dear. She was. Your husband knew. I was coming back from a meeting at the Town Hall and saw him chase her across the road and pull her into his car, with her kicking and screaming like a banshee. Such excitement. I thought at first he was chasing some bit of skirt, because Diana was plastered with make-up. Then I recognized her. He saw me looking too. He asked me afterwards not to worry you with it, because he'd had a word with Diana and she'd promised not to go out like that again. I don't know if she did or not. Anyway, she straightened out, more or less, didn't she?'

More or less. Less rather than more.

Ellie said, 'Diana's brave and bright and she's got a flair for interior decoration. I know she's other things as well.'

'Yes, dear. We all have our crosses to bear. Now, do you need to write down what we've discovered? Lana's working at the travel agency — I think I've seen her there, but I wasn't sure because she's cut and dyed her hair and lost a few pounds in weight. Now she's got a husband but no children, right? Trudy's a teacher at the High School, with a partner but still no children.'

Ellie didn't feel inclined to investigate any further. What if the Cullen girls had more bad news about Diana to impart? 'We've discovered that both of them and their particular girlfriends are still alive, so that's a dead end. We don't have to talk to either of the girls.'

'Don't we?' Mrs Dawes was disappointed.

'What would be the point?'

Mrs Dawes sagged.

A lady of vast proportions, when she sagged she was a dead weight. Mrs Dawes could be on her feet all day when organizing a flower exhibition or judging one, but her bad leg would make her pay for it afterwards. Perhaps you needed to be reasonably mobile to make a good detective. Ellie was pleased to see the minicab waiting for them on the corner.

* * *

After dropping Mrs Dawes back at her home, Ellie took the cab on to the big house Diana had converted into flats, stopping on the way to pick up some bits and pieces from the shops.

Standing back to get a good look at the house, Ellie still considered it looked bare and unwelcoming with all the garden stripped away to provide car parking. There were no For Sale notices outside, but Diana seemed to have managed without having to pay an estate agent.

Whether she'd been wise to go it alone was another matter.

Ellie found Diana inside, showing another couple around the ground-floor flat. It was much like the one Diana was occupying, though slightly larger, as the house was an irregular shape.

Both Diana and the customers appeared pleased with themselves. Diana was still looking pale but was back in her working gear. Ellie went through to the garden flat to unpack the food she'd brought. It was going to be another beautiful evening with a splendid sunset, and Diana had the French windows open on to the garden outside. She'd even got a tiny fountain playing in a stoneware pot on the patio.

Ellie started putting supper together. Diana came in and threw herself down on the settee, saying she still felt awful. 'I know I look all right, but I'm not. You've no idea what it's like.'

'Haven't I?' Ellie kept her temper. 'You forget that I went through it five times.'

'Oh. Well. Yes, but not as badly as this.'

Ellie refrained from saying it had been worse to lose babies when they were five or six months. What would be the point? 'Supper'll be half an hour. Are you still showing people round? I thought you'd sold the lot.'

'You can never have enough interest. Someone may drop out. Besides, once this lot is all through, I'll have to start all over again on another project. By the time I've paid the bank charges and the mortgage, I'll be lucky if I can clear enough to buy a two-bedroomed semi for my next effort. You don't know of an old wreck that needs doing up, do you?'

'You'd be better off buying a terraced house that's sound, and modernizing it.'

For once Diana didn't dismiss a suggestion of Ellie's out of hand. Instead, she nibbled a forefinger. 'You may be right. Would you help me?'

Ellie considered this idea. On the one hand, she could afford to invest in some housing and Diana had proved she could modernize and appeal to a certain market. On the other hand, Diana was not above cutting corners to make a quick killing. 'I'd have to think about it. Could I trust you?'

'What a thing to say!' Diana had reddened. 'Of course you could trust me. Now I've found something I feel happy doing, I won't need to skimp on detail. I haven't here, have I?'

'I don't know, dear. I'm no expert. To change the subject, I went to see Ms Cullen this afternoon. You remember her mother lived next door to us and you used to play around with her grandchildren?'

'They were older than me. That Trudy . . .' Diana laughed. 'As wild as anything, out with her friend all hours, but butter wouldn't melt, to look at her now. Teaching somewhere, isn't she? Boring!'

'I heard it was you who were the wild one, out all hours in the town centre, smoking and drinking, when you were supposed to be in bed.'

Diana shrugged. 'There was a crowd of us. Lana and Trudy and a whole gang from the High School. Looking back, I think how innocent we were, but at the time we thought we were so daring! We bought cigarettes and shared them out and took them to school to show how cool we were. Lana pinched some of her gran's make-up — would you believe, at her age, her gran was still trying to look glamorous? — and we shared that out, too.

'I remember I pinched some stuff from Woolworths, false eyelashes and mascara and stuff. Sometimes I see Lana sitting behind that desk in the travel agency and think how lucky I was to escape all that. Poor cow, she'll probably be there till she dies . . . unless they throw her out for a younger, prettier model.' Diana smiled to herself, remembering. 'You never had a clue, did you?'

'No, dear. Your father knew how poorly I'd been, and he protected me. He realized how much it would have worried me.' Yes, Frank had protected her and he'd been right to do so. She'd never have been able to cope at that time, recovering oh so slowly from the hysterectomy and still working full-time.

Diana shrugged. 'Well, I grew out of it, didn't I? By the time Stewart came along, I knew there had to be more to life than sitting behind a desk all day.'

'Poor Stewart,' said Ellie, wondering if he and Maria had found anywhere suitable to live yet. 'Now, Diana. Tell me straight. Are you thinking of going back to him?'

'No way. Maria's welcome to him. And before you ask, Derek has been ringing me, trying to make up. I've told him to get lost. Maybe we'll still have the odd few hours together—' And here Diana ran her hands down over her breasts and smiled — 'but now I've lost the baby, I'm free to look around me again. Next time I'll choose someone who'll back me no matter what. Don't look so disapproving, Mother. I'm a free agent.'

'You do worry me, Diana. A self-centred life is no recipe for contentment.'

'Oh, if you're going to preach the Bible at me . . .'

'Remind you, yes. God's laws are wise and, if we disregard them, we pay the price. You conceived a child by a man with whom you'd had a passing affair, and when you were threatened with a miscarriage, you made sure the baby would die.'

'It wasn't a baby. It was just a . . . a collection of cells.'

'How soon will it be before you think of the baby you lost, think of its little arms around your neck, loving you? I still grieve for all those babies that I lost.'

Diana flounced. 'Well, I won't.'

'You promised before God to take Stewart as your husband as long as you both shall live . . .'

Diana flushed scarlet. 'Well, I wasn't to know that he couldn't—'

'He was a good man, Diana, and he truly loved you. He went on loving you long after you'd broken your marriage vows. You almost destroyed him . . .'

'I did nothing of the kind!'

'You reduced him to a wreck, you destroyed his self-confidence and his manhood. Perhaps even worse, you tried to corrupt him into your sneaky ways, using inferior contractors because they would give you a backhander. No, of course I don't approve of divorce, but I felt like cheering when Stewart found out he could still function as a man and discovered that Maria was interested in him. What's more, I'll dance at their wedding.'

'Well! I suppose you'll back them in keeping little Frank, too?'

'I did think I would, yes. But now, I really don't know. You love Frank and he loves you. But he also loves Stewart and Maria and his childminder and me and Roy and everyone. Most of the time, anyway. I see you in him sometimes, when he gets into a tantrum. Stewart and Maria love him, yes. But will they let him get away with murder? That would be very bad for him. On the other hand, are you the sort of mother who gives in to her child just because he takes after her? And would that be good for Frank?'

'How dare you!'

'I never thought I'd say this, Diana, but I don't much like what you're becoming. If you're not careful, you'll end up a hard, selfish woman whom nobody loves, because you don't love anybody but yourself. And that's enough of a sermon. Supper should be ready by now. Shall I lay the table?'

'Go to hell!' Diana made for her bedroom and slammed the door behind her.

Ellie unstuck herself from her chair. She was trembling. Had she really said all those terrible things to Diana? Granted, Diana had had it coming to her, but . . . her legs were shaking, they really were.

And — sniff — supper was going to spoil if she didn't attend to it straight away. She'd put some minted lamb chops in the oven and cooked some potatoes and broccoli on top of the stove. Yes, everything was done. She dished up for the two of them and called to Diana that supper was ready.

Diana did not respond. So Ellie found herself a knife and fork, sat down at the table and ate her supper. Still no Diana. Perhaps she was waiting for Ellie to rush to her side saying she didn't mean all those things she'd just said, and would Diana please forgive her. Ellie did nothing of the kind. She put clingfilm over Diana's plate and left it beside the microwave. She washed up everything else, called out to Diana that she was off now, and left the flat . . .

. . . only to come face to face with Stewart and Maria, with Frank, on the doorstep.

'Why, hello, Mrs Quicke,' said Maria. 'We didn't expect to see you here. We've come to look at the ground-floor flat that's for sale.'

CHAPTER FOURTEEN

Ellie walked all the way back home to tire herself out. She couldn't remember when she'd last got so churned up. Fancy telling Diana off like that! Had she gone too far? Probably. Had Diana deserved it? Certainly, but . . .

Did it ever do any good to rant and rave?

No, of course it didn't. The gentler approach was always better.

Except, of course, that the gentler approach had never worked with Diana, who'd always made it clear she thought her mother weak.

Coming face to face with Stewart and Maria had been another shock. They'd seen the advertisement for the flats on the Internet, and had had no idea that Diana was involved. Miss Quicke had given Stewart details of two houses which she'd said they could rent from her, but both needed a great deal of work doing to them. They'd continued to look at other flats and houses as they came on the market, but so far had seen nothing they could afford or even liked.

They hadn't liked the look of Diana's big monster of a house, but they'd thought there was a garden flat which might suit them. When Ellie told them that Diana was keeping the only garden flat in the house, they said they'd go on to the next house on their list. Ellie wished them luck, kissed little Frank and waved them off.

Little Frank had been yawning. It was way past his bedtime. Ellie wondered if she should point this out, but didn't. After all, how could that busy pair look round houses together, unless they took Frank with them?

By the time she got home again, Ellie was scolding herself for an interfering busybody. She ought to have been more understanding with Diana. After all, the girl had only recently miscarried. Her hormones must be all over the place. Ellie ought to have made allowances.

The house seemed very empty. Ellie still wasn't tired. She hoovered the sitting room. She always had to do that after the gardening club had been in for coffee. How was it that men couldn't eat a biscuit without leaving half of it on the floor? She even polished the furniture. She used up a lot of energy.

All the time she was remembering scenes she hadn't thought about for years. Pushed to the back of her mind. Stupid, stupid to think about them now. To let them upset her.

Diana, ten years old, defiant, swinging the bag with her swimming things in it. Frank, white with fury and shame. The headmistress, saying that she had to consider involving the police . . . the other girl's parents, one crying, the other so angry he could hardly speak.

Diana hadn't meant it. It had been a bit of playground fun that had got out of hand. Diana would never deliberately . . . no, of course she wouldn't. The fact that the other girl had ended up in Casualty had been . . . well, it had been an accident. Of course it had.

Diana wouldn't. No. Of course not.

It had taken quite a lot of hushing up, though. The other girl had never returned to that school. Frank had had to pay her first term's fees at a private school, but luckily she and her family had moved away from the area and the whole nasty incident had been forgotten.

Except that . . . except that . . .

No, Ellie couldn't manage to recall exactly what had happened that evening on their return from school when . . . when . . .

She wept.

For the child that had never been born. Five months she'd carried their child that time and she'd hoped, oh how she'd hoped that this time, surely . . . five months, over halfway. It should have been all right.

Only, as they'd returned from their interview with the head, Frank had lost his temper and shouted that this time he was going to teach Diana a lesson she'd never forget. Diana had cowered, afraid of him perhaps for the first time in her life, and then Frank had advanced on Diana, who'd turned and run screaming up the stairs, pushing past Ellie as she'd just come out on to the landing and . . .

Thrusting Ellie away from her and . . .

Ellie heard herself wail.

She'd fallen awkwardly, five months pregnant.

She'd heard Diana screaming defiance at Frank. Frank had cried out in horror, rushed to Ellie's side and tried to pick her up and . . .

The pain!

. . . and the doctor had said, 'I'm so sorry, but this time I'm afraid there's nothing for it. Hysterectomy.'

It was absurd to weep for something that happened twenty years ago.

* * *

The businessman was using his mobile, pacing up and down outside the end house in Endene Close. The Close was deserted, all the workmen gone for the day. From this vantage point he could watch the backs of the houses that interested him. He saw lights switched on in various houses — but not in the one that he was watching. He saw cars rounding the Green and turning into the side roads, parking, people hefting their laptops, locking their doors, walking to their front doors, which often opened as they approached. Welcoming them home.

'. . . I tell you! I've been backwards and forwards all day. There's been people coming and going, quite a crowd this morning, and then she went off with that big woman I told you about, the local gossip. She only got back a short time ago . . .'

'I don't understand. Why haven't the police arrested her? You can't have done it right.'

'I did, I did. I have to go home now. My wife's been ringing me. Father's worse. If he has to go to hospital . . .'

'I'm booked solid all this week. I can't get down again so soon. Tell him . . . reassure him. You know what to say. We can't have him worried by this now.'

'It's easy for you to say. I'm at my wits' end . . .'

* * *

After a while Ellie mopped herself up, switched on some lights, and went to draw the curtains. The evenings were drawing in.

A couple of shadowy figures were standing at her gate, looking up at the house. Kate and Armand?

Ellie threw cold water over her face and went down her own pretty garden to see if they wanted to talk.

It was Kate and Armand, he with his arm around her. Perhaps Kate had been crying? Armand was very quiet, for him.

Kate said, 'Isn't it absurd, Ellie? I was just wishing we'd never thought of having a water feature. Not because of the murder hunt and all the trouble that's caused, but because she must have been so peaceful, lying there covered by wild flowers.'

'Weeds, too,' said Armand.

Kate and Ellie did their best to laugh.

'Listen!' said Kate. They listened to the birds going to roost in the trees around the church, the distant traffic, the cheery 'Hi!' of a commuter using the alley to reach his home further along. A bus passed by on the main road. A frog, or perhaps it was a mouse, rustled in the undergrowth. A moth swooped past.

'I can't help thinking she had found a good place to rest,' said Kate. 'Peaceful, yet with happy folk around her.

Covered over by nature. Birdsong. No one has claimed her, poor thing. And now she's been dug up and made an object of interest and put in a freezer without a name or anyone to mourn her. She was better off in the ground.'

Armand gave her a hug. 'Kate, I didn't know you could be so poetic.'

'Neither did I,' said Kate, with a return to her normal commonsensical manner. 'Sorry about that, folks.'

People took different paths to come to terms with death. Kate had mentally turned a sordid murder site into something rather beautiful. Ellie didn't blame her for it. If possible, Ellie admired Kate even more.

'If no one ever claims her,' said Ellie, 'perhaps we could jointly pay for her to have a Christian burial. Perhaps put in a particularly beautiful shrub or rose or something where she was found, in her memory.'

'Yes,' said Kate. 'I think I'd like that.'

So they'd decided to stay. Good.

* * *

DC Honeywell arrived next morning as Ellie was having her first cup of coffee in the conservatory, having fended off Midge, who wanted to sit on her lap.

'May I have one too?' He seated himself, and Midge immediately jumped on his lap.

Midge knew when visitors liked him. Ellie fetched more coffee and the biscuit tin. She'd never yet met a man who didn't like chocolate biscuits.

'How are you doing?' he asked.

She was surprised. Did the tears from the previous evening still show? They didn't usually. 'I'm fine. Lots to think about, looking back, wondering if I'd done this or if that had happened . . . stupid, really.'

'Good coffee. I must apologize for your having to put up with me. There's been another incident on the other side of the borough, which has mopped up resources. And the boss is still off. Antibiotics, and all that.'

Ellie shook her head in sympathy. 'Teeth! You're too young, but just you wait!'

'I know. My partner suffers, terribly. Me, I'm lucky.'

'In more ways than one,' said Ellie. 'You have an even temperament.'

He grinned. 'Do you mean I'm shallow?'

They both laughed.

He put down his cup. To business. 'Have you thought any more about the past?'

'Yes, I even went with a neighbour to see Ms Cullen yesterday. We wanted to check out her daughter's friends, to see if one of them could be the body in the garden. But they weren't. I still couldn't think of any link between me and the body, though. What makes you think there is one?'

'After every murder, the police get crank calls claiming they did it, or that they know someone who did it. That's one of the reasons why we never disclose all the particulars to the press. But among the host of calls this time we had two emails. That in itself is odd. Cranks usually write in, or phone. The first email accused your husband of having killed a young girl he was having an affair with.'

Ellie winced.

'Yes, it was laughable, but we had to check it out. It would have been convenient if it had been true. There we were, looking for a murderer . . . and what do we find? A dead man. Lovely. Case over. Most satisfactory. Get on with the next job.'

Ellie said, 'You got an email which tried to involve Frank? But . . . is it someone with a grudge against him? A neighbour?' Would Mrs Coppola have gone to such lengths? No, surely not. In any case, Mrs Coppola would have pointed the finger at Ellie, and not at Frank.

He had an engaging grin. 'That's what we wondered. But no sooner had we dismissed it as coming from a spiteful neighbour, than the second one came. This time they pointed the finger at you, Mrs Quicke, claiming you killed the girl because your husband was having an affair with her.'

'What?' Shock, horror. 'But . . .'

'As we were ninety-nine per cent sure that your husband hadn't been having an affair with anyone, we assumed this was from the same spiteful neighbour. But we also considered that it might be an attempt to divert attention away from the murderer himself.'

'Let me get this straight. You think the murderer might have sent these emails himself? Or herself? Why?'

'In the first place, because they weren't sent from an ordinary home computer. A spiteful neighbour would have used their own home computer, or perhaps another local machine which they could easily access. But this person has gone to considerable trouble to avoid being traced. Now, I'm the patient sort, Mrs Quicke. I like looking at photographs. Do you?'

'You've lost me.'

'Whoever sent those emails thought they couldn't be traced. Wrong. We have men and women who can track an email down to a machine in Outer Mongolia if necessary. The first email came from the rank of computers used by all and sundry at the public library in Ealing Broadway. We can pinpoint the machine and the exact time the email was sent. There's a whole row of computers, and people book time on them. They come and go throughout the day, signing in, using the computer, leaving. The records are kept properly, but a squiggly, indecipherable signature is pretty common. Addresses are required, but sometimes not accurate. You follow?'

'Sounds pretty foolproof to me. You can trace the email back to a machine, but no further.'

'Well, yes and no. What the first email gave us was a list of people who might have been using that computer at that time. Many of them are students who come regularly. Some of them notice who's sitting beside them. We've got a policeman at the desk in the library now, watching out for people who might have been using the computer at that time. What our man or woman didn't know was that there's a CCTV camera trained on the main library entrance all the time. So we have a piece of film showing everyone who went in and out at about that time.'

'There must be dozens of people.'

'Of course. But then we got the second email, which was sent from a different library in the borough. Same MO. He went in at a busy time of day . . .'

'You say "he"? Are you sure it's a man?'

'Pretty sure, yes. There's one particular person showed up on film twice. Would you like to see him?'

'A local man?'

'No. I don't think so. But you see, it must be someone who's had contact with you some time or other. Possibly some considerable time ago. Otherwise, why mention you or your husband in the emails?'

She was bewildered. It wasn't Mrs Coppola. In any case, Mrs Coppola knew very well that Frank was dead. Ellie couldn't think of anyone who it might be. Unless, twenty years on, the two young lads next door might for some reason . . . ? Oh, nonsense. 'How old is this man?'

His eyes sharpened. 'You've thought of someone?'

'Well, no. Not really. There were two lads next door when we first came. Only youngsters, though older than Diana, of course. They were both under ten when we moved in. Say, eight and seven. Something like that. When they left, the eldest was in the upper sixth at the High School, his brother a year younger. So now they'd be about thirty-seven, thirty-eight. Oh, it's absurd.'

'Their name was Spendlove, wasn't it? The father worked for the council? Is that the right people?'

'Yes. They were here for ages. Nice neighbours. The father was great, always joking, very laid back. He'd been in a road accident. He was on his bike at the time and a lorry turned left without seeing him. When we first came, he was still in a wheelchair, but he graduated to crutches and then a stick. By the time they left, he was walking without a stick but he still had days when he could hardly move, and the stairs were a trial to him, which is why they eventually moved on to a big flat somewhere on the other side of the park.'

'You knew them well?'

'No, not really.' She found she was clutching her mug of coffee so hard that her fingers had gone white. She unstuck herself from the mug. It was stupid to get so upset about something that had happened twenty years ago. It really wouldn't hurt to tell the policeman why she hadn't been a good neighbour, all those long years ago.

'I should explain that we came here when I was pregnant with Diana, my daughter. We'd been living in my tiny flat and we used the sale of that to provide the down payment for this house. But it was a terrible struggle to make ends meet. And the pregnancy didn't go easily.

'Next door — Mrs Spendlove — she didn't understand that I found her boys noisy and destructive. They weren't bad boys, but they did use to kick their football against the fence at the back and, every time, it boomed.' Ellie tried to laugh. 'It sounds so stupid, doesn't it? I wasn't used to boys, that's all. And I did need to take it easy. But every time I sat down to rest, they seemed to . . . Well, they did have a problem. They needed space, growing boys like that, and they didn't have it.

'You see, with their father pretty much disabled, he couldn't do much with the garden and she had a part-time job in the library on the other side of the Green, and wasn't interested, anyway. For a while he managed to keep the top of the garden more or less clear, so that the boys could play cricket of sorts, and a spot of football.

'As soon as Diana could toddle, she was out in our garden, calling to them through the fence to play with her, but of course they were much older and didn't take any notice. Within a year or two, the boys were old enough to go off to the park to play. But I . . . I had a problem. I kept having miscarriages. I'm really not sure how many, now. Five for certain, but maybe others, too. Yet I had to go out to work somehow, to cover the mortgage repayments. So, I really didn't have time or energy to socialize, and after they left, we lost touch.'

He was sympathetic. 'That's why you didn't want to talk about that time?'

That and Diana's behaviour. She nodded. 'Is it one of the Spendlove boys?'

He relaxed. 'No, this man is much older.'

'Not Mr Spendlove?' Ellie was upset at the thought.

'No, no. I can't tell you why we don't think it's him, but it isn't. Now, would you like to come down to the incident room? We've got the CCTV films to show you and they're trying to improve the quality of the picture so's we can get some individual pictures as well.'

Ellie mentally reviewed everything she was supposed to be doing that day. The plants would be arriving for Endene Close in an hour and a half's time, and she must be there to supervise their placing in the right positions. She was supposed to be meeting Rose at the Sunflower Café for lunch — a weekly date which both women enjoyed.

'Yes, I'll come right away.'

* * *

The CCTV film footage from the main library was blurred. A policeman was fiddling with the controls, trying to make it clearer. 'This is the worst tape, and I'm still working on it. What we've done is run the tape from about half an hour before the email was sent, till half an hour after, to allow time for him or her to wander around, find the computers, and maybe have to wait for one to be free before he could use it.'

He ran the tape a little way. Ellie concentrated hard, but could hardly make out what the individual figures looked like. The policeman ran it back. Did some more fiddling. Was this better? Yes, it was. She watched figures jerkily enter the library. She thought she could just about make out a woman tugging along a reluctant child. Two students in jeans, sex unknown. Someone in a baseball cap, presumably a man. A woman in a sari helping along another woman, large, having difficulty walking. A couple of men who might be Somalis? Pakistanis? A teenage(?) girl in a cropped top.

After a while Ellie shook her head. 'I'm so sorry, but it's too difficult. How can you identify anyone from this?'

'Sometimes you can recognize people by the way they walk and hold themselves. We're refining our techniques all the time. The other tape's better. But let's try again.'

More fiddling. They ran the tape back and tried again. Now the pictures were clearer. Ellie could see that it was definitely a woman tugging along a child, who was probably male. The two students were probably one man, one girl. The baseball cap wearer was definitely a man. The two women in saris were both elderly, but one more so than the other. The men were definitely from some ethnic minority, though she couldn't be sure which. The girl was definitely a teenager.

The tape went on and on, revealing a cross-section of the multicultural society that was Ealing. The elderly, the young. The middle-aged. Those with shoppers and those without. Women in a hurry. Ethnic people in saris, turbans, headscarves. Students of all nationalities, Chinese, Japanese, Javanese . . . Africans, Somalis, Australians . . .

Ellie lost concentration. 'I think I've seen a couple of people I know to talk to, though I don't know their names. Both women who live around here, and I may have met them at some function, possibly at a big meeting at the Town Hall. But I can't possibly be sure. I'm so sorry.'

'Let's try the other tape. I think the images are sharper. This one is taken from a camera trained on the High Street in Acton, but it covers the library entrance.'

They were sharper. A middle-aged woman helping an elderly man along, a boy who probably ought to have been in school. One student, male. An elderly Pakistani. Three foreign students, gesticulating. A woman with a toddler in a pushchair. More students, more women, more . . .

She began to blink. The effort to keep concentrating was hard. When it finished, she said, 'Run it through again.'

'You recognize someone?'

'No. But . . . No.'

DC Honeywell said, gently, 'I don't want to lead you, but you did see somebody you recognized, didn't you?'

Ellie shook her head. 'Can I see the first tape again, please?'

They ran it through for her till they came to the two darker-skinned men. 'Stop. I can't be sure, but is one of those men the same as in the other tape? Or am I imagining things?'

'You recognize him?'

'No, I don't think so.'

'Think hard.'

Ellie threw up her hands. 'I have never to my knowledge spoken to or seen this man, but that's the only one I've spotted so far who looks the same in both tapes. I follow your reasoning. It's possible for someone to use both libraries, but not usual. Which doesn't mean it doesn't happen. I mean, someone might go into Acton library and find that the book they want is only available at Central, so they'd go on to Central to take the book out there.'

'It was the other way round,' said the policeman. 'He visited Central first, and Acton afterwards.'

'Perhaps he lives in Acton, but happened to be shopping in Ealing Broadway and that's why he went to Central first?'

'We've thought of that, too. Mrs Quicke, believe me, we have another very good reason for wondering whether this could be our man. Look again.'

Ellie looked. Shrugged. 'I'm sorry, but I don't think I've ever seen this man before. Anyway, how could a complete stranger know anything about me or my husband? No one from Pakistan or India has ever lived in the house next door, or even — so far as I know — in our road. It just hasn't happened.'

'Think hard.'

Ellie snapped at him. 'I am thinking. There was a lovely family of Pakistanis lived opposite my friend Mrs Dawes at one time, and of course we knew quite a lot who came into the charity shop in the Avenue when I was working there. But they were all women. They were always so polite and helpful, though they did sometimes let the boys have a little too much of their own way. But that's their culture, isn't it?'

'Go on.'

'Well, there's the people who ran one of the newsagents in the Avenue. They were great. Their children went to our school here, and everyone spoke well of them.'

'You said "ran". Did they leave, and if so, why?'

'They lived above the shop, and when they retired they sold to a cousin, I think. Someone else from their extended family, anyway. The new people are still there, husband and wife and two lovely boys. Why don't you show this photo to them?'

'We'll do just that. But we've still got to track down the link with you. For instance, do you get your newspapers delivered from that shop?'

'No, they come from the bigger newsagents at this end of the Avenue, the one which is also the post office. The two shops divide the newspaper rounds up between them, you see. At our end the newspapers are delivered from the post office one, and the other side of the Avenue is delivered by the other newsagent. I buy the occasional magazine or chocolate egg at the other shop if I'm in a hurry and the post office is crowded. They're nice people, very friendly.'

'Who runs the post office, then?'

'Not Asians. It's part of a big chain of newsagents and they put in their own managers. Some of the staff there are Asian, but they come and go and, as far as I remember, they're all youngish.'

Ellie looked at the video which they were still working on. The picture was much sharper now.

'What are you thinking, Mrs Quicke?'

Ellie was puzzled. 'He looks . . . I don't know . . . like a professional man.'

'All right. I'll buy it. Where would you expect to meet this man in the community?'

Ellie closed her eyes and let her mind grow blank. Nothing happened. She waited for a while, but could only think of bus drivers, which was no help at all, because this man didn't look like a bus driver. She didn't know what he looked like. A teacher? Possibly.

'I'm sorry. I can't think of anything. I wish I could. I don't like the thought of some man out there knowing about me, and my not knowing anything about him.'

'If you see him anywhere locally, will you let us know? And remember, he may be dangerous.'

'As if I haven't enough to worry about!'

DC Honeywell asked if he could drop her anywhere, but it was only a short walk across the Green to Endene Close, and it was a beautiful clear day, so she decided to walk — keeping an eye out for Asian men of a certain age.

CHAPTER FIFTEEN

The ambulance arrived as the businessman turned into the road in which he lived.

His wife was crying, his father only semi-conscious. The paramedics took control efficiently, talking in loud voices, being cheerful and positive.

The businessman got out of his car and scrambled into the ambulance, shedding thoughts of the meeting he should be attending at that very moment, and the people he'd arranged to see that afternoon.

He tried to reach his father, to reassure him that everything was under control, but the paramedics pushed him aside, made him sit at the back. When he tried to use his mobile, they told him off.

* * *

Ellie was well aware that there are days when everything goes wrong, even when the sky is blue and the air is warm. Things shouldn't go wrong on such days, which were intended for people to enjoy themselves in.

But there it was. She arrived at Endene Close just in time to see the large van from the nurseries drive off, and a furious site manager contemplating a hundred plants in pots, which had been unloaded in a thoughtless manner and were now completely blocking the driveway.

Ellie had arranged that the nursery should supply someone to plant out the things she'd ordered. But no; a scribbled note on the delivery sheet informed her that they were short-staffed, so hadn't been able to help her out on that.

The site manager wanted the plants cleared off the driveway immediately, as he was expecting a delivery and, no, he couldn't let her have access to any water that day, since the plumber had cut everything off to deal with an unexplained leak!

What to do? She wasn't wearing gardening togs, and anyway had neither spade nor trowel with her. Even if she started moving pots by herself, it would take her ages to get them off the driveway, and then . . . it was a warm day. The plants must go into the earth at once, but would need watering in.

She tried charm on the site manager, hoping he'd be kind enough at least to help her move the pots, but he was the sort who stood on his dignity, and said it wasn't his job to shift plants and she ought to have made proper arrangements to deal with them, shouldn't she! She asked for Roy and learned he'd gone chasing after some special fitment or other and wasn't expected back till late afternoon.

The site manager was enjoying this. Ellie wasn't.

Who could she ask to help her? Maria Patel ran a cleaning firm — very efficiently. Would she have any gardeners on her books? Not very likely. Ellie tried Maria just in case, but it was no good. Unexpectedly, Maria wanted to talk. Stewart had found them a possible house and they wondered if Ellie could spare the time to come and look at it with them? Ellie promised to ring her back later.

The site manager was tramping up and down, looking at his watch, muttering about women who couldn't organize their way out of a paper bag.

Ellie rang Rose, to see if she might be able to spare a half hour to help before she started getting lunch for Aunt Drusilla. Rose squeaked in surprise, but said she'd be right over and would bring a flask of coffee for the workers, just give her half an hour to finish making a cake for Miss Quicke.

The pots needed to be moved *now!*

Ellie asked the site manager if she might put her handbag in his works caravan and could he lend her a pair of gloves? He rolled his eyes, but allowed that. Ellie got down to it.

She'd ordered lavender bushes, skimmias, some of the very bright yellow euonymus, and pierises. For focus plants, she'd ordered buddleias and red-stemmed dogwoods. The idea had been that everything could be pruned back just once a year, with a mulch several inches thick over all, to keep the weeds down. A row of variegated ivies were supposed to drape themselves over the low front wall.

The mulch was there, in sacks, and all but two of the lavenders she'd ordered. She marched to and fro, heaving the larger plants roughly into position, discarding her jacket, going back for more . . .

Tum-Tum came past carrying some shopping in plastic bags. 'What on earth . . . ? Ellie, my dear. Let me shift that for you.'

Ellie had been trying to tug the largest of the dogwoods into position at the time and gladly let him help her. Once she'd explained what she was doing, he said he'd drop his shopping back at the vicarage and come back to help her.

Ellie wiped her forehead with her forearm. 'You haven't a couple of watering cans, have you? The supply's been cut off here and we need to water everything in.'

He told her to sit down and rest till he came back, but the site manager was hovering and becoming increasingly unpleasant as time drew near for the lorry to deliver whatever it was he wanted. So, Ellie continued getting pots off the road and on to the pavement till Tum-Tum arrived back, suitably clad and pushing his wheelbarrow with all his tools in it.

Then Rose arrived, bearing an enormous basket containing all her gardening tools, plus coffee and slices of deliciously scented cake. Tum-Tum hailed a couple of neighbours who helped out occasionally in the garden around the church, and half chivvied and half charmed them into joining in.

Soon after, the plumber popped up to say the water was back on and would they like him to connect up his hosepipe for them, since it was not going to do those plants any good to sit around in the hot sun.

The lorry which the site manager had been expecting still hadn't turned up, much to his fury. Ellie never did get back to her house to fetch her own tools, but concentrated on getting all the plants in the right positions and facing the right way. And treading them in properly, which amateur gardeners never did, thinking they were going to damage the roots, whereas a real gardener knows you have to tread down properly or the roots won't make contact with the soil. Tallest plants at the back and trailing ivies at the front . . . and no, that dogwood was too obtrusive there and must be moved round the corner . . .

Dear Rose might twitter and fuss, but she was a dab hand with a trowel and nattered happily away as she put the plants in. The cake and coffee she'd brought helped everyone stay in a good temper.

At noon, Tum-Tum popped back down the Avenue for fish and chips all round, and they took a break in the sun, sitting on the low wall and chatting away to all who passed by. One helper said that, with reluctance, he must get back, as the gas man was calling. But a woman who sang in the choir came along to take his place.

By two o'clock all the plants were in and watered, and they were beginning to spread mulch over everything. Ellie seized a broom and started to tidy up. Rose got out her secateurs and snipped a dead leaf off here and there. Tum-Tum started a chorus going, which Ellie feared might turn out rather . . . well . . . raucous. But it was all right. Just. You never quite knew with Tum-Tum, respected vicar though he might be. There was just a touch of 'Yo-Ho-Ho' and 'Heave Away, My Hearties' in Tum-Tum.

They were just stowing the last few tools away when Roy drove up with his head sticking out of the window, shouting, 'Wey hey! Fan–tastic!'

The site manager was even more angry now. 'That something delivery hasn't come, and they promised to be here by eleven this morning!'

Roy said, 'Have you got on to them, then? It'll put us back a couple of days if we don't get those fitments today.' He parked and got out to admire what the gardening team had done. 'This makes all the difference. I've no sort of head for garden design. I couldn't imagine how it could look, but this contrast of foliage and shapes is just right! Ellie, everyone! A thousand thanks. Ellie, I owe you one. I was going to take you out tonight, but something's come up and I need to make up a foursome, so supper at my place tonight? Eight o'clock? Can you get over by yourself?'

That was Roy all over: he always expected Ellie to fall in with his wishes. But at least she wouldn't have to cook for herself that evening, and that was a bonus.

The site manager came up to break the bad news to Roy that the lorry had broken down somewhere on the M25 and wouldn't make it today.

Ellie looked down at herself. Her light shoes were ruined. Her skirt and blouse would wash, but the shoes were beyond repair . . . and what had she done with her jacket and handbag? Dear Rose looked as untidy as Ellie. 'Ellie dear, we've missed our usual lunch at Sunflowers. Shall we make it tomorrow instead?'

Tum-Tum, wearing a navy T-shirt over heavyweight drill trousers, was surprisingly clean. Rose sagged. She was tired, but pleased with their efforts. Ellie summoned a minicab to take Rose home, but hung back to have a word with Tum-Tum.

He seemed to be having the same idea, for he took an age to settle his various tools in his wheelbarrow.

She held out her arms, which were muddied to the elbow. 'Look at me! I need putting in the washing machine with my clothes. Join me for a cuppa in a while?'

She thought he might refuse. He was a widower and half the parish invited him round for a meal. But he nodded, and trundled off over the Green to the vicarage, pausing on the way to have a word with a young mother whose toddler was misbehaving.

Ellie retrieved her handbag and jacket and made her way home. The house seemed very silent. As was next door. Were the birds not singing today? She stopped in her garden by the sundial, and listened. All that summer, the sky had been busy with house martins swooping and tittering away. They didn't nest under the eaves of her house, but in some of the houses further along. Now the sky was empty. Had they already gone to their winter quarters in the south? It was a sign that autumn had come with a vengeance despite the warmth of the sun that day.

Heavy shadows lay across next door's garden and even across hers.

Midge bounded out from where he'd been hiding under a weigela, and sniffed at her legs, which were spattered with water and earth. A shower and a change of clothes was a priority.

* * *

Tum-Tum was good at listening. And eating. Ellie left the chocolate biscuits out and he put three into his mouth whole. After which, he took it more slowly.

She said, 'I don't know where to start. People always say that, don't they? It must irritate you no end.'

He shook his head, smiled and took another biscuit. Judging by his comfortable figure, he must be feeding himself properly. He drained his mug of tea and handed it to her for a refill. She made him another cuppa. With her back to him and her hands occupied, it was easier to start. He knew that, of course.

She said, 'Can houses retain a sense of evil? A while back I'd have said that of course they couldn't. People have lived in houses which are supposed to be inhabited by ghosts, and never noticed anything. I thought it was all in the mind. I mean, if you were told that someone had committed a murder in your house, you'd start worrying about it and imagining all sorts of things, but if you hadn't heard, would you suspect anything?'

She handed him his mug. 'I've read about people sensing bad things in a house and I've put it down to draughts, or their disliking the colour of the wallpaper, or . . . just not liking the way the kitchen's laid out. Or damp. The smell of damp could put you off, easily. Then there's the way a house is built. Is it full of light, or not? A light, airy house full of sunshine would lift your spirits, a dark gloomy one would depress you.

'I've always been amused when people say that my living room is restful. One person even said she thought I must pray a lot in there. Well, I do, but not that much. At least, I wouldn't have thought it would make any difference. The fact that the walls are a restful pale green, and that everything else is in keeping . . . surely that's the reason people think it's restful?

'The house next door is a reverse image of this one. The rooms are arranged slightly differently, in that they still have two reception rooms, whereas I have one big through room. Their kitchen is larger than mine, because I have a kitchen *and* a study, where they only have one big kitchen. The bedrooms are the same size, as is the bathroom. That house has been decorated in many different styles over the years, and sometimes I've liked the colours and sometimes I haven't, but that doesn't explain what's happened there. And I'm not just talking about the murder.

'I've lived here thirty-odd years. Frank and I have had our share of troubles. I wasn't well for a lot of that time. Diana had the usual rebellions. For a long time we were really short of money, and I was always anxious about paying the bills. The walls were painted this green when we came. We liked it, and renewed it from time to time.

'The kitchen is old-fashioned, I know. As is the bathroom. My pride and joy was the garden, and I suppose you could say that looked good. It's given me enormous pleasure over the years.

'I'm struggling to express myself properly. The question is: why is next door so different?'

He peaked his eyebrows. Took another biscuit, but this time ate it slowly, almost daintily.

She sighed. 'When we first came, the garden next door was a bit of a mess. Mr Spendlove had had a tragic accident and the boys were, I suppose, a little wild. But I never thought anything of it. Then the Cullens came. He faded away, and she was eventually confined to the house. Her daughter and grandchildren looked after her but . . . and here's where I begin to get uneasy. Did she die naturally, or was she pushed? The family wanted to get their hands on the house. They didn't let anyone see her. Oh, no! I'm making too much of it. They looked after her. She was miserable. She died. Full stop.

'Then another tragic couple came and there was possibly a criminal twist to the way they left. He died of cancer and she was courted by a man who said he'd been a friend of her husband's and took her for a ride. He persuaded her to sell the house and said they'd marry and go to New Zealand or Australia. He didn't marry her, but took the money and ran. She's now living alone on the South Coast.

'After them there was Shirley and Donald, who had terribly noisy parties. Mrs Dawes couldn't sleep, even though she was two streets away. We were all kept awake. They were a relentlessly jolly couple, if you know what I mean. They drank, they partied, they didn't give a damn about anyone else. I suppose they were the happiest family who'd lived in that house for a long time, but I wonder now if all that noise was a cover for dissatisfaction with their lives? Anyway, they went off to Spain where he died, and the house next door was turned over to the social. Bosnian refugees, grieving for the loss of a husband and son. Then a poor creature with runny-nosed children, who neglected their pets quite horribly. She had a series of men, the children were taken into care . . .' Ellie shrugged.

'Then Kate and Armand, who are my very good friends. They didn't know anything about the families who'd lived there before, but within weeks Armand was physically abusing Kate.'

Tum-Tum gave a great start but Ellie held up her hand. 'It's all right. All over. She stopped thinking it was all her fault and he came to realize that he'd miss her if she walked out on him. They've settled down nicely and he won't try that again, because he knows that if he does Kate will have his guts for garters. Anyway, they ripped everything out of the house and redecorated and, though they hadn't thought much about the garden to begin with, they did eventually decide they wanted a low-maintenance garden with a water feature and . . . that's how they found that poor girl.'

Tum-Tum frowned. 'You think her ghost has been giving grief to everyone who lives in that house?'

'No, I don't. I've seen where she was found and it was a quiet and peaceful grave. Kate and Armand think so, too. They don't know all the bad bits that have happened in that house before. I–I suppose I toned it down when they asked about it. They were at first revolted, thinking the murder had taken place in their house. They wanted to move, straight away. But now they know the girl never lived there, was probably never even in their house, well . . . they want to give her a Christian burial. I said I'd help. What do you think?'

He scratched the side of his face. And thought about it. 'You want me to go into that house and bless it? Just in case?'

Ellie sighed. Shrugged. 'I think a spot of prayer wouldn't do any harm.'

'That's one thing you can count on. Prayer always helps. But it's their house and they're not churchgoers.'

'If I suggested it and they agreed?'

He nodded. 'You deny that you're sensitive to atmosphere, though I know you're sensitive to your surroundings. The way you've done up this house and garden proves that. Is there an atmosphere next door now?'

'No, I don't think there is.'

'Good. Well, let me know if they could do with my help. Or you may be able to deal with it yourself. You say you've had your ups and downs while living here, but the face you show to the world is one of hard-won peace.'

Ellie blinked. 'You mean I'm showing my age?'

He laughed. 'I meant that your practical Christian loving-kindness shines through.'

'Oh.' She flushed. She didn't think she was much of a person. She certainly hadn't been much of a good neighbour. In fact, when she thought about all that had gone on next door, she felt nothing but guilt. But she couldn't confess that, when he'd just paid her such a compliment. 'I'm not always calm, you know.'

'Neither am I.'

He stood up to leave, and so did she. She used his proper name for the first time. 'Thank you, Thomas.'

As she waved him off, she wondered if she would dare to talk to him about the ethics of abortion some time. He'd have heard about Diana's miscarriage from other members of the choir, but Ellie hadn't raised the subject, so he hadn't, either. It seemed he trusted her to deal with things. It was a compliment. Probably.

He also seemed to think she could deal with Kate and Armand's problem.

There was one thing she could do, and that was track down the year in which their shed had been burned down. She kept all her old diaries at the back of the big drawer in Frank's desk. She'd never been one for writing a journal, but she did jot down appointments and reminders to herself and kept them because you never knew when they'd come in useful. Like checking back when she'd last seen an old friend and when so and so had got married. She got out the plastic bag in which she kept the diaries and discarded them one by one, denying herself the temptation to dip into this one or that.

What she was looking for was some appointment with the insurance people about the shed having been burned down, which would probably be within a couple of weeks of their return from holidays.

Summer vacations had to be taken in the school holidays while Diana had been growing up. For some years they'd shared a holiday cottage with another family. Frank had grown up and been to school with the man, his wife had been delightful, and their daughter about the same age as Diana . . . though they'd been very critical of Diana not helping with the chores around the house, but . . .

No. The year the shed had burned down, they'd gone alone to a tiny place, renting a house on Dartmoor, where it had rained and rained and . . .

No. It hadn't been that year.

Think, Ellie, think. It must have been after they'd stopped sharing a house with Frank's friends. Before or after the holiday on Dartmoor? The diaries weren't in the right order. She must have missed one.

Finally she found it. Diana had invited a friend to join them that year, and they'd stayed at a B&B near Brighton. Near enough to get down to the beach when they wished, but quiet enough in the evenings. One week after their return to London, she'd scribbled down an appointment for someone to come from the insurance company.

1984. The worst year. No wonder she hadn't wanted to remember. She'd been five months pregnant. Diana accused of bullying and worse. Diana thrusting her down the stairs, the fall . . . the pain . . . the loss of the long-hoped-for child . . . the hysterectomy.

Frank had worried that she might not be able to cope with going away on holiday so soon after, but she'd dragged herself out of the horrible black place into which she'd fallen, and said they'd all been looking forward to it for so long, they must make the effort and go. When they came back in September, they'd start afresh. Put it all behind them.

So they'd gone down to Sussex and it hadn't been a bad holiday in many ways, though she'd been very tired and prone to tears. She'd tried to smile and not cry before the others, because they hated to see her give way. Diana's little friend had been delightful: a strongly built girl without imagination, a perfect companion for Diana, who never tried to bully her. A pity that child — what was her name? — had moved away from London the following year.

They'd returned in good spirits, mostly. Frank had certainly benefited from the rest, had collected an attractive tan. Diana seemed to have forgotten the past, and was looking forward to the new term and getting some new clothes. Ellie had been feeling deathly tired still, and worried that she wouldn't be able to cope with going back to work and running the household.

They discovered the shed had been burned out in their absence. Their neighbours, the Spendloves, had unfortunately moved away while they'd been gone, but someone crossing the Green had spotted the flames and called the fire brigade. There hadn't been much left. Some bits and pieces which had once been metal tools, half a charred old cupboard. Some wellington boots, melted. Frank had been accustomed to keeping one or two half-used pots of paint in the shed and they'd added to the fury of the flames. The smell lingered till the autumn gales.

The insurance had paid up, though not enough to get a new shed. Someone on the allotments on the other side of the park had been throwing out a toolshed which had seen better days, and Frank had picked up some second-hand tools from a car boot sale. They'd managed for some years till they could afford to get a new, solid, purpose-built garden shed with a padlock on it.

So, it was in 1984 that the shed had burned down, and presumably that was when that poor girl had been killed and buried. Ellie shuddered. She has glad she hadn't known about it before.

But now she did know, and what was she going to do about it? Her shilly-shallying, her refusal to look up the dates, must have put back the police investigation. If she'd only been sensible and faced her memories down, they'd probably have found the culprit by now.

She still couldn't remember having anything to do with an Asian man around that time. No? No. Nothing.

She phoned the police station and enquired for Inspector Willis, only to learn she was not on duty. Ellie wondered whether the poor woman was still off sick with her abscess. Probably. Would it be appropriate to get her a get well soon card from the post office and drop it through the police-station door? Um, well. Probably not. It might look . . . well, as if she were crawling to the police. Which she definitely was not going to do.

She left a message for DC Honeywell instead. Now it was up to him to track down the murderer.

There wasn't anything else she could do to help. Was there?

CHAPTER SIXTEEN

Well, of course there was something else she could do if she wanted to poke and pry into other people's business. She could look up the Spendloves — if they were still around — and see how they were getting on. It was clear they'd never had anything to do with the murder, but while she was about it, she wanted to know exactly what had happened to all the people who'd once lived next door to her. She now knew what had happened to nearly all of them. Only the Spendloves still remained on her list.

She would look on it as a sort of spring cleaning, for her memory. Another way of putting it was that she wanted to see if she were in profit or loss as far as being a good neighbour was concerned. She rather feared it was a loss.

She got out the phone directory but found there were no Spendloves in it. Not one. That was strange. The father might have died by now, of course. Or gone into a home. He'd recovered pretty well from that awful road accident, but once you start breaking bones like that, you find yourself with arthritis and other problems at an early age. His wife had been delightful, hadn't been a Londoner but had come from . . . the Midlands? Shropshire? If her husband had died, she'd probably have gone back there.

So what about the two boys? They'd been nice lads, both of them. Bright enough to aim for university. Ellie hoped they'd both made it. They would be, what, thirty-six and thirty-seven by now? Probably married with two point four children. But neither of them were in the Ealing phone book.

She put the directory away. She'd done what she could, and now . . . now she must think about what she should wear to Roy's that evening. Who else had he invited? She had intended at first to wear an ordinary summer dress, but if he'd invited another couple, perhaps she ought to look out something a little better?

Ellie was still uncertain of her taste in clothes. Kate had shown her how much better she looked in well-made clothes that hung well, and in the sweet-pea shades that suited her colouring. Could she ask Kate to help her choose something appropriate? No, surely not. Kate and Armand had enough on their plate without bothering about dressing Ellie up for a supper party.

Before she did anything else, she had a mental apology to make to her husband's memory. She'd been thinking of him rather harshly, imagining that he hadn't really understood how awful those early years had been for her. She wondered if all widows went through these mood swings. One minute she missed Frank because he'd always taken such good care of her, and the next she wished he'd let her do more for herself.

Recently she'd seen him as — almost — as selfish as Diana. Now she'd learned that he'd protected her from the knowledge of Diana's wild behaviour and she was grateful to him. She couldn't have borne to know about it at the time.

And now? She was glad she'd learned what Diana had been up to then, because she could see that her daughter wasn't consistently awful. She'd done bad things, yes, but she did seem capable of learning from her mistakes. At least some of the time.

Of course, it would be better if Diana didn't feel obliged to make those mistakes in the first place, but the fact that she never made the same mistake twice did give Ellie a tiny glow of hope for the future.

She wondered if Diana was going to forgive her for her harsh words the previous evening. There'd been no message from her on the answerphone today, which was bad news. If Diana had as much as a slight sniffle, she was on the phone to her mother asking — no, demanding — to be looked after.

At that point in Ellie's musings, the phone did ring. It wasn't Diana, but Jean from church, asking — no, demanding — that Ellie should prepare the coffee and tea for Women's Hour the following evening. Someone had dropped out for a Very Good Reason, said Jean, insinuating that Ellie's defection after church the previous Sunday had not been for a good enough reason, and had to be atoned for.

Ellie wondered what would satisfy Jean by way of an excuse.

Death, presumably? A car accident requiring hospitalization? An atom bomb dropping on Ealing?

No, Jean would consider an atom bomb dropping on Ealing a very good reason for us all to Get Out There and Pull Our Weight. She would exhort her team to Pull Their Socks Up.

'Of course I'll do it,' Ellie promised, and remembered too late that Stewart and Maria had asked her to babysit that evening. And wasn't she supposed to be going out to supper with someone?

She rang Stewart at the flat and caught him just as he and Maria were giving little Frank his bath. Ellie smiled, thinking how adorable little Frank looked in his bath, surrounded by all his brightly coloured toys, many of which she'd given him.

'So sorry, Stewart, you asked me to babysit on Thursday but I've got a church "do" on and I can't get out of it. Can you get someone else?' Stewart relayed this to Maria, manlike, leaving her to cope.

Maria came on the line, sounding cheerful. 'Yes, of course, Ellie. You mustn't think you have to drop everything just to help us out.' Which meant that Maria did really think Ellie ought to drop everything to help them out. Didn't it? Or was she being oversensitive?

Maria continued, 'We're popping out in half an hour to see a house Stewart found, which we thought you might like to see as well. Someone at work told him about it. Stewart had a quick look at it this morning and thinks it worth a second visit, so one of our neighbours is going to look after little Frank, which is kind of her. Would you like to come, too?'

Ellie was in a quandary. If she said yes — and she would like to say yes — then, if Diana rang and needed her, she'd be out. 'I'll see if I can disentangle myself from something else I promised to do, and ring you back, all right?'

'You're brilliant, Ellie.'

Am I? thought Ellie, grimly. You want something, my girl, if you're prepared to stoop to flattery. You want me to help you buy a house and, yes, I've already said I would. You also want me to back you and Stewart in keeping little Frank, and now I'm in such a muddle about that that I can't think straight.

'Pull yourself together, girl.' That's what her husband would have said. He used to say that when she got into a state about silly little things. Like the shed burning down.

He'd had no idea there had been anything sinister about it. 'Kids!' he'd said. 'Playing around with matches, just to see what would happen. If I'd caught them, I'd have tanned their backsides for them.'

He'd gone ballistic about the shed burning down, but he hadn't suspected the Spendlove boys, had he? They were hardly 'kids' at the time, and as far as she knew had never been involved with any of the petty vandalism which occasionally resulted in arson or graffiti in the neighbourhood. Tod hadn't been living in their road then. Had there been other bands of youths roaming around after dark at that time, creating chaos? She didn't think so. She'd heard of it happening in other parts of London, but not here. Or not recently, anyway.

The phone rang again. It still wasn't Diana, but a long-time friend who was now living on the far side of London, suggesting a date for them to meet up in town and have lunch, perhaps take in an exhibition. Ellie didn't mention the problems they were having locally, or Diana's miscarriage. Her friend was a respected councillor and dealt with problem people all day long. Though she'd listen patiently, and even with sympathy, it wouldn't be right to burden her with Ellie's particular set of troubles.

Once that phone call was over, Ellie decided to ring Diana, even if Diana hadn't rung her. Maybe Diana was still so angry with her that she wouldn't answer. There was no way Ellie was going to apologize for what she'd said, though she now wished that she'd been more tactful.

The phone rang and rang. At last Diana answered, very abrupt.

'Oh, so there you are at last! I've been ringing and ringing. I need you here, right now.'

Contrary Ellie. As soon as Diana wanted her, Ellie wanted to be anywhere else but.

'I'm on my way out, but thought I'd just check how you were getting on.'

'What do you think? I'm still bleeding. How long does this go on for? Are miscarriages usually so bad?'

Ellie felt like saying that Diana hadn't experienced anything yet. Just let her wait till she was four or five months gone before she miscarried! But she didn't say it. 'It varies, Diana. Have you checked yourself out with your GP yet?'

'Have I time for that? How quickly can you get round here? I've got another couple coming round to look at the flats in half an hour, and I'm really not up to it. And I thought you could take over for me tomorrow evening, when I've got two of last Sunday's people coming back to take another look, and I've got a dinner party I simply have to go to . . .'

Thursday evening? Oh no. How many people wanted a piece of Ellie on Thursday? She'd stopped counting. 'Sorry, Diana, I'm already booked . . .'

'But I need you! I can't trust anyone else to—'

'No, Diana. Sorry, but no. Now, if you'll let me get a word in edgeways . . .'

'You don't understand. I can't be in two places at once and—'

'Neither can I. If you want to sell your flats privately and not through an agent, then you'll have to find someone to help you . . .'

'I thought you'd be proud to—'

'No!' Silence from the other end of the phone. 'Now, Diana, listen to me!'

The phone crashed down at the other end.

Ellie hung up her own phone, feeling limp. Without letting herself reconsider, she phoned Maria and Stewart back and said she'd be happy to meet up with them to go house-hunting, if they'd give her where and when.

'You're sure you can spare the time?' asked Stewart, who really was a dear. 'I know how busy you are.'

'Never too busy for family,' said Ellie. 'And we really must set aside one afternoon a week, say, in which I can have little Frank all to myself. It's been a moveable feast so far, sometimes this day and sometimes that, but I'd like to settle on a definite day of the week — if you agree.'

'Ellie, you're a marvel. The babysitter's just come, so we'll pick you up as soon as we've got Frank settled. In about half an hour's time, if that's all right with you?'

* * *

The house Stewart and Maria took her to see was shabby but had potential. As the agent pointed out, it was a well-built three-bedroom semi in a quiet, leafy street. An elderly lady had lived in it without making any attempt to renew faded decoration or furnishings, but the structure itself had been well maintained. Now the owner had gone into a home, and the house was up for sale. It looked as if it wanted to apologize for its hangdog appearance, but they could all see that with a little tender loving care it would be a perfect family house.

'Very possible,' said Maria. 'I can see us living here. We'd have to have the central heating and boiler checked out, of course. And does the wiring need renewing?'

'Looks all right to me,' said Stewart, who knew about such things. 'We could perhaps put in a loft conversion some time in the future. I see most of the houses in this road have got one, so we shouldn't have any difficulty in getting planning permission.'

While the estate agent hovered, Stewart tested window frames, squinted at drainpipes, gutters, and roof tiles. 'I can't see anything very wrong. A missing tile at the back. That manhole cover needs replacing. We'll have to have a full survey done, of course. The garden's neat enough if dull, but I see she's had someone coming in to mow the lawns and cut the hedges. Once the place has been painted, it'll look quite different. All in all, I think it's worth the money they're asking.'

Maria said, 'If we got someone to paint the outside and put in a new bathroom and kitchen — I've been looking at catalogues and they can be very reasonable — then the rest of the house just needs a lick of paint, which we could do ourselves.'

Ellie agreed. 'It's in a good area, not far from the shops and in the catchment area for the primary school on the Green. Can you afford it, though?'

Stewart looked worried. 'I think so. We've had an offer for Maria's flat already, and accepted it. Then there's the money from my half of the house Diana and I bought up north, and we've both got jobs, so we shouldn't have any difficulty getting a mortgage. Also, Maria's people said they'd help out. They said they'd come round and see the place tonight if we were that keen on it.'

'I'll help, too,' said Ellie, wondering how Diana was going to take the news, and deciding that she didn't care.

'I'll put in an offer for you, shall I?' asked the estate agent. Stewart and Maria went into a huddle with the estate agent while Ellie wandered out into the garden. She remembered that this was what she'd done long ago when she and her husband had been looking for something to move into and they'd discovered their present house. It had been dark then, but she'd stepped down the garden while Frank had haggled with the estate agent.

Stewart and Maria had more money to spend now than Ellie and Frank had had years ago, but property prices had moved up since. This garden was peaceful. A blackbird sang. Good.

The house would be a good buy.

Maria came out of the house and lifted her face up to the sky. She looked radiant, a picture of good health and good looks, with her superb carriage. 'It's good here, isn't it?'

'Yes, dear.' Ellie looked sideways at Maria and decided that, yes, the girl was certainly pregnant. A number of questions occurred to her, such as, would Maria still want to look after little Frank when she had a child of her own, and when were she and Stewart planning to marry? And how long did Maria propose to work? Ellie decided she wouldn't ask any of them.

Maria was smiling to herself, walking around the garden, which was big enough for a reasonable lawn, with a space for children's bikes and perhaps a swing or a slide. There was even a reasonably stout-looking shed at the end. And no water feature. Water features and small children did not mix.

Maria laughed out loud. 'Ellie, I've never had a garden of my own before. My mother never had time to attend to our garden while I was growing up, so it was really a playground for my brothers and me. It was a dustbowl in summer, and mud in winter. You'll have to tell me what to plant and how to look after it. Should we have a sandpit for the children, do you think?'

Children. Ah. Frank plus one. Or maybe two?

Ellie said, 'My treat. You'll need some kind of cover on it for wet weather. Otherwise the sand gets claggy.'

'I love your way of putting things,' said Maria, taking Ellie's arm and walking round the garden with her. 'That's a new word to me. "Claggy". It sounds just like what it means. Wet and saggy.'

'Like children's nappies.'

'Mm. Wet towels at bath time.' Without missing a step, Maria said, 'You've guessed we're having a baby ourselves? Next spring.'

'But you want to keep Frank?'

Maria didn't frown exactly. She didn't go in much for frowning. But she stood still, and looked grave. 'It was a difficult decision to make. Stewart adores his son. It would tear him apart to lose him. You and I, we're level-headed enough to know that Stewart would probably get over losing Frank, if he had one or two more of his own to look after. Only, would that be the best thing for him?

'We didn't plan for me to get pregnant so quickly. In fact, we thought we were being very responsible and taking precautions. But it happened. My family was horrified. I was, a bit, too. I would never want to bring a child into the world without a proper family to love it. Of course, we'll marry the moment the divorce is through.'

Ellie folded her mouth over all the questions she'd still like answered.

Maria was looking up at the blackbird in an old apple tree. 'You mustn't think we're taking this lightly. We're not. I feel some shame — well, not a lot, but some shame — about helping a man to break his marriage vows. He feels even worse about it than I do.

'Stewart believes in marriage as a sacrament. He married in church, believing that it was for life, that he was making his vows in the presence of God. Then Diana . . . and well, somehow we got together and before we knew it . . . no, no excuses. We behaved badly.

'I was brought up to go to church now and then. Stewart, too. We talked it over and decided that we needed help, so we went to see your vicar . . .'

Ellie blinked. Tum-Tum hadn't said anything about seeing Stewart and Maria. But then, perhaps he wouldn't.

'. . . Stewart said that he was an understanding sort of person, and indeed he was. We talked everything through with him. We plan to go to see him again soon, and we're going to go to church on Sundays in future.'

Ellie tried to keep up with this turn of events. 'If he doesn't feel able to marry you because of the divorce, he'll probably give you a service of blessing after you've got married in a registry office.'

'Yes, that's what he said. Now, one of the things that may hold up the divorce is if we have to fight Diana for Frank. In many ways it would be easier for us to give in, let her have him. Stewart and I'd miss him terribly, of course we would. But then, we'll soon have our own child to love. Only — and here I'm trying to be absolutely fair to everyone — wouldn't it be better for little Frank to be brought up by me?'

She blushed. 'That sounds awful. I know Diana loves him. At least, I think she does. But does she love him wisely? Will she correct and guide him? He's got a wicked temper and Stewart's far too easy-going, indulges Frank all the time. That worries me. How does Diana cope when he throws a tantrum?'

Ellie sighed. 'Diana does love him. She was prepared, almost, to give him up to you last week, but then . . . things happened to make her change her mind. She's got a ground-floor flat with a garden and she's been taking Frank there for some time, because he used to get in Derek's way. She's broken with Derek, she says. Maria, I don't know what to say. You may be right, and little Frank would benefit enormously from calm, consistent loving care. But he does love his mother and she loves him. Can't you agree to share?'

'I'd go along with that if Diana will agree. You understand how it is?'

'Yes, dear. I understand, and I will talk to Diana if she'll let me. At the moment we're a bit . . . well, not quite as happy families as we might be.'

'Bless you, Ellie.' To Ellie's surprise, Maria kissed her, and then went into the house, leaving Ellie to wonder what other complications God had in store for her.

* * *

Only one more that evening. DC Honeywell had dropped in a photo of the elderly Asian who'd been caught on CCTV visiting both the Acton and Central libraries in Ealing about the time the damaging emails had been sent.

'Bother,' said Ellie, holding the photo up to the light and deciding that, no, she still didn't know this man. 'I'd have liked to show this to Maria. Maybe she knows him.' She put the photo in her handbag, thinking she'd show it to everyone she knew who'd lived locally. Rose might know him, or Aunt Drusilla. Roy wouldn't, though. He'd been around for less than a year.

Which reminded her that Roy was expecting her for supper at his place that evening to make up a foursome. Who else had he invited? What on earth should she wear? She pulled one or two things out of her wardrobe and dithered. The blue with the cowl neck? No, it would be too warm for a summer evening.

Something casual but attractive? A cream top with a spot of self-embroidery on it, and a cream skirt? Not formal enough.

Her shoes . . . ugh! She'd ruined her best cream-coloured shoes that morning. She'd scrubbed them and left them on the draining board. Perhaps, with a good coat of cream polish . . . ?

She was working on them at the kitchen sink when Kate strolled up the garden path, waving to attract her attention.

'Are you busy, Ellie? Armand's not going to be back till late this evening, and I thought you might like a drive out into the country, supper at a pub somewhere.'

Was Kate ducking out of staying in the house by herself? Could be.

'What it is to be popular. Come in, my dear. I've already been invited out for supper and can't think what to wear. And just look at my shoes! Do you think they'd be all right? It's a dinner party, I gather.'

Kate inspected the shoes and shook her head. 'No way. Show me what you were planning to wear. We'll all go out tomorrow night instead, shall we?'

How many invitations did that make for Thursday evening? And she had to go to a talk in the church hall, which would probably turn out to be the most boring evening out, and then make coffee and wash up . . . !

'I wish I could. At the weekend, perhaps? While this beautiful weather lasts?'

She showed Kate what she'd picked out to wear.

'Definitely not!' Kate dived into Ellie's wardrobe and picked out a lacy top and silken swirly skirt in old rose, which she'd made Ellie buy for a friend's birthday party and never worn since. 'Delicious against your silvery hair and pretty complexion. And high heels, Ellie! I'm not letting you walk out of here in flatties.'

'I'll take a cab, then. It's a bit far to walk in those high heels. Are you sure I have to wear these things? Isn't that top too revealing? I've only worn it once. Doesn't the skirt make me look a bit tarty?'

'They make your boobs and your legs look fabulous. So don't argue. I'll drop you wherever it is you're going.'

'Bless you, dear. That would be good. It's only at Roy's. He'll bring me back, I expect.' She found a small evening bag and emptied her own handbag out on the bed.

Kate didn't think much of Roy, but confined herself to a grimace while picking over the jewellery from Aunt Drusilla's cigar box, which had finally made it up the stairs into Ellie's bedroom.

'Hello, this looks like a good brooch.' She held it up to the light. 'Ah, yes. It breaks up into two clasps. Marcasite. Nineteen thirties, at a guess. Where did you get it?'

'My aunt decided to bestow various bits and pieces on me. They belonged to Frank's mother, who died aeons ago. I objected but Aunt Drusilla said they weren't costly and I could insure them for a few hundreds. Only, I still haven't done anything about it. The thing is, they're not quite my style.'

Kate threw herself on the bed, trying the effect of various necklaces and rings on her own fingers. Kate was wearing shades of tobacco this evening, extremely plain and shrieking money.

Ellie glanced at Kate sideways, amused by the way the younger woman had assumed their friendship extended to dressing Ellie up for a night out. 'Did you use to dress your mother up for a night out like this?'

'She's only interested in the bingo. I've almost been disowned since I married Armand. She says he's a snob and he's taught me to become one, too.'

'You aren't a snob.' Ellie was indignant.

'I probably am, you know. I find bingo boring.' Kate picked up a necklet of seed pearls. 'This is pretty but perhaps not quite "you". These earrings are for pierced ears and you haven't had yours done. Will you sell them? They might fetch a bit, and then you could buy something you really liked for yourself.'

'As they were Frank's mother's, I couldn't possibly get rid of them.' Ellie caught sight of Kate's outstretched body in her mirror and thought, Is she pregnant? No, no! I'm imagining things. Just because Maria and Diana were . . .

'Cameo brooch,' said Kate. 'Just the right touch. Expensive, tasteful, unusual.'

'A bit old-fashioned, like me?' Ellie pushed lipstick, a comb, a handkerchief and some money into her tiny evening bag.

'What's this?' Kate had found the photograph of the elderly Asian.

Ellie explained, brushing out her hair, smoothing her eyebrows, putting a dab of powder on her nose, which always got shiny, no matter what she did with it.

Kate held the photograph away from her and then brought it close to. 'Are the police sure? It seems such an odd thing for a man like that to do.'

'A man like what? Where would you place him in society?'

'I don't know. Not a manual labourer. Not a small shopkeeper.'

'I thought he might be a professional man.'

'Have I met him through work? No, I don't think so. I can't place him on the other side of a table in committee . . . and yet. No, I don't know. What sort of car does he drive? That usually tells you a lot about a man.'

'I really don't know. I don't think anyone's connected him with a car, yet. But there is one other thing, Kate.' Careful, thought Ellie. I don't want to give Kate the impression that everyone who lived in their house before had a bad time.

Ellie continued, 'Mrs Dawes dragged me over to see Ms Cullen, whose mother used to live in your house, and she was talking about her two daughters. Well, boasting, really. And complaining, too. One of them works in the travel agency in the Avenue. That's Lana. But there was a younger sister who trained as a teacher, and Mrs Cullen said she was at the High School. Her name's Trudy. Could you ask Armand if he knows anything about her?'

'Will do. I think I've met the girl at some do or other. She's not a teacher, though. A classroom assistant, something in the science line, I think. Ellie, you are not going out in those flatties, I won't have it!'

Ellie, who'd hoped to do just that, gave in and put on the high-heeled sandals Kate had picked out for her. They did make her taller. And made her stand up properly. Kate stuffed the photo into Ellie's evening bag and handed it to her. 'Knock their eyes out, girl!'

* * *

The businessman sat in his car outside the hospital. The cost of the car parking there was astronomical, but there was nowhere else to park for miles. He rang his brother.

'He's a little better but very frail. There's not much they can do for him, he's on a drip, antibiotics, painkillers. My wife's with him, and my elder daughter. The others are coming later.'

'I'll take leave, cancel my appointments . . .'

'It would be good. He's been asking for you. He wants . . .' He broke off with a sob.

'He needs to know we're going to look after him. You told him we would?'

'Yes, of course. But how? We've done everything we could to protect him . . .'

'And ourselves, remember. If the truth comes out, it won't only be him in the dock. Think what would happen to your family? And mine? Our sons . . . our daughters' marriages . . . the grandchildren's education?'

'Yes, yes. I know. He's not really conscious, but he was trying to ask me about it. It's giving him no rest!'

The surgeon's voice hardened. 'You know what to do.'

'No, no. I don't.'

'Then I'll tell you . . .'

CHAPTER SEVENTEEN

Roy had only moved into the Gate House last weekend but he'd worked hard to make it into a home. To Ellie's eyes his new quarters looked a little self-conscious, as if posing for *House and Gardens,* but it was undeniably stunning. Now that he'd hung his contemporary pictures on the walls, the balance of the decor had tipped from ancient to modern. He'd arranged spotlights to focus on this and that piece of art, he'd cleared all the removal men's boxes away, all the media bits and pieces were in working order and he could host a dinner party without a qualm.

Ellie wondered how many man hours Rose had put into helping Roy get things straight, and hoped he'd given her a good present in return.

Two other guests arrived at the same time as Ellie. One guest Ellie recognized immediately as the mega-thin woman in marketing who she'd met at the wedding of Rose's daughter a while back. She'd been a cousin of the bride and had made a dead set at Roy. What was her name? Helen something?

The other guest was Bill. Ellie was delighted to see Bill. And then she wasn't at all delighted, because it looked as if she were being pushed into his arms all the time and at the moment she didn't want to be pushed into any man's arms.

Helen was wearing a halter-necked black dress which did nothing for a figure that really hadn't had anything to boast about to start with. Except thinness, of course. She advanced on Ellie, smiling a little too widely, showing a little too much teeth.

'Eggy, isn't it? I think we met at my cousin's wedding.'

'Ellie,' said Ellie. 'And you're Hedda.' If Helen could get her name wrong, then so could Ellie.

Helen's smile vanished. 'Helen, actually.'

Ellie continued cheerfully, 'Of course. Silly of me. Yes, we met then. A beautiful wedding. Are you down for a few days? I thought you lived up north somewhere.'

'Indeed she does,' said Roy, playing the part of hearty host. 'She's down for a conference in town and rang me on the off chance, which gives me the opportunity to show off my new pad.' He handed Ellie a glass of her favourite sherry and asked Bill what he'd like.

'I'm driving,' said Bill, twinkling at everyone, blandly ignoring any undercurrents in the room. 'So something soft, if you will. I must say I like the way you've done this place out. It used to be a decrepit old coach house, didn't it? What do you think, Ellie?'

'I like it,' said Ellie. 'Though I gather your mother, Roy, expected you to make it an all-glass, minimalist sort of place.'

'Oh, mothers!' said Helen, with an expressive twist of her shoulders. Ellie reflected it was lucky Helen had worn a halter-neck, as it was only the tie at the back of the neck which kept the dress from falling off her.

'My mother's something else,' said Roy, standing up for her. 'I'm devoted to her — and her brilliant brain! Here's to her!'

Ellie and Bill raised their glasses accordingly.

Helen wasn't accustomed to hearing people praise their mothers, and only tipped her glass up a fraction. Unwisely, she decided to make a joke of Roy's devotion. 'I'd never have put you down as tied to your mother's apron strings!'

The idea of Miss Drusilla Quicke with apron strings struck her listeners as so bizarre that conversation was suspended until Bill recovered enough to change the subject. 'The word is that your town houses in Endene Close are attracting a lot of interest. When do they go on the market?'

'Any day now. We've been held up waiting for some light fitments, but they've promised to deliver tomorrow. If I can get the electricians back to fit them the next day, then . . . but there's always this and that needs tidying up. Cupboard doors without their knobs, floors needing polish. It won't be long now, though.'

Helen perked up. It was news to her that Roy was responsible for a development of town houses on the Green. Ah, now she could see him as a suitable prospect for her wiles. Ellie wasn't so sure how Roy felt about Helen. At the wedding he'd been all over her, but now . . . ?

Helen moved over to stand a little too close to Roy. Roy moved away. So he wasn't that keen on her now? Ellie sipped her sherry in demure enjoyment of this little bit of byplay.

Bill pulled out a chair for Ellie and she sat, remembering to display her pretty, high-heeled shoes. Helen was also wearing high-heeled shoes, but the varnish on her toenails was chipped and her heels red. Ellie began to be sorry for Helen, a little.

Helen might be twenty years Ellie's junior and many pounds lighter in weight, but she was no fool and her quick, bird-like glances to and fro were telling her that both men were on affectionate terms with the older woman.

Roy was enjoying himself. He didn't seem to realize Helen wasn't. 'To tell the truth, Endene Close is selling itself. I've had a man pestering me all this week, wandering in and out, measuring up, wants to make me an offer as soon as he can decide which he wants, the one nearest the road or the one farthest away. The estate agents — not Jolley's, I'm happy to say — were pressing me to put the houses on the market even before the cupboard doors were on. Only one of the houses has been decorated so far, and yet . . .' He shrugged. 'Well, time's money in this business, so maybe I'll let them start showing people round early next week. Now Ellie's worked her magic on the gardens, I must say the whole development looks good.'

Helen arched impossibly thin eyebrows. 'Oh, you do gardening, do you, Eggy? Mow lawns, trim hedges, that sort of thing? I've heard there's always jobs for people like you.'

Ellie heard the note of scorn in Helen's voice. Bill heard it, and looked down into his glass. Roy wasn't sure that he'd heard aright. He treated Helen to a puzzled look.

'General dogsbody, that's me,' said Ellie, satisfied that she didn't look the part of dogsbody in that rig-out. Bless Kate for making her wear it. 'And now, Roy, is there anything you'd like me to do for you in the kitchen?'

'My dear girl, no! You've done more than enough, helping me settle in. I made a trip to Waitrose and picked up everything we need. It's all cold, so, if you'd care to come to the table . . . ? You sit on my right, Ellie. Helen, you're on my left. Bill goes between you. And in a trice, I turn myself into a waiter and supper is served!'

He brought in a tray on which rested four starters of smoked salmon and thinly cut brown bread and butter, with a garnish of radishes cut into flower shapes. Ellie decided that he certainly hadn't arranged the food himself. Perhaps dear Rose had popped across to help him out and take back titbits of gossip to Miss Quicke?

Helen languished at Roy. 'Clever old you.' She picked up her fork and began on a long tale of a recent weekend away with friends, which was meant to impress Roy with her sophistication and knowledge of the high life. Bill listened politely. Roy smiled with the fixed half smile of one whose thoughts are elsewhere.

'. . . and there he was,' said Helen with relish, 'with his trophy wife! And he even had the nerve to call her "Candy".' Then, explaining to those who might not be expected to know, she added, 'They call the young women who hang on the arms of older, powerful men, "arm candy".'

'Indeed,' said Bill, being courteous.

'Well, there it is,' said Helen, confident she was putting herself over well. 'I'm afraid older women don't stand a chance nowadays. Powerful men, men who've made their way in the world, will always go for youth.'

Ellie was amused. 'I heard that older men are flocking on expensive cruises looking for only slightly younger women who'll stick with them, nurse them through to their graves. Not that I fancy someone with one foot in the grave.'

Helen looked sour.

Bill twinkled at Ellie. 'What would you look for, Ellie? A toy boy?'

Ellie giggled. Bill grinned. Roy looked worried. He wasn't enjoying himself much, was he?

The meal progressed, with Ellie becoming more and more sure that Roy regretted having invited Helen, and that he had not prepared the food by himself. Slices of game pie arrived, with tiny new potatoes and a mixed salad.

Helen talked at everyone about the conference she'd come down to attend.

'Fashion statements for next year. I don't suppose you'd know anything about that, Eggy.'

Ellie corrected her without rancour. 'My name's Ellie. I'm afraid I'm no good at shopping. I have a personal shopper nowadays. Is that what you do?'

Helen lost her temper and slapped her napkin down on the table. The men looked at her in astonishment. Ellie, too. Had her random enquiry struck home? Was the girl really nothing but a personal shopper in a big store? And not a great fashion buyer?

Roy pushed back his chair. 'A glass of water, Helen? Has something gone down the wrong way?'

Helen rushed from the table with Roy showing her the way to the toilet.

Bill stolidly went on eating. 'Do you think she's bulimic? Gone to throw up?'

'Heavens, Bill! I never thought of that,' said Ellie, slightly ashamed of herself, but still wanting to giggle.

Roy came back in a little while, escorting a pale-looking Helen. Roy said, 'I'm afraid Helen's got to leave us. She hadn't realized it was so late. Luckily she's got her own car outside.'

Ellie and Bill made suitable noises of regret and Helen left. Roy resumed his seat and poured out more wine for everybody.

Ellie said, 'I'm afraid I was a little hard on her.'

Both men smiled.

Roy said, 'I'm really sorry about all that. She rang up late last night after I'd gone into a really deep sleep, woke me up. Said I'd promised to take her out on the town and she was taking me up on my promise . . . which, by the way, I can't remember making. She reminds me so much of my ex-wife. I can still see why I was attracted, but the moment she turned up here this evening, I knew I didn't want to go through all that again. I'm sorry I dragged you two into it.'

'Not at all,' said Bill. 'I enjoyed Ellie's performance immensely.'

Roy picked up Ellie's hand and kissed it. 'So did I. You're worth six of her, Ellie Quicke.'

'Yes, I've heard old men like to marry money second time round,' said Ellie, tartly. 'Now, shall I help clear the table? Has Rose gone back to her own place yet?'

'I can't keep any secrets from you, can I?' Roy took out their plates. 'I thought I might as well cater for six as for four, so that she needn't cook tonight. I could have managed to dish up by myself but she wouldn't have it. She insisted on helping me put everything out on plates, but she's gone back now. Ice-cream gateau with caramelized pineapple slices for afters. And then Ellie can tell us all about her latest murder case.'

Ellie protested. 'You make me sound like a proper detective, but I wouldn't mind you having a look at this.' She pulled the photograph out of her handbag and passed it to Bill.

Bill produced a glasses case — half-moon type — and set them on his nose. 'No, I don't know him. Ought I to do so?'

Ellie explained about the emails and how the police had spotted this one man at both venues. Bill shook his head, and without thinking, passed the photo to Roy. Roy took something that looked like a fountain pen from his pocket, and opened it to remove the slimmest pair of glasses Ellie had ever seen. He'd be too vain to wear glasses to correct his long sight normally, but these would do to read a theatre programme or a menu, if you wanted to maintain a fashionable image.

'You won't have come across him, Roy,' said Ellie. 'This affair goes back twenty years.'

Roy stabbed at the photo. 'But I have! This is the man who's been hanging around Endene this last week. The man who says he's going to make an offer when he can decide which end of the terrace he wants to buy! Didn't you come across him today when you were planting the garden? No, come to think of it, I didn't see him today.'

'What's his name?'

'Patel.'

'There are lots of Patels,' said Bill. 'It's a very common name. There are a couple of pages of them in the Ealing directory alone.'

Ellie licked her spoon clean. The dessert had been delicious. 'Maria is a Patel. I must ask her or her father if they know him. Extended family and all that.'

'More like a tribe,' said Roy. 'Thousands of them.'

'What are his initials?' asked Bill. 'What does he do? Where does he live?'

Roy hit his forehead with the heel of his hand. 'I don't know. He said he hadn't got a card on him because he was in the process of moving down to London from the north. He said he wants a house near his brother, who lives somewhere down by the river. He said he'd been cruising around the neighbourhood looking for something suitable, happened to spot our development and thought it was exactly what he's looking for. He said he's still got to sell his family house up north — Leeds, was it? — but that was only a formality. I said he'd have to talk to the agents, and he said that was all right, if I didn't mind him hanging around a bit. He was waiting for his wife to come down to have a look at the place, wanted to make sure she liked it.'

'What sort of car does he drive?' asked Ellie, thinking of how Kate judged a man by the car he drove.

'A Mercedes.'

Silence.

'It doesn't make sense,' said Ellie. 'He sounds so genuine. A businessman, driving a Mercedes? He can't be the one who's sending the emails. The police have made a mistake. It must be someone else.'

'Unless,' said Bill, putting his glasses away, 'he's got an ulterior motive in hanging around Endene Close. You can get a good view of the back of your house and garden from there, can't you, Ellie?'

Ellie gasped. 'You mean, he could be hanging around there just to watch me? But I've never met the man in my life. Why is he targeting me? I don't understand why he's doing this. It's . . . scary.'

Roy put his glasses away, too. 'The first thing to do is to tell the police about him hanging around Endene. Then we've got to work out how to protect Ellie from this man.'

Rose knocked on the door. 'Miss Quicke says, would you like to join her for coffee?'

'Dear Rose,' said Roy. 'You are the light of my life. How did you know I haven't been able to get my coffee machine to work since the move?'

* * *

Miss Quicke was waiting for them in her drawing room. You couldn't call that room a 'lounge'. It was much too grand. Fine coffee had already been made and was sitting in a thermos waiting for them, while the best tiny cups had been laid out with three different kinds of sugar, and some petit fours. Miss Quicke liked to do things in style, and Rose appreciated the chance to use good china.

Ellie bent to kiss the older lady, who said, 'You're looking very pretty tonight, Ellie. Careful you don't trip over the rug in those high heels, though.'

Roy also kissed his mother, while Bill gave her a little bow of appreciation.

'I gather you got rid of the bimbo,' said Miss Quicke.

Roy laughed to hear his mother use that term.

'Arm candy,' said Ellie, enjoying herself.

Miss Quicke admonished Roy. 'You can do better than that.'

'So I can,' said Roy, looking at Ellie.

Miss Quicke accepted a cup of milky coffee from Rose. 'Now, bring me up to date on Ellie's murder case.'

Ellie protested. 'It's not my case, and I don't know how I came to get mixed up in it, but this is what's been happening recently . . .'

When she'd finished, there was a thoughtful silence.

Miss Quicke said, 'Twenty years ago. I was about your age then, Ellie. I remember I'd overreached myself in purchasing . . . well, never mind that, now. But money was tight. I'd the greatest dread of bankruptcy. I'd mortgaged everything to pull off this one big coup. The problem was that the planning department at the Town Hall were being extremely stupid about what I'd done with another house in the same block. Wanted me to pull down the extension I'd built at the back. Such nonsense. Without it, my tenants wouldn't have had a modern bathroom or kitchen. Yes, that was a worrying time.'

Ellie smiled. 'You sound just like Diana, sure you know best and maybe overreaching yourself in the process.'

'Hm, yes. Remind me to have a word with you about Diana later. Now, where was I? Ah yes. My nephew Frank was not as helpful as he might have been at the time. Some problem with your hormones, I gather. I told him, I don't approve of interfering with the bodies the good Lord gave us. But he didn't agree.'

'That was when I had to have a hysterectomy?'

'I asked him to help me with my applications to the planning department. He said he'd got too much on to do anything, but he put me in touch with a man named Spendlove who lived next door to him and worked at the Town Hall.'

'You knew him, then?' Ellie was surprised.

'Yes, of course I did. I went to see him at the Town Hall and explained my position. He wasn't in the planning department but I thought he might know someone who was. Nice man. On crutches. He told me he was looking at the prospect of spending the rest of his life in a wheelchair.'

Silence.

'Yes?' Roy prompted her.

His mother raised her eyebrows, and did not reply.

Bill chuckled. 'Came to an arrangement, did you?'

Miss Quicke handed her cup to Ellie to put on the tray. 'Of course not. Nothing needed to be said, and nothing was said.'

Roy began to grin. 'Nothing in writing, either? So, what was the deal? You found him a ground-floor flat with disabled access, and he got your plans passed?'

Miss Quicke did her best to look shocked. 'Really, Roy. Nothing of the sort. It's true I did happen to mention that I had a flat which could be adapted to his needs, that it was either for rent or for sale, and that I'd send him particulars. We both deplored the cost of sending his boys to university, although I think one of his sons was perhaps not up to that. He had to cut our meeting short, as he was having lunch with one of his colleagues.'

She accepted a refill of her cup from Rose. 'He was an honest man. I half expected him to want the flat rent-free, but no, he paid the market price for a long lease when he sold his own house. And I made sure the necessary alterations were made so that a disabled person could live there.'

'You got your planning permission?'

'Of course. I told you, there really were no good grounds to refuse me. So everyone was happy.'

Ellie wondered whether everything really had been as straightforward as Miss Quicke had indicated. From the sceptical looks on the faces of Roy and Bill, they were thinking so, too. Miss Quicke looked serene.

Ellie asked, 'Is Mr Spendlove still alive? He's not in the Ealing phone book.'

'Gracious, of course he is. Why, he can't be more than sixty-five, if he's a day! Pays his ground rent on the nail.'

Ellie said, 'You think I might learn something if I visited them?'

'You might. He's in Wembley, so of course he won't be in the Ealing phone book. Grove Avenue. Number eleven, if my memory serves me right. The boys are both off and away, of course. Married or whatever equivalent it is that they go in for nowadays. One of them is in the planning department at the Town Hall. A useful contact.'

'Mother, you never fail to surprise me,' said Roy. 'But you're looking tired. Shall we leave you now?'

Miss Quicke did her impersonation of a nutcracker. 'I know what you boys are like. You're going outside to fight over who takes Ellie home.'

Ellie laughed. 'Aunt Drusilla, you are appalling. And I love you dearly.' She kissed the old lady's cheek and looked around for her handbag.

'You left your bag at my place,' said Roy. 'I'll run you home, shall I?'

'No need,' said Bill, smooth as silk. 'I've got my car outside. I'll wait for you in it, shall I, Ellie?'

'Thanks, Bill.'

As she picked up her handbag and put the photo of Mr Patel in it, Roy took her by surprise. Putting his arms round her from behind, he kissed her cheek and then, turning her round, kissed her on the lips.

She quite liked it. But drew back. 'No, Roy. Really. We're such good friends and I want to keep it that way.'

'But you don't mind my trying?'

She laughed and went out to where Bill was sitting in his car. 'Lovely evening,' she said. 'Isn't Miss Quicke amazing?'

'She gave us a sanitized account of the Spendlove affair, don't you think? I wonder what the truth is.'

'Maybe it wasn't so far from the truth. She told me she'd learned long ago that honesty was the best policy. I'll find out tomorrow.'

He drew up outside her house and before she knew it — she was so slow this evening — he'd put his arm around her, said, 'My turn, now!' and given her a kiss. She liked that, too. Really, she was becoming far too partial to all this kissing. And dear Frank not dead twelve months yet.

She drew back. 'Dear Bill, I love you, and I love Roy and I still love Frank. You understand how it is, don't you? This whole nasty business has brought everything back, the good bits and the bad of my marriage. I'm all mixed up and it's going to take time for me to sort myself out. If ever I do. Bear with me?'

He took it well. Saw her into the house, waved goodbye and drove away.

Only when she had closed the outside door did she wonder if she ought to be afraid of spending the night in a house which was being watched by a strange man.

She went round the house making sure all the locks were on, and the doors bolted.

Those two boys . . . ! Well, they really were only boys to her, even though both were older than her. Aunt Drusilla had them down to a T. She put it all down to wearing those high-heeled shoes, which she now took off with a sigh of relief.

She was happy enough as she was, going up to bed when she wanted to, having a late-night snack if she wanted, or not.

And no washing-up that evening.

* * *

The old man opened his eyes. His hand tightened around his son's.

'Promise! Promise!'

'Don't agitate yourself, father. Nobody's going to hurt you. My brother is on his way down . . .'

The old man was fretful. 'He shouldn't . . . he's such an important man . . .'

'So are you. Of course he's coming.'

'If they find out . . .'

'No one will find out anything. I'll see to it. I promise.'

'You promise?'

'Yes.'

The old man's eyes closed again, and he slept.

CHAPTER EIGHTEEN

It rained in the night. Not much, but enough that Ellie didn't have to worry about watering the busy lizzies and pansies in the top bed by the conservatory. That was the worst of those particular flowers; you couldn't leave them without water in dry weather or they dried up and died.

Wonder of wonders, there was only one message on the answerphone and it was from Armand and not from Diana.

Armand was in a hurry, as usual. 'Kate says you wanted to know something about Trudy Cullen? She does work at the school, though not for me. General dogsbody in the science department. Kate wasn't clear why you were asking after Trudy, but if you need to contact her, she lives in one of those pretty old houses just at the back of the Broadway round by St Mary's Church. They haven't been there long, and I don't think they're in the phone book yet, but I could get her phone number for you if you want it.'

He'd ended the call there.

So Diana hadn't called back. Oh well. Plenty to do. People to see.

Ellie made out a shopping list, remembering to include some biscuits for the coffee after the Women's Hour that evening. Last time she'd washed up at church after that meeting, there hadn't been a clean tea towel in sight. She put a couple out to take with her.

She rang the police station to say that Roy had supplied a name for the man in the photograph, but neither DI Willis nor that nice constable Honeywell were available, so she left a message for them.

Walking across the Green, she checked to see if the mystery man were hanging around Endene Close, but there was no one to be seen. Not even the lighting fitment people, or the electricians. Roy wouldn't be pleased about that, would he.

She waved to Tum-Tum but he didn't see her. He was leaning on his rake, pretending to collect up some of the leaves which were beginning to fall from the trees, but actually having a good gossip with a passer-by.

Before she started her shopping, she climbed the stairs to Maria's office at Trulyclean Services. Maria was there already, cup of coffee in hand, talking to a client on the phone while calling up information on her computer.

When the client had gone, Ellie said, 'Before anything else, did your parents approve of the house?'

Maria beamed. 'Yes, they did. They said it was just like their own first little house and they'll help us with the mortgage. And, the estate agent rang back last night to say our offer has been accepted!'

'I am so pleased for you, my dear. Now, a couple of things. Am I allowed to take little Frank out this afternoon?'

'Oh.' Maria looked upset. 'Not today, no. You won't believe this, but since he started at the toddlers' group, he's had invitations to two birthday parties, and this is one of them. Of course, I said he could go, and I completely forgot you wanted Thursdays in future. What about tomorrow?'

'Fine. And—' here Ellie took the rather mauled photograph out of her handbag — 'Do you by any chance know this man? The police think it was he who sent them an email saying I was mixed up in that murder case. He told Roy that his name's Patel, though I do realize there are hundreds of

Patels around. All we really know about him is that he drives a Mercedes and said he was interested in buying a house in Endene Close . . . though I don't know if he was serious about that, or just wanting to keep an eye on the back of my house.'

Maria took the photograph to the light. She shook her head. 'No, I don't think I know him. If you can wait a minute, though, I'll fax a copy to my father and ask if he knows the man. Being on the council, he knows a great many business people around here.'

So Maria assumed he was a businessman. Interesting. Competent as ever, she ran off a covering note and sent it with a copy of the photo. 'Coffee while we wait?'

Ellie looked at her watch. 'I'd better not. I'm having lunch with Rose at Sunflowers and I've got lots to do first.'

The fax machine whirred back. Maria rescued the message, and shook her head. 'My father says he doesn't know this man. Do you know what line of business he's in? Are you sure he's local?'

'No, I don't think he is. It was a long shot. Thanks for trying, anyway.'

So that was that. Walking along to the grocer's, Ellie hesitated outside the travel agency. Was that girl at the desk inside Lana Cullen, whose grandmother had died next door in questionable circumstances? Now was it she who was married or was it her sister? Lana was wearing a too-bright red blouse and black skirt. Her hair had been blonded but the roots showed dark. She was wearing a lot of heavy-looking jewellery, including a wedding ring, but it all looked as if it had been bought off a market stall.

Ellie pushed the door open, and went in. The girl looked up with a bored smile, and then recognized her. 'Hello, Mrs Quicke. You went to see my mum with Mrs Dawes, didn't you? She was on the phone to me last night, saying how kind it had been of you to call on her, but that you'd only stayed a minute or two. She said you'd promised to come back to see her another day. I do hope you can. She gets lonely. What can I do for you? Perhaps a cruise?'

'Perhaps.' Ellie took a seat opposite the girl. Business seemed slow. There was only one other desk manned, and the youth behind it seemed to be playing Free Cell on his computer. 'I could do with some brochures on holidays abroad, and I'll pick them out in a minute. It was good to see your mother again and catch up on old times. I hadn't realized you knew my Diana so well.'

Lana laughed, crossed her legs, leaned back in her chair twiddling with a pen. 'Well, yes. In a way, I suppose. She used to try to hang around with us in those days. But you know what teenagers are, all mouth and no trousers, as the saying is. We used to dare one another to do things, but . . .' She shrugged. 'I suppose all teenagers are like that. Gran used to go on at us like anything. "I've got my eagle eye on you," she used to say. And "You give me lip, my girl, and I'll give you something to remember me by." She was a funny old thing, wasn't she?'

Ellie tried to fit this portrait of old Mrs Cullen into what she remembered of the woman and then with what she'd surmised, perhaps wrongly. 'I remember you coming to the door and not letting me see her.'

Lana laughed, a trifle too loudly. But then, that was her style. 'She told us not to let anyone in, because she'd got mouth ulcers and couldn't bear to wear her false teeth. What a scream that was, us trying to mash up her food so's she could get it down her.' She sobered up. 'She went off quickly at the end. Gave us a fright, that. My sister wondered if she'd taken too many of her painkillers and we looked for the bottle, but it was all right. They were all there. She fell on the landing, on her way to the toilet, you know. It was bad luck we weren't there that night, any of us. Poor old thing. We would have liked her to have died in her bed, but there . . . she died with her boots on, as she would have said.'

'Yes, indeed.' Ellie couldn't think of any other questions to ask. Lana's manner was so open, it was clear she was telling the truth. Ellie'd been wrong about the manner of Mrs Cullen's death. She pulled the photo out of her handbag. 'You don't happen to know this man, do you? His name's

Patel. He's been hanging around, may be connected in some way with the girl they found murdered near my house.'

Lana looked and shook her head. 'He looks a bit like our boss, but it isn't him. Have you asked Mr Patel at the baker's?'

Ellie said she'd do that, collected some brochures at random, and wondered about hopping on a bus to the road in which Mr Spendlove lived. It was certainly too far to walk. She waited five minutes. And then another five. She was just on the point of phoning for a cab when a bus came along and she got on.

She'd looked up Grove Avenue in the A to Z and got off at the nearest point en route. They were in a very select part of Wembley. There were spacious detached houses in their own gardens, all built around the turn of the previous century, with semi-circular driveways and heavily frowning porticoes over the front doors. Most were divided into flats, as was the house to which Miss Quicke had directed her.

There was a ramp up to the front door, and a bell push gave the name of Spendlove beside a speaker entry system. Ellie rang the bell and waited. Someone was playing music nearby. Classical music. Rachmaninov? Very loudly. She pressed the bell again, and the music was muted. A man asked who was there, Ellie gave her name, and was admitted.

A wide hall, parquet floored. A door on the right admitted to a large ground-floor flat, and Mr Spendlove was holding it open for her. His hair had turned white and thinned since she saw him last, and he was in a wheelchair, but otherwise looking much the same as ever. A music centre was still pouring out music. Someone behind him shut it off, and called out to know who was there.

He called back into the flat, 'It's all right. I've got it.' Footsteps retreated and a door slammed shut.

Mr Spendlove frowned at Ellie. 'Why, hello! I thought you were someone from the church. Do I know you?'

'I'm Ellie Quicke, who used to live next door to you? Remember?'

He passed a fretful hand over his forehead. 'It comes and goes. It comes and it goes. You lived next door to us, did you? Not here, though. Was it?'

She shook her head. Was his memory going?

He said, 'If you're from the church, you can come in and take a seat.'

Ellie followed him in and took a chair. The flat was light and airy, with wooden floors and furniture kept to a minimum to allow for free passage of the wheelchair. Another door led to the back of the house. Someone was playing a radio in there, not loudly. Whoever it was stayed the other side of the door.

Ellie said, 'We've been talking over old times when you and the boys lived next door to me, so I thought I'd look you up.' It sounded weak to her ears, but he didn't seem to mind. 'Is your wife in?' She looked at the door to the back.

'She's out. It's only the Home Help in there,' said Mr Spendlove. 'Do you play chess? Have you come to give me a game? I play all the time.'

A chess set was laid out on a table in the window. Ellie was amused. 'I'm afraid I never learned.'

He twirled his chair around to face her. 'Sometimes they send someone down from the church to play with me. Did you come from the church?' He lost his alert look, the lines of his face became slack, and he grew fretful. He passed his hand across his eyes and looked around the room as if he'd never seen it before.

Ellie wondered if he was altogether aware of her sitting there. She said in her most commonsensical voice, 'Do your boys play chess with you?'

He brightened. 'My boys? No. They've got their own families to look after now. Oh, they come round regularly enough, I suppose. They were only here . . . yesterday?' He'd lost the plot again, looked vague.

Ellie wondered when his wife would be back.

His wandering eye lit upon the music centre, and he wheeled himself over to it, saying, 'My wife doesn't like noise, you know. Likes everything kept very quiet and regular. Me, I like a bit of loud music now and then.'

'I remember.' Ellie was amused. 'My husband said he always knew when you were out, because there was silence from your side of the wall.' Would Mr Spendlove remember Frank?

'Ah. Your husband. He was called . . . what was he called?'

'His name was Frank.'

'Frank! Yes, I knew I'd remember it in a minute.' Mr Spendlove was pleased with himself for remembering the name. 'How is he getting on nowadays? He's a good bit younger than me, of course.'

There was no point in telling him the truth. Ellie steeled herself. 'No, he's not that old.'

Mr Spendlove pummelled his left hand with his right, watching her out of the corner of his eyes. Had he forgotten who she was already? She saw with pity that he had indeed aged a lot. His knuckles were knotted, and the skin on the backs of his hands mottled.

'At least your boys do come to visit you,' she said. 'I've been talking to the Cullens . . .'

'Who? Who did you say? I don't know you, do I? Did you say you'd come from the church?'

She didn't think it would be any use, but she produced the photograph of Mr Patel. 'Do you by any chance remember this man?'

He looked but didn't take the photograph. Was that a flash of recognition? No, probably not. He looked vaguely around the flat. 'I think my wife must have gone out for a bit. She's usually here. Have you come for a game of chess?'

She shook her head and he didn't seem to mind. He seemed even to have forgotten she was there. Now she saw that there was dust on the chess board and some of the pieces had fallen over and not been replaced. It was a long time since this man had played chess.

He went over to the music centre and turned the sound up.

Definitely Rachmaninov.

It was all deeply depressing. Ellie put the photo back in her handbag and left.

* * *

Lunch at the Sunflowers Café with Rose had become something of a ritual. Ellie got there first, dumped her shopping in the corner behind their favourite table, and tried to decide whether she preferred chicken and mushroom pie to beef stew. Could she manage soup as well?

She patted her stomach. Best not. She ought to go on a diet, of course. But not just yet.

Dear Rose staggered in, pushing a large shopping basket on wheels ahead of her. Rose was wearing a smart new navy-blue jacket and trousers, and her hair had been freshly permed, but set in looser waves than usual. Ellie didn't know how Aunt Drusilla had managed it, but Rose never seemed to appear in public with her buttons done up wrongly nowadays. She looked, in fact, surprisingly well turned out.

They settled down to a delightful chat about the appalling behaviour of the manageress of the local charity shop, which was where they'd met some years before. 'Madam', as her staff called her, had a flair for upsetting people, and since Ellie and Rose had left, hardly any of the old-timers remained. Ellie maintained that Anita at least would see Madam out, but Rose feared the worst.

'Perhaps they'll have to close the shop, if Madam drives everyone away.'

At which thought, both women sighed and shook their heads.

When their food came, Rose said how lovely it was of Roy, giving her and Miss Quicke unexpected treats like their supper last night, and she was really glad that Helen had left early, because, little as she wished to criticize, and not all her daughter's friends were quite so self-centred, she'd never been able to take to that Helen girl, though why that was, she really couldn't say.

'I quite agree,' said Ellie. 'And how do you like your quarters in the big house?'

'Lovely, dear. The new shower unit took a bit of getting used to, because I've never had anything like that to deal with before, but I got the upper hand of it eventually. Dear Miss Quicke insists I have a little rest in the afternoons and go out and about every day, and she won't hear of me doing any cleaning, and now dear Maria has found us a really good cleaner that I can trust, I really don't need to do anything more than flick a duster occasionally and change the flowers.

'Sometimes we sit and chat — well, gossip, dear, really — and sometimes if I want to be quiet, I go off by myself and she's insisted on paying me an enormous wage, just for cooking her a light meal once a day and a bowl of soup at lunch time. She's making me take taxis everywhere when I go shopping . . . which reminds me that she really doesn't care for cooked celery. I don't think there's anything else she doesn't like.' She always says "Thank you" nicely when I do the tiniest thing for her. And she never rings for me in the night nowadays.'

'You've done wonders, Rose. I should think you've added ten years to her life expectancy.'

Rose blushed. 'But it's such fun, dear! I was a bit lonely up in my council flat with no one to look after, and now I have company when I want it, and my own beautiful rooms and a proper garden to look after, which, by the way, she insists she's going to get a gardener in to do the heavy work for, and she'll pay all the bills! And do you know, Miss Quicke says she's never been so well looked after, though it's really her who looks after me, if the truth were but told.'

Ellie grinned. 'I understand you've taught her to sit still and appreciate the garden. How on earth did you manage that?'

'My dear Ellie! You don't know the half of it! She wants to build on a big conservatory at the back, just for me to potter around in. If I weren't a church-going woman, which I am, of course, I'd say I was in heaven. To think how I longed for a tiny patch of land to grow things in the old days when I lived in that high-rise flat . . . and now . . . !'

'I'm so pleased for you.' And Ellie really was. Not to mention what a relief it was that Miss Quicke had someone to look after her . . . well, it was more than that, really. Ellie was truly happy for them both.

Dear Rose had always needed someone to look after, and had had a flair for homemaking without having had anyone on whom to lavish her talents. Miss Quicke had always been able to make money but not friends, and had been sinking into an acid-tongued, selfish old age until Rose came along to show her what a great difference a little loving care could make to her life.

Since then, Rose had become more self-assertive and had even put on a little weight. Miss Quicke was still a scrawny old dame, but she was beginning to taste the delights of doing something for other people, perhaps for the first time in her life, and her health had certainly improved.

Ellie said, 'How do you find it with Roy living so close?'

'He's a lovely man and really thoughtful, you wouldn't believe, always thinking of things to make life easier for his mother and for me, too. Though you'd have had a fit if you'd seen him trying to change the fuse in the steam iron. In the end I had to take it off him and do it myself. Some people just seem to have been born without any idea how to do anything practical, which Miss Quicke had said came from his father, but she wasn't going to hold that against him.'

From all of which Ellie learned that the three of them were settling down very comfortably together, aware of one another's failings but very willing to put up with them. Which was really all you could expect of any family, however loving.

'It was such a lovely party last night, wasn't it?' said Rose, enjoying herself mightily. 'As dear Miss Quicke said, there's always fun and games going on around dear Ellie, and she's right, you know! I said how pretty you looked last night, and she said she didn't think Roy stood a chance, but there

. . . you need time to sort yourself out when your husband's passed away, don't you?'

From which Ellie gathered that Miss Quicke thought Bill had the edge as a suitor. She shook her head and laughed. 'Rose, you're wiser than my aunt. I do like Bill and I do like Roy, but only as dear friends. I can't get over Frank's death so quickly. Sometimes I wonder if I ever will. I don't think my aunt understands that, but you do, don't you?'

They exchanged nods, over their pot of tea. Two widows, indulging themselves over a fattening lunch. Sometimes carbohydrates are the only thing which help.

* * *

The businessman resigned his place at his father's bedside to his brother. The favourite son, the one who was a famous surgeon. The elder brother knew he only had second place in his father's affections.

But now was his chance to redeem himself. He was going to save his father, and not only his father, but the whole family.

He thought through every step of his plan. First he had to go home and find some of his wife's pills. He had a crate of bottled drinks in the back of his car.

Then he'd have to watch for an opportunity to get into the house when the woman was out. Luckily, she didn't seem to stay at home for long.

* * *

When lunch was over and Rose had twittered herself away, Ellie felt she couldn't put it off any longer, and phoned Diana.

Predictably, Diana proceeded to put her mother in the wrong. 'Where are you, mother? I've been phoning all morning. Why didn't you pick up the phone?'

'Well, I've been out and—'

'I don't suppose you ever thought of me, stuck here without being able to get to the shops, with the phone ringing and people coming round every half hour!'

Ellie composed herself. 'Would you like me to bring you in some shopping?'

'Well, of course. Why do you think I called you? Some fresh fish, preferably a wing of skate, I could just fancy that; not salmon or any of that nasty greyish stuff . . .'

Ellie made notes, thinking she'd better take her own shopping back, then return to the Avenue to do Diana's list.

'. . . and you can see if my cleaning's ready. You know the shop I go to, not the one with all the advertisements in the window but the other . . .'

Yes, Ellie thought. I shall definitely have to take my stuff back home before I start on this list. Or I could gather everything together, get a cab, drop my things off at my house and then go on to Diana's.

'I'll be there as soon as I can, dear. It will probably take me about an hour.'

'Oh, for heavens' sake, mother. It can't take that long.'

Ellie shut the phone off, wondering why the words 'please' and 'thank you' had never made it past Diana's childhood. They might never have existed, for all their appearance in Diana's life. Perhaps with her peer group she behaved better?

CHAPTER NINETEEN

Diana's car was parked outside the big house, but there was no other vehicle in sight. Everything looked freshly painted and rather bare. There were still no estate agents' boards outside, but Diana had organized a professional-looking For Sale notice with two telephone numbers on it. The ground-floor flat on the left had a Sold notice in the window, as had the one above it.

Ellie reflected that Diana did know how to run this sort of operation. If she hadn't inherited all of her great-aunt's qualities, her business sense seemed to have descended intact.

Ellie tugged her bags of food and Diana's cleaning out of the cab and struggled to the front door with them. Dropping Diana's newly cleaned dress in its plastic sheath, she managed somehow to get an elbow to the doorbell. Diana came to the door frowning, and the frown deepened into a scowl when she saw her cleaning on the floor.

'Oh, mother, really! Look what you've done to my best black! And where have you been? I expected you half an hour ago.'

Without waiting for a reply, Diana picked up her dress, smoothing out the plastic cover, and walked off into her flat.

Ellie stood there with her laden plastic bags of food and considered her options. She would very much like to throw the bags into the hall, slam the front door and leave Diana to it. There were some eggs in one of the bags. They would make a lovely smashing sound and mess up all the rest of the food. It would be so easy to give way to impulse, and it would serve Diana right if she did it.

It would, of course, be a really childish gesture.

Well, why not?

Or, she could just dump everything in the hall where she stood, and leave. That would be a grand gesture — of sorts. Not a brilliant one, but it might make Diana think for a change.

No, it probably wouldn't. Sigh. How ever had this state of things come to pass? Did it all date back to Diana's childhood, when Ellie had been just about holding on to life? She understood that Frank had been weak with Diana because she'd been their only living child. Had she herself also been to blame, allowing Diana too much leeway?

Ellie thought about Maria, clear-sightedly deciding that — love apart — little Frank needed a firm parental hand. If someone like Maria had had the handling of Diana, would the girl now be so . . . difficult?

Perhaps it really was all Ellie's fault that Diana was like this, never speaking to her except in a hectoring tone, always finding fault? It was almost as if their positions were reversed and Diana was the exasperated, scolding parent and Ellie the child.

'What's the matter with you?' Diana's voice cut through Ellie's thoughts like a cold wind through a cotton T-shirt. 'There's a terrible draught if you leave that outer door open.'

Ellie thought of saying, 'I'm not your servant.' But she didn't. She took a firmer grip on her bags and carried them through into the flat. She put the food in the fridge and switched the kettle on.

Diana was talking on the phone, fluently describing the beauties of a top-floor flat to a prospective customer.

Ellie opened the French windows and walked out into the garden. The afternoon had clouded over but it was still very warm. Perhaps it would rain. She must remember to take an umbrella to the meeting in the church hall tonight. There were some scarlet geraniums in a pot just outside the door. Ellie automatically deadheaded one plant and plucked a couple of dying leaves off another. The scent clung to her fingers, soothing her.

'Kettle!' shouted Diana from within.

Obediently Ellie went to make tea for herself and coffee for Diana, who was on the phone again, stabbing with her pencil at a pad as she talked.

Ellie took a seat and waited for Diana to finish.

At last Diana threw down her pencil, stretched, yawned, and switched the machine over to answerphone. 'It's been non-stop today. It looks like I could have sold these flats twice over. I'm wondering about bumping up the price. I thought you could take a spell on the phone for me tomorrow, while I get my hair done before I fetch little Frank for the weekend. Though, come to think of it, I'm going to need some cover this weekend, with so many people to show around.'

Ellie kept her voice pleasant. 'You'd better ask the child-minder, then. See if she's got time to help you out.'

A quick shake of the head. 'She'd charge me double.'

'And I won't?'

Diana opened her eyes wide. 'Honestly, mother! Sometimes I wonder if you know what you're saying.'

'You owe me twenty-eight pounds forty-two pence,' said Ellie. 'That's just for this afternoon's shopping. I won't charge you for the cab fare.'

'What on earth's got into you, mother?'

'I might ask the same of you, dear.'

'You act as if I've committed a crime. No matter what I do or say, you always disapprove. I can't remember when you last smiled at me as a mother should. No, you always look anxious and it makes me want to scream!'

Ellie thought about that. Was it true? Yes, very possibly it was. 'You'd agree that I have reason to be anxious about you?'

'I'm no different from anybody else. I have to try things out, see what works for me.'

'There is one thing in your favour,' said Ellie, who perhaps wouldn't have said it if she hadn't exhausted her usual reserves of tolerance, 'you learn by your mistakes.'

Diana looked shocked, and then gave way to a great crack of laughter. She laughed till she choked, blew her nose, coughed. Shook her head. Sipped her cup of coffee. Smiling, she said, 'Yes, I try not to commit the same folly twice. I broke with Derek for good, by the way. Gave him back his ring, told him I didn't want to see him again. And if I can close a sale on just one more of these flats, I'll breathe more easily.'

She frowned at a broken fingernail and reached for a nail file. 'But you're wrong if you think I'm giving up this developing game.'

'It isn't a game, Diana.'

'Oh yes, it is. I'm good at it, too. This place was a bit of a gamble, I'll grant you that, but it's going to pay off. Next I'm going to go for rundown two- and three-bedroom semis, buy them cheap, install new bathrooms and kitchens, decorate, do something about the gardens and sell them on. Now I know how to sell on the Internet, I won't ever need to use an estate agent again.'

'I can see your great-aunt lives again in you.'

Diana scowled. 'She should have backed me from the start, when I told her what I wanted to do.'

'You weren't straight in your business methods then, or she might have done. She's interested in what you're doing now, anyway. I don't suppose for a minute that she'd back you with capital, but she might come to see what you've done here some day.'

'I don't want her capital,' said Diana, sullenly. 'I'm going to make it on my own, thank you very much.'

Ellie was quietly pleased. For the first time ever, Diana was talking to her adult to adult. Perhaps now was the time to give Diana a little praise. 'You have done well. I congratulate you.'

Diana saw an opening and took it. 'So you'll help me out this weekend?'

'Don't push your luck.' Ellie stood up. 'I must go. I'm doing coffees this evening at church and I've got a lot to catch up on first. I'm having little Frank tomorrow afternoon, and will bring him round here afterwards.'

'I hate being without him,' said Diana, frowning again. 'But I don't know how on earth I'm going to manage to show people around with Frank needing attention.'

'Get an au pair. Or go back to Stewart.'

Diana shook her head. 'No, I can't go back. That's over.'

'Well, I need to get on. By the way, I've been looking up some of the people who used to live next door, trying to remember who lived there over the years. I went to see Lana Cullen . . .'

'Oh, her. Married her childhood sweetheart and settled into a dead-end job in the travel agency. She's never going to set the Thames on fire.'

'And I saw Mr Spendlove . . .'

'Got early dementia, they say. Hard on the boys.'

'And on his wife, too, I should think.'

'Oh, she left ages ago. The social services send round people to look after him, but he's going into a home soon. It's a valuable property, that flat. Should fund his bills for quite a while.'

'You seem to have kept in touch with them.'

Diana shrugged. 'Those that are still around, yes. I see them at parties sometimes. I used to see quite a lot of Trudy Cullen. She was much the livelier of the two sisters. But then I got married and moved away and she latched on to Gerry. They've not bothered to marry as there's no children. He's got a good job, though. Something at the council. She did a lot of temping, working for all sorts, abroad and here, but she got fed up with that eventually, and now she works at the High School as a lab technician. They used to have a big flat across the river, heavenly for parties, but they've moved back into Ealing recently. They sent me a change of address note and asked me to pop round, but I haven't been able to go, because I couldn't get anyone to look after little Frank. If only you hadn't been out so much, I could have gone.'

Ellie ignored the implied rebuke. 'So, that's why they aren't in the phone book? The other side of the river isn't Ealing, so they'd be in the Twickenham and Richmond phone book, instead. Someone said Trudy was now living near Ealing Broadway.'

Diana read off an address from her Filofax, and Ellie made a note of it. 'I'm surprised you kept in touch all this time.'

'I should have married one of the Spendloves. They've both done better than Stewart. But there was such an age gap, it didn't work out. Do you know the younger one has a flat in Docklands? Something in the City, he is. Stewart and I were invited over when we came back down from the north, but Stewart didn't want to go, so . . .' She shrugged. 'We've lost touch.'

* * *

Ellie stood in the forecourt of Diana's house and looked at her watch, wondering if she had time to visit Trudy Cullen before she had a bite to eat and went over to the church. She could just about do it. She phoned for a cab, which deposited her at the back of the Broadway near St Mary's Church.

School was out, and the roads and pavements were busy with pupils returning home. The university term hadn't started yet, but there was always a problem with parking in that area. The pretty houses around St Mary's had probably been designed as workmen's cottages, but were now going upmarket in a big way. It wasn't far from the High School, so Trudy might well be home by now.

Ellie rang the doorbell, and waited. Nothing happened. Probably Trudy wasn't home yet. She was just turning away when a man who seemed vaguely familiar came up behind her and inserted his key in the door.

'Hello there,' he said, all hearty. 'I know you, don't I? Mrs Quicke. Remember me? We used to live next door to you.'

At first she couldn't place him, and then she did. 'Gerry Spendlove! What are you doing here?'

'I live here. Didn't you know? Come on in. Trudy'll be back any minute, I expect.'

Gerry Spendlove showed Ellie straight into a pretty sitting room, which was small but rather charming. What's more, it still had all the old features, such as cornices and ceiling roses, which Diana so despised. There was a mixture of furniture from all periods, which looked as if it had been picked up in auction houses and handed on from relatives. Ellie could see that they'd just moved in. Samples of wallpaper were Blu-Tacked to one wall, and unpacked boxes had been half hidden behind the settee. A group of framed photographs stood in the fireplace, waiting to be hung.

Gerry dropped an expensive-looking laptop on the floor. 'Have a seat. Like a coffee, or a cuppa?' He must now be about thirty-seven; a thin, pale man who looked very much as he had at seventeen, except that he was now wearing slightly more fashionable glasses. He looked solid and reliable, possibly not very adventurous.

He revealed a nice flash of self-deprecating humour as he removed some slightly risqué videos from the coffee table. He saw Ellie had noticed the titles of the videos, but was self-possessed enough not to excuse their presence. She liked him for that, too.

He made his way through a far door, where she could hear him whistling as he switched on a kettle. He'd been ungainly as a child and youth, she remembered, with legs longer than he knew what to do with. He seemed to have changed very little. There was a photo on the mantelpiece of him and Trudy Cullen with arms around one another on a bleak hillside somewhere. Perhaps it had been taken on a camping holiday? That would seem to be their style. It was the only thing on the mantelpiece so far.

He brought in a couple of mugs of tea and set one down in front of her, collapsing on to a worn armchair himself. 'How are you, then? I hear some of the gossip from Trudy's friends and from Diana, of course, though we haven't seen her for some time. She told me your husband died last year. So sad.'

'Yes. I went to see your father today.'

'Ah, yes.' He shook his head. 'He's being well looked after, of course, but . . . they say there's nothing to be done. We've got him a place in a good home, and hope he'll settle there. We've been trying to move him for years, but he clings to that flat. Only, just lately he's been deteriorating rather fast, so we've had to make arrangements for him to move. I wish there was an alternative, but he needs twenty-four-hour care now, and with us both working . . .' He shrugged.

He said, 'Sometimes when I go he seems quite normal, and at others, he doesn't seem to know me at all. He keeps telling me that mother has just gone out to the shops. It doesn't seem kind to disillusion him, so we don't. Anyway, he might not take it in. We keep her informed of what's going on, of course, but . . . she married again, you know? Living down in Crawley, Sussex. I thought I'd hate having a stepfather at my age, but, you know, he's really nice and they're very happy together.'

'I'm so sorry about your father, though,' said Ellie, sympathetically. 'Will you be able to manage financially?'

'We can sell the flat and that'll see him through for a few years. Luckily mother doesn't need to claim her half of the value, because our stepfather is what they call a "warm" man. Funny, you don't hear people say that nowadays, but I always think it's rather a good description of someone who keeps the wolf from the door. If the money does run out eventually, well, my brother and I have both got good jobs. Perhaps it's lucky that Trudy and I haven't had any children, or that might have been a different matter. Good of you to visit him, Mrs Quicke.'

'You and Trudy? How did that come about?'

'Unexpected, don't you think?' Again, that self-deprecating charm. For the man had charm, definitely. 'Who'd have thought that jet-setter Trudy would ever settle down with a stick-in-the-mud man who works for the council? We were at school together, although she was some years behind me. I hadn't seen her, or even thought about her, until one day I walked into a party and there she was. She recognized me, we got talking and realized we'd both lived in the same house at different times. That's the way it started. We didn't set out to make it a permanent arrangement. Trudy didn't seem the type and there's quite an age gap. But we've been together now for quite a while. Yes,' he said, smiling to himself. 'Quite a while.'

'That's good,' said Ellie, liking him. 'Did you hear that the police found a body in your garden?'

He looked shocked. 'What? But . . . ! No, I . . . We don't get the local paper, just listen to the news at night last thing, and . . . are you sure? Who was it?'

'I thought you might know.'

He reddened. 'Me? You're joking.'

'No, I'm not. She died about twenty years ago, a young girl in her teens.'

He spilt his coffee. Stared at Ellie.

He said, 'No!' There was horror in his eyes and voice. He'd made some kind of connection between himself and the dead girl.

Ellie took some tissues from a box on a shelf nearby and mopped up the coffee, giving him time to assimilate what he'd just heard.

A key turned in the lock. 'I'm home!' Trudy Cullen stood there, pretty and perky and not very tall. Like the girl in the grave.

Gerry rose to his feet in a series of jerks. He was ashen-faced. 'Trudy. This is . . .'

'Mrs Quicke, isn't it?' Trudy advanced with outstretched hand. 'Mum said you'd been round to visit her and promised to come again at the weekend. That was very kind of you. She can be, well, difficult.' She looked at Gerry and registered that something was wrong. 'What's up?'

'I . . .' He sat down as suddenly as he'd stood up. Pressed both hands over his eyes. 'A bit of a shock. Mrs Quicke said someone had died, someone I might have known, years ago.'

'You mean, one of your old girlfriends?' Trudy wasn't really worried. She was concerned, yes. But not worried. She said to Ellie, 'You wouldn't think it to look at him now, but when we met I had to beat off all the women who wanted to get into bed with him.'

He held out his hand to her and she took it, patted it. Became more concerned for him. Sat down beside him. She said, in a soft voice, 'What is it? Whatever it is, it can't be that bad.'

He gulped. Grabbed at his self-control. Still holding Trudy's hand, he turned to Ellie. 'For a moment there, I thought . . . but of course it couldn't be . . . !'

Ellie said, 'You thought of someone just now. Some girl you knew once, a long time ago. When you were about seventeen? The year you left the house next door. Tell me about her.'

He spoke to Trudy. 'Well, yes, I did know someone, but it was a schoolboy thing, came to nothing. You remember — no, perhaps you don't — but in our last year in the sixth form, some of us paired off. It was what we all did in our last year at school. You did it, too. I remember you told me how you went out with that boy who went on to music college.

'Well, Jasreen was doing much the same subjects as me. Like me, she was aiming for university. She was the prettiest thing, dark and vivacious and, well, straightforward. We knew her parents didn't approve of her seeing me, but it didn't worry her and it didn't worry me. We went to the disco a couple of times, though she never stayed late. I took her to the pub, but she didn't drink, of course . . .'

'Why, "of course"?' asked Ellie.

He looked surprised. 'Because she was Muslim. Her family came from Pakistan and were very religious, though Jasreen wasn't. I mean, she didn't pray or wear the headscarf or anything. She was interested in Christianity, because she said it was the only religion she knew where people were asked to look out for one another. We talked about that quite a lot. About everything. She was very bright. Beautiful, actually. We were applying to the same university and planned to go down by train together for the interviews. It was after that, that the trouble really started.

'She came into school one day and said her family didn't want her to go to university or even to take her final school exams. I couldn't believe what I was hearing. I thought she was exaggerating. But she changed. She'd say she'd meet me at the cinema and then not turn up. She started cutting classes at school. One minute she was excited about going to uni and the next she was listless, would hardly talk to me. I had a friend who was also Muslim. He said perhaps her family wanted her to marry someone back in Pakistan. I couldn't believe that she'd go along with that.

'The last time I saw her, she walked home from school with me to my house, where we could be quiet and talk without anyone interrupting. My parents and my brother were out. Now, I don't want you to get the wrong impression. We didn't make love or anything. We hardly knew if we were in love or not, but I said that if she didn't want to go back to Pakistan, then she needn't, that I'd look after her.

'I asked her to trust me, I said I would marry her if that was what was needed, and that if her family wouldn't let her, then she must move in with us, that my parents would look after her till we went to uni, and after that she'd be independent and could make up her mind whether she wanted to marry me or not. I said I wouldn't pressurize her in any way, but the offer was open. She wouldn't say yes, and she wouldn't say no.'

Ellie said, 'Where did all this happen? In the garden?'

'No. We were in the back room together though — yes — I believe I may have opened the French windows, because it was so hot.'

'So anyone could have heard your offer.'

He stared at her. 'I suppose so. But it was so innocent. You must believe me, Mrs Quicke.'

'I do believe you, but others might not. Tell me what happened after that.'

'It was getting dark, and my brother came in with my parents. They'd all been out for the evening to the cinema. When they came back in, she said she'd see me next day and ran out of the house . . .'

'Did she go out of the front door, or down the back garden? Did your family see her go?'

He nodded. 'Down the back garden, because then all she had to do was cross the Green and she'd be at the bus stop. Yes, of course they saw her. You can ask my brother or my mother. Jasreen called back to me to say that she'd give me her answer the next day at school . . . but she never came back to school. I never saw her again. I rang her parents, but they said she'd gone back to Pakistan to be married and that it was no business of mine. I was upset for quite a while, but then I thought she'd made her decision and I could picture her in Pakistan, married and a mother. Tell me it isn't her in the garden!'

'I don't know,' said Ellie. 'Did you kill her?'

'No!' He turned to Trudy. 'No, Trudy. I didn't. Believe me. I wouldn't!'

'I believe you.' Trudy took his hand in both of hers.

Ellie said, 'Did you see her leave the garden?'

He gulped, understanding what she meant. 'Well, no. I don't think I did. My parents had brought in some pizzas for our supper. They called me to eat while they were still hot. I didn't think to watch her leave. Anyway, you couldn't see the bottom of the garden from the house, because it was terribly overgrown, as we never did a thing to it. There were bushes and shrubs and nettles, which my mother liked because they attracted butterflies. And to think my mother's turned into a keen gardener now! There was a sort of track down the garden to the alley, but I suppose anyone could have been hiding there behind the bushes, waiting for her.'

He was beginning to understand what might have happened. The lines of his face sharpened. 'Do you think they were watching? Do you think they'd followed her? I thought she was being paranoid when she said they were watching her all the time, but . . . do you think that they caught up with her in our garden?'

'What time of year was it?'

He took a deep breath. 'September. We'd just gone back to school at the start of the September term. Most people were back from their summer holidays, but I think you were away next door, weren't you? And, of course, we moved a couple of days later to the flat where my father is now. Because of his needing to be in a wheelchair. I don't suppose any of us ever went down the garden after that. We wouldn't have any cause to. It is Jasreen, isn't it? In the garden?'

Again Ellie said, 'I don't know, Gerry. But I don't suppose you'll be able to rest now, till you've told the police.'

He put his head in his hands, and was quiet for a while. The two women waited.

He said, 'Yes, I've got to tell them. It might not be her, but . . . I can't take the risk of it not being her. Oh, Jasreen! To think of you lying there, all this time.'

'Where did her parents live?'

He stood up, looking lost. 'Somewhere over towards Perivale way, I think. I never went to her house. I had her phone number once, but . . .' He gestured helplessly. 'Long gone.'

'What was their name?'

He sought for it in his memory. 'It's so long ago. Iqbal? Yes, I think it was Iqbal.'

'Not Patel, then?'

He shook his head. He looked around at the pretty home which he'd been making with Trudy, and then he looked at Trudy. 'I suppose you want to know if you reminded me of her, and yes, I suppose you did, in a way. You're like her, and not like her. I didn't love you because you looked like Jasreen, if that's what you're thinking. I love you because you're you.'

Trudy stood up, too. The top of her head reached his shoulder. 'I know you like small, dark women. That's your style. But I'm not letting you go as easily as Jasreen did. I'll come with you to the police station, Gerry. And if necessary we'll get your brother and your mother to meet us there, too.'

A pulse twitched beneath his eye. 'I'm in for a rough few hours though, aren't I? They're bound to think I did it. But I didn't. I swear it.'

Ellie said, 'Shall I get my solicitor friend round to help you?'

He looked at her without really seeing her. 'You know, Mrs Quicke, if you'd not been away on holiday, you might have seen what happened.'

Ellie nodded. She'd worked that out already.

She rang Bill and filled him in on what had been happening, and saw Gerry and Trudy off to the police station. It seemed to her that, now the girl's identity had been discovered, the murder would soon be solved. In any event, she needn't worry about it anymore. So, she could go back to worrying about the usual things, such as Diana. Maria and Stewart. Roy and Aunt Drusilla and . . .

And getting to the church hall on time to set out the cups and saucers for coffee that evening. She looked at her watch and thought of summoning a cab, but it wasn't far and the bus went nearly all the way home. And yes, there was one coming, which she could catch if she ran for it.

CHAPTER TWENTY

Arriving on the Green, Ellie looked around her. There was still an hour and a half before she had to be at the church hall, but though there were plenty of people about, there was no Tum-Tum — whom she really must begin to think of as 'Thomas' — plodding across the green with his wheelbarrow full of gardening tools. Would he be at home?

She'd never yet called at the vicarage unannounced. Lots of women did, of course. Thomas had a way with him of total concentration on what you were saying. Most flattering. And somehow he'd not yet been entangled in any of the snares which the widows and spinsters of the parish had been throwing his way. Of course, many of these callers had good and sufficient reasons to demand his attention. Some didn't, though, and it was those whose names were thrown around by the gossips of the parish.

If Ellie Quicke marched into the vicarage, there would be talk. 'Did you hear who was the latest to cry on his shoulder? That Ellie Quicke, no better than she should be, and with all those men hanging around her. I wondered how long it would be before she joined the queue to his door . . .'

She knew there'd be talk, but she couldn't resist going, just for once.

She rang the doorbell in the gaunt porch and wondered why they didn't pull down this damp-smelling, awkward-to-heat old house and build something modern.

Tum-Tum . . . Thomas . . . opened the door, drying his hands on a rough towel. He'd been gardening, of course. And probably listening to the woes of half the parish all day. She really ought not to intrude on his hours of leisure.

'I've been hoping you'd call,' he said, throwing the towel on a hall chair and ushering her into his surprisingly light and well-equipped kitchen. At least the parish had done something about the kitchen when he moved in, though they'd neglected to replace the central heating. 'Coffee? Tea?'

'Do you greet all your visitors this way?' Ellie was feeling and sounding awkward. Even aggressive.

'Only those who need to talk. The others I keep standing on the doorstep. There's a wicked draught there; it often makes them decide not to wait.'

She laughed because he expected her to. He handed her a mug of tea and gestured her to take a seat at the kitchen table. A casserole was cooking in the eye-level oven, and vegetables lay prepared on the table, ready for the pot.

Thomas scooped up vegetables and dropped them into saucepans on the stove. 'And don't say, "I don't know where to begin."'

She laughed again. 'Oh, I know where to begin all right. Mea culpa. Is that a good start? It was all my fault. Or not all, but . . .' She sighed. 'I could have done a lot to help my neighbours and I didn't. It's no excuse to say I was poorly, although I was. There were times in between pregnancies when I was all right. Or more or less all right. I could have helped my neighbours, anyway.'

Bright eyes watched her over his mug. 'Did they ask for help?'

'Well, no. But I could at least have offered. I know that my husband didn't want me to get involved with them, but ought I to have gone along with that?'

Thomas — there, now, she had actually thought of him by his correct name — drummed his fingers on the table top. 'Do you want me to tell you that you're a bad woman?'

'What?' Whatever she'd expected from him, it hadn't been that. She didn't think she was a bad woman, precisely. Not terribly good at times, but not really bad.

'Tell me what you were doing all those years when you think you ought to have been running round looking after your neighbours.'

'Well . . . I wasn't well for a lot of that time and we were really short of money, so I did what secretarial work I could at home while Diana was little, and then when she went to school, I had a regular job. I suppose you'd call Frank one of the old-fashioned kind. Supper had to be on the table at six thirty every evening, there always had to be clean shirts and clothes, clean house, everything just so. He liked everything neat and tidy. He was a neat and tidy man . . . oh, perhaps I shouldn't have put it quite like that.'

'Why not? I've heard about him from other people. "Meticulous" was the word they used for him. And "family-centred". They said he thought of you equal first with his job, his daughter and his aunt second, and the church third. Would that be about right?'

'It seemed like I came last in his list of priorities most of the time, but . . . there! It's understandable. His aunt and Diana were so noisy! I tried to keep the peace, keep the house going, keep the bills paid.'

'Ellie the Peacemaker,' said Thomas. 'That's what I've heard. Ellie, who could always be relied upon to do all the jobs that nobody else wanted to do. Ellie, who put up with a bad-tempered aunt who treated her like a skivvy. Ellie, who took Mrs Dawes' washing home every week and did the ironing for her, too, when her leg was bad. Ellie, who befriended those tiresome elderly women whom nobody else would visit. Ellie, who cared for a boy from a single-parent family when his mother couldn't have cared less. Ellie, who always tries to see the best in people even when they aren't particularly likeable. Ellie, who always thinks she hasn't done enough to help other people.'

'Oh!' said Ellie. 'But, I mean, who . . . ?'

'Or do you prefer "Ellie, the Bad Samaritan"?'

'Well, no. But . . .'

'Didn't you keep the peace at the charity shop for years? Since you left, I gather they've all been at one another's throats.'

'Yes, but . . .'

'Haven't you given unconditional love to all the difficult people around you? To your aunt and your daughter, for instance?'

'Yes, but there's only so much I can do to—'

Thomas stood up, smiling. 'Goulash suit you? I must warn you I like it hot and there's cream going in at the last minute.' He busied himself at the stove, while Ellie thought about what he'd said.

'So you think I'm not so very bad, after all?' she said, as he put a large round soup bowl in front of her, topping it with vegetables. She sniffed. 'Wow. Can I have the recipe?'

'No, you may not. I'm auctioning it at the next bazaar, when you can bid for it if you wish.'

She ate in silence. Had a second helping. He did the same. She reflected that this was the first time a man had ever cooked for her. It seemed vaguely wrong to let a man cook for her. Only, she didn't think of Thomas as 'a man' really. Although, he was, of course. A man.

And a fine figure of a man in his own way. There was a bit of the old-fashioned Navy Cut type sailor about him. All that gardening had slimmed him down a bit, although the amount of cream he'd poured into the goulash couldn't have helped keep his weight down. Or hers, either.

'A selection of cheeses for madam.' Brie, stilton, a mature cheddar. Nothing particularly unusual about the cheeses. She had some, though. Followed by some very strong after-dinner coffee.

'Which reminds me,' she said, feeling guilty, 'I must get along to the church hall, put out the coffee cups and saucers for the meeting this evening.'

'You're feeling better?'

'Thank you. Yes. Sometimes I get things out of proportion. Frank was always telling me about it. I'm a bit stupid that way. Let me help you wash up first.'

'You're not stupid, Ellie. And your sense of proportion is better than most people's. And no, you're not washing up. Go on home, woman, and do your bit for the community.'

She nodded, suddenly feeling rather shy. 'Thank you.' She wanted to shake his hand, which on reflection didn't seem at all the right thing to do. She thought about kissing him on his cheek and decided against that, too.

He showed her out and waved her off across the Green. She looked at her watch. Had she time for a quick shower before she went over to the church hall? She must change her clothes, collect the biscuits and the tea towels . . . and what else?

Midge was sitting on top of the sundial in the middle of her patch of lawn. He never did that. In fact, he was such a large cat that she wouldn't have thought he could balance on it. She wondered how he'd fitted himself around the gnomon of the sundial.

She paused with the key to her back door in her hand, looking at him. Midge was an intelligent cat and any departure from his routine was worth at least two thoughts.

Midge wasn't looking her. He was looking up at the house.

Could someone have got in while she was away? Diana? Well, it was true that Midge didn't like Diana and never willingly stayed in the same room with her, but surely Diana was all tied up with selling her flats at the moment? No one else had a key, did they?

Ellie scanned the back of her house. The conservatory looked as it always did, though she rather thought the blue plumbago was drooping a bit. Mrs Dawes had warned her about that plumbago, which needed a lot of water. She ought to have given it some this morning before she went out.

The kitchen looked the same, as far as she could tell. As did the lounge through the conservatory. But hadn't she left the French windows from the lounge into the conservatory open, because it was such a humid day?

She glanced across the boundary hedge, but there was no sign of life from next door. Probably Armand was working late at school — and Kate? Kate could be anywhere, still at work in the city, or out with a friend.

'Good evening, Mrs Quicke.' A strange voice. 'I found the back door open, so took the liberty of entering your delightful conservatory. I trust you don't mind?'

A Pakistani gentleman was holding the door of the conservatory open for her to enter. Was this 'Mr Patel'?

He was urbane, educated, charming. Possibly in his early forties. Muslim, probably. Where had he left the Mercedes? In the road outside her front door?

Should she run for it? No. Why should she? He wasn't at all threatening. He wasn't even very tall, probably not much taller than she was. Midge didn't seem to be alarmed. In fact, Midge had plopped down from his perch on the sundial and was loping up the steps into the conservatory.

'Did I really leave the door unlocked? How very remiss of me.' She ascended the steps behind Midge.

Mr Patel pulled out one of her own conservatory chairs for her to seat herself, just as if he were the host and she the visitor. That amused, rather than annoyed her.

She could understand why Roy had accepted this man as a bona fide customer for one of the town houses at Endene Close, because he looked the part of a wealthy businessman. He was wearing an expensive suit with immaculate shirt beneath, gold cufflinks, excellent shoes.

She half glanced down at her watch. She didn't have long before she must change her clothes and get herself across to the church.

Meantime, she supposed she could find out as much as she could about this man. 'We haven't met before, have we? Forgive me if I don't offer you any refreshments, but I'm due to go out shortly.'

He inclined his head towards her. 'It is for you to forgive me, calling on you unannounced like this. I, too, have many calls on my time and would not normally have forced myself upon you, but there was some urgent business I needed to discuss with you.' He waved a hand at the inner doors leading into the living room. 'Perhaps you'd prefer to sit inside in the cool?'

'No, not really.' It occurred to her that though not many people did use the alley, those who did would be able to see them in the conservatory, but wouldn't be able to see them if they went further inside the house.

He smiled. 'Then you must let me provide you with some refreshment.' He retrieved a briefcase from the floor beside him and extracted two bottles of what looked like lemonade. The labels were unfamiliar to her but looked as if they were written in Arabic. 'One of my interests is in a soft-drinks firm and this is a new line for us. Lime, with a hint of herbs. We are marketing it for the hot weather next year. These are samples only, of course. I am taking them round with me, asking everyone to give me their opinion.'

He unscrewed the lids and looked around. 'Do you have some glasses?'

Ellie was in fact rather thirsty after all that goulash so she fetched a couple of glasses from the kitchen and placed them on the table. He poured for both of them and leaned back in his chair, lifting his glass towards her and taking a long swallow. 'Do tell me what you think.'

If he'd drunk some, it must be all right. She took a cautious couple of mouthfuls. It was pleasant enough, she supposed, though she didn't much care for the hint of herbs he'd mentioned.

'Refreshing on a warm day, no?'

'Yes, it is.' She drank some more. 'I'm sure you would do well with this. So what may I do for you?'

He wiped his mouth with a handkerchief. 'You have a beautiful view from this house.'

Yes, yes, she thought. Flannel, flannel. So, what does he want? He sat there, bowing and smiling. Irritating her. Midge had polished off the food she'd left out for him in the kitchen and now came yawning and stretching back out into the conservatory.

She said, 'I'm afraid this house is not for sale, if that is what you were thinking, Mr . . . ?' Was his name really 'Patel', or perhaps . . . 'Iqbal'? It would be best, perhaps, not to mention the name 'Iqbal'.

'Oh, no. I have a very pleasant house of my own, you understand, which I have no plans to leave. My eldest son is interested — not in this house, no — but in a town house in a new development. That is why I came around to have a look at the neighbourhood. There are some very pleasant houses in this district, are there not?'

'Yes, indeed.'

Midge jumped upon the table and hunkered down, his whiskers enquiring whether the drinks on the table were suitable for a cat. Ellie moved her glass away from Midge, who was perfectly capable of knocking it over if he felt like it.

Her visitor sat opposite her, quite at home, smiling, watching her over steepled fingers. Ellie noted the gold rings the man was wearing. His hands were plump, the nails well cared for. Definitely a businessman.

Midge shifted to stare at Mr Patel, which seemed to disturb him. Perhaps he wasn't accustomed to having cats in the house? Mr Patel flapped his hands at Midge and said, 'Shoo!' Midge continued to stare, unblinking. Mr Patel shifted his chair to face away from the cat.

Ellie said, 'Forgive me, but I am in rather a hurry . . .'

He continued to smile. 'This won't take a minute. You are on your way out?' The smile disappeared and the words hung on the air, containing a double meaning. Was there a threat there? Ellie decided that, yes, there probably was. Yet, apart from the fact that he'd entered her house without permission, she did not feel particularly threatened. Midge, certainly, was showing no signs of fear. Midge was watchful, yes. But not angry or afraid.

She said, 'May I ask . . . Mr . . . ? I'm afraid I don't know your name.'

'Patel.' Again the smile, the slight bow.

A lie, she thought, still more amused than afraid.

'Mr Patel, how can I help you?'

'If only the garden had been left undisturbed, none of this would be necessary. You would have been able to enjoy your widowhood in peace, our poor sick father would not be fretting his life away in hospital, and my brother and I would not be driven to distraction.'

Ellie said, 'You refer to the body of the girl found in next door's garden? You think I was in some way involved . . . ?'

'You knew nothing, Mrs Quicke. We were aware of that. Virtuous women should be protected, and we have protected you all these years.'

'Thank you very much, but—'

He raised his hands. 'How could we tell you what had really happened? It would have destroyed you. Your husband would have been sent to prison for life, and your daughter ruined in the eyes of society. Believe me, our family understands what it means to have a daughter disgraced in the eyes of the world.'

Ellie shook her head to clear it. 'You think my husband killed that girl? Nonsense. And if it were true — which it isn't — then why didn't you report him to the police?'

'You must understand that twenty years ago we had not been very long in this England. We still spoke Punjabi among ourselves. My father worked very hard to give his children a good education. Our family ties, the culture we brought with us, they kept us separate and proud in this land, so far from our home.

'My father was very strict, very devout, and in turn he revered our grandfather back in Pakistan. We still had very close ties with the rest of our family, with my cousins, uncles and aunts. We still do, of course, but . . . it is not quite the same now. One of my cousin's daughters has rebelled against the marriage that has been arranged for her, and wants to train as a solicitor. My own children wish to adopt Western dress. It is not the same.'

Ellie said, 'It is only natural, surely, that you adapt to Western ways?'

He spread his hands. 'To carelessness with morals? To stupefying yourself with drink and drugs? To our daughters flaunting their bodies, inflaming men's worst desires? That girl brought her death upon herself. If her shame had been made known, not one of our family would have escaped censure. Everyone would have pointed the finger at our father. The arrangements for myself, my brother and my sisters to marry would have been cancelled, for who would wish to ally themselves with a family without duty or respect for their parents? We would all have been held up to ridicule for allowing her to behave so badly.

'We could not accuse the murderer without calling attention to our shame, so we gave out that the girl had gone back to Pakistan to be married, exactly as had been arranged. To our cousins in Pakistan we said she had died of a fever.'

'What relation was she to you?'

'She was our sister.'

He pushed her glass slightly towards her. Automatically she picked it up and lifted it to her lips. She was still thirsty. She hadn't liked the drink much, but at least it would quench her thirst.

It felt unreal to be sitting in her conservatory, listening to a stranger accuse her husband of murder. It made her want to laugh. With one part of her mind, she could hear herself laughing inside her head. With another part, she wondered how soon she could set the police on to the track of this man who seemed to have regarded his sister as 'disposable'. And with a third part . . . how could you have three parts to your mind? What was the matter with her?

The man was still talking. 'I do not care for what I see happening to the next generation of our womenfolk. They cease to observe our times of prayer. They dance in public to indecent music. They disobey their elders. Where is their modesty? How can we arrange good marriages for them if they behave without respect for their elders?

'My brother is a respected surgeon, and I have many interests in the food industry. Our remaining sisters married respectable men from back home, both of whom now work in my organization. Our father is still alive though very frail. My sons and daughters will not be forced to marry anyone against their will. Oh, no. But they will be guided by their elders, as is only right and proper. All was well . . . until my brother heard that our sister's body had been discovered.'

Ellie rubbed her forehead. Had the central heating switched itself on by mistake? She felt very warm. 'You don't live locally, do you? So how did you — or your brother — find out?'

'Successful surgeons move around the country. My brother's wife has always kept in touch with a colleague's wife who used to live near him up north, but has since moved back down to London. She phoned my brother's wife to tell her the news, just gossiping, you know. That's how he knew the body had been discovered. He understood at once that action must be taken.

'He arranged to take leave from the hospital and came down to consult with me. The news has put my father in hospital again, and I fear . . . the prognosis is not good. What should we do? At first I was all for leaving sleeping dogs alone. What good would it do to disturb the way things have been for so long? How could we ever be connected with a body in someone else's garden?

'But my brother was eaten up with worry. He said we must keep in touch with police proceedings. But how? It is not like back home in Pakistan. We know nobody here in the police force. We have not so much as a parking ticket between us.

'I consented to drive around this way. I saw the police tape and the tent in the garden, and realized that I could watch what happened from the houses that were being built on the Green. My brother said we must watch from there, see what happened. My business affairs require me to be in touch by phone all the time — you cannot trust anyone else to make a decision quick quick, like that. But I have spent some time at the houses, saying I was looking for a place for my eldest son, and also at the newsagents and the dry cleaners, who all knew what was going on. It was I who sent the emails to the police, telling them what your husband had done.'

Ellie wiped the back of her hand across her forehead. 'I really don't know why you should think Frank was involved.'

'I am sorry for you, indeed I am. I saw him with her. It was all arranged that she should return to Pakistan to marry a cousin that summer, but she had got into the wrong crowd at school and some of her so-called friends were giving her bad advice. She refused to fall in with the family's plans. My mother beat her, and my father reasoned with her. We all reasoned with her. My younger sisters wept, for who would marry them if Jasreen disgraced us by refusing to marry the man selected for her? So my brother and I took it in turns to follow Jasreen home from school . . . and that was when I saw her with your husband.'

Ellie knew what had really happened. Gerry Spendlove had told her. She was feeling unaccountably tired. She let herself sink further down into her chair. Midge shifted to look at her with great, golden eyes. She said, 'I don't have to listen to these lies. Would you please leave now?'

'Not till we've got this all absolutely clear in our minds. Your husband was called Frank. You had a daughter called Diana, who was very badly behaved. If she had been my daughter, I would have taken a strap to her. I saw you that evening at the bedroom window with your daughter. The window was open and I could hear everything you said. You were packing to go away on holiday. Your husband mowed the lawn and put the machine away in the shed. You called out to him to come in for supper, but he shouted back that he had to find some wire first to secure the door of the tool shed.

'I saw everything. My sister had walked back from school with a boy from her class. They stood at the bottom of the garden, talking. Then he went on up into his house, saying he'd see her in school again the following day. All the time your husband stood there with his mouth gaping, watching her as she walked along the alley and across the Green to the bus stop.

'I'm telling you, he didn't take his eyes off her once! And she, the little whore, rolled her hips and swung her hair, knowing that he was watching.'

Ellie could see it all. Frank gazing after the young, nubile girl. A beautiful girl with long, dark hair. At that time, Ellie had been not much to look at, worn out with all that had happened to her physically and mentally. It left a bad taste in her mouth to think that he'd yearned after that beautiful young girl. She couldn't blame him for having done so. But he'd been faithful to her. A sigh.

She said, 'Men look, but don't often touch.'

'Men like that look first, and then they touch. The next afternoon, my brother and my father followed Jasreen to make sure nothing happened. But they were too late. He'd killed her and left her body in the garden. She had dishonoured us all. The shame of it haunts us to this day.'

'I understand what you're saying, but—'

'We decided not to make it known how we'd been shamed. We went back later that evening — there was a fine moon — we took tools from your husband's shed and we buried her where we'd found her.'

'You got it wrong,' said Ellie patiently. 'We — my husband, my daughter and I — all left on holiday the morning after you saw him mow the lawn. Jasreen was seen alive and well, and leaving next door's house the following evening. The Spendloves all agree to that. I do not know who killed her but it was certainly not Frank.'

'You are a liar. All women are liars.'

She tried to get to her feet and failed. What was the matter with her? She said, trying to sound stern, 'That's enough of that. Now would you please go?'

'Your husband looked at my sister with greed in his eyes. She inflamed him with her rolling walk and flirting ways. He knew she was returning to that house the following day, so he waylaid her and killed her. There is no other possible explanation.'

'I'm afraid there is,' said Ellie. She felt very tired. 'Your brother and father saw Jasreen leave the house the following evening. She'd spent some time alone in there with the Spendlove boy. The French windows were open, and they were in the back room. He was urging her to resist your family's arrangements for her. He offered to marry her, even. That must have alarmed your father enormously. The rest of the Spendlove family returned from their evening out, and Jasreen left by the garden . . . only to be waylaid by your father and brother. She never left the garden. There were bushes and shrubs providing perfect hiding places.'

There was a long silence.

'You think my father . . . ? No, no. It was your husband.'

'We'd left London by that time. You know that it was either your father or your brother who killed her. Do you know — do you even care — which one it was?'

'If it happened that way, then it was an honour killing. We could not have lived with the shame of our sister refusing to obey us.'

'Which one? Your father or your brother?'

'It would have been . . . if what you say is true . . . it must have been my father. But he was justified!'

'Was he? Then why didn't he go to the police and confess what he'd done?'

'Your laws are—'

'If you want to live in this country, you must abide by its laws. But you knew that very well. So the following night the three of you used our gardening tools to bury the body, and then set light to the shed to hide all traces of what you'd done. The Spendloves moved away. When Gerry Spendlove rang your house, he was told Jasreen had left for Pakistan. Do you still live in Perivale?'

He gave a great start. 'What do you know about—?'

'Gerry Spendlove told me that was where Jasreen lived. He also told me that one of his school friends had warned him Jasreen was due for an arranged marriage. Was that you? Will he recognize you when he sees you again?'

'It was your husband who killed her. He's dead. Let it go at that.'

'Nonsense. Frank might have looked but he'd never have touched.'

He stood up, went to look down the garden. 'My brother was right. You are a difficult woman and I should not have wasted my time explaining things to you. If you had had any sense at all, you would have agreed with me, the police would have taken the matter no further and my father would be left to die in peace. As it is, we will have to proceed to Plan B. Here . . .'

He reached across the table for her glass, but Midge suddenly turned himself from snoozing cat into pouncing kitten, and batted his hand away with his claws out.

The man yelped and drew back, blood streaking his hand. 'You . . . !'

He swiped at Midge, who knew exactly when to make himself scarce. Midge leaped from the table, knocking over Ellie's glass and one of the bottles.

The man screeched with fury, trying to right the bottle and the glass while pulling a handkerchief from his pocket to staunch the wound on his hand.

Ellie said, 'Oh, dear.' Trained to clean up household mess, she aimed for the kitchen door to fetch a mop, but the man caught her arm. 'Where are you going?'

'To fetch a . . .' She couldn't understand what was the matter with her legs. They didn't seem to know what they were there for. She clung to the door frame. 'What did you put in my drink?'

'A mild sedative only, to help you relax. But now!' He was angry. 'I was to take the bottles away with me, wash the glasses . . . now what am I to do? My brother will not be pleased to have his plans so stupidly wrecked. Well, there is no help for it. I have brought your suicide note with me, just in case. Where is it? Didn't I put it in my wallet? See how you have upset me. I am shaking with nerves. I have never killed anyone before, you see.'

He unfolded a piece of paper, and held it up for her to see.

She read, *I can't bear the shame any longer. Frank did kill the girl.*

She knew it wasn't really funny, but for some reason she wanted to laugh. How absurd! No one would believe it for a minute!

It had been stupid to laugh, because it made him angry.

His face darkened. He caught hold of her arm and swung her back into her chair. The sticky liquid from the bottles swelled into little pools, and began to move slowly to the edge of the table. One drop fell on her skirt. Another on to her leg.

'Make yourself comfortable,' he said, producing a sharp knife. He lifted up her right hand. She tried to pull away. He was much stronger than her.

He closed her fingers around the knife.

He laid her left hand, palm upwards, on the table. He forced her right hand — still holding the knife — to hover over her left wrist.

'No!' She tried to scream. No sound came out.

'And now, dear lady, let me help you to slash your wrists . . .'

* * *

There was a crash as the door to the garden was thrown open and Mrs Dawes, scarlet-faced and perspiring, thrust herself into the room. Her magnificent chest heaved with the effort she'd made in hurrying across the Green.

'Ellie, whatever's the matter with you! You should have been over at the hall fifteen minutes ago, and . . . you! What on earth are you doing? Drop that knife, sir!'

The man had already proved he didn't think quickly on his feet. He froze, the knife poised. Then he made the wrong decision. Instead of running out of the house by way of the front door to the road, he tried to push past Mrs Dawes. That lady was in no mood to be brushed aside. She'd just been through a difficult half hour, trying to excuse Ellie's failure to turn up to do the coffee — yet again! Finally she'd rushed across the Green and up the sloping garden to give her friend a piece of her mind, only to find her calmly seated in her conservatory, with the evidence of bottles and glasses still around to show that she'd been drinking with a strange man.

Mrs Dawes refused to be pushed around anymore, thank you!

The man was strong and forceful but not over medium height.

Mrs Dawes weighed in at fifteen stone in her stockinged feet and was a fraction taller.

No contest.

'Woman, out of my way!'

'Not so fast, little man!'

The man screamed with fury. Mrs Dawes brought up her knee. He gagged and doubled over, clutching her dress. She tried to shake him off. He clung, keening to himself. She tried to shake him off, he curled up on the floor, on her feet. She tried to kick him away and lost her balance. She toppled over.

On top of him.

Ellie forced herself to her feet. She felt as if she were walking through cloud. He'd given her far more than a light sedative. But there was one thing she knew about sedatives and that was that you could beat them and remain conscious, if you wanted to badly enough. She wanted to.

Mrs Dawes was thrashing around, screaming at the man to get off her, though really it was she who was on top of him. He'd stopped moaning and was now lying ominously still.

Ellie lunged for the chair opposite and tried to help Mrs Dawes back on to her feet. She failed. Ellie almost fell on top of Mrs Dawes and the man. Ellie thought about that. Mrs Dawes was purple in the face, shouting for help. Ellie pushed a chair towards Mrs Dawes and tried to help her turn over . . . on top of the man, but that couldn't be helped. Mrs Dawes, panting and straining, managed to get herself connected to the chair. She hung there, her legs beneath her at an angle, shouting at Ellie to help her up. Ellie pushed the chair further under Mrs Dawes. Mrs Dawes heaved and somehow got herself half off the floor and half into the chair and hung there, panting, her improbably jet-black hair coming down. Her eyes closed, sweat on her forehead.

Ellie prayed Mrs Dawes wouldn't have a fit. Her blood pressure must have gone through the roof. The man lay still, his face a curious ashen colour.

'Stay there,' said Ellie. 'I'll get help.' She wandered into the hall, bouncing gently off walls as she went. She found the phone, lifted the receiver, and then couldn't think what number she wanted.

She could hear Mrs Dawes gasping for breath.

Midge jumped up by the phone. He was ruffled. Began to wash himself with furious haste.

There were fragments of glass on the floor in the hall. And one of the panes of glass in the window by the front door was missing. The man must have got in that way. Ellie shook her head. So she really hadn't left the back door unlocked, had she?

She rang for the police and an ambulance.

CHAPTER TWENTY-ONE

It was early October but hardly any leaves had fallen from the trees as yet. The late flowering roses were looking blowsily content with life. The herbaceous border was at its best, purple and scarlet shrieking at orange flowers.

Ellie was helping Kate and Armand to plant up their newly landscaped garden. Their previous plans had been tacitly forgotten. There was to be a water feature, yes, but no deep tank where a body had lain for so many years.

The new water feature was to be on the upper terrace, which had been paved with brick setts in concentric patterns, shaded by a pergola which would eventually be covered by a vine and a golden hop. The water feature was set to one side under a childproof mesh. It would bubble up through a millstone and gently dissipate itself through large pebbles, down through a grid to a pump and up again through the millstone.

Armand was digging a hole large enough to accommodate the vine, while Ellie was showing Kate how to site plants on either side of the brick path which slanted this way and that down the slope. This garden was even steeper than Ellie's, but at the lower end by the alley, a terrace of three large raised beds had been built up in which Kate intended to grow a variety of fruits and vegetables.

Kate was carrying pots in containers down the garden, and Ellie was helping her. Ellie wanted Kate to 'own' her plants, so encouraged her to decide where this hebe or that lavender bush should go. Packets of spring bulbs lay nearby, to fill in any gaps.

Once they'd agreed on where everything should go, Ellie showed Kate how to transfer the plants from pots to ground.

'You dig a hole a little bigger than the pot which the plant is in,' said Ellie. 'And slightly deeper. Then you put some of this good compost in — though really the topsoil here is pretty good. Then you pick up the plant pot with your fingers spread across the top and upend it . . . like this. The plant should fall out of the pot into your hand, but if it doesn't, then you tap the edge of the plant pot sharply against something hard . . . like this. The whole plant should now be free of the pot. Drop it carefully into the hole you've dug and stand back to see if it's showing off to its best effect.'

Kate followed these instructions and stood back, hands on hips, head to one side. Armand was huffing and puffing as he dug away at the top of the garden, digging a hole far larger than necessary.

Kate hadn't said anything yet about being pregnant. Maybe she was, and maybe she wasn't. Maybe she was just going about smiling to herself because she was happy that the man who'd murdered that poor girl had died in his hospital bed, and that those who'd covered up the crime had been arrested and were awaiting trial. Maybe that was it. Maybe Armand was taking extra care of her because it was a fine autumn day and he felt like it.

Ellie didn't mind, so long as they were both content with the way things were going for them. She knew they'd had long talks with Tum-Tum — Thomas — and that he'd visited them and stayed for some hours. Perhaps they'd asked him to bless their house. Perhaps their own happiness would do the trick. But prayer always helped, and Ellie had certainly put in her two pennies' worth of that.

She prayed again now for them and for her spiky daughter Diana, still waiting to sell the last of the flats she'd renovated. Ellie also prayed that the court would make the right decision as to who should have care and control of little Frank. She prayed for Maria and Stewart, settling into their new home, looking forward to the day when his divorce would be made final and they could marry. For Roy and Rose and Aunt Drusilla; who'd have thought that they could all live so close together in harmony?

She prayed for the girl whose life had been cut short in a clash between cultures.

* * *

Kate had started off by saying she didn't think she knew if a plant looked right or not. Now she bent down and twisted the lavender a couple of degrees to the right. Then stood back again. Nodded. Started to infill the hole around the plant with compost. Smiling to herself.

Ellie turned her attention to the raised beds, taking handfuls of the topsoil that had just been tipped into them and letting them drift through her fingers. Good soil. Even with the winter coming on, they could plant fruit bushes, perhaps some cordon apples and pears, and a clump of rhubarb. Some people set broad beans to overwinter and get a head start on next year's growth. This was a sheltered spot, so perhaps it would amuse Kate to try some. It wouldn't worry her too much if the frost got them.

Armand, now, was going to be as competitive about gardening as he was about everything else. He'd take it as a personal insult if his broad beans didn't do better than anyone else's.

Midge arrived from nowhere to investigate what Ellie was doing in someone else's garden. Ellie stroked his head but he wasn't interested in being caressed today. He made his way delicately to the middle of the nearest bed, turned his back on her and squatted down, tail poker-straight out behind him, ears flexing. Concentrating.

'Oh dear,' said Ellie.

'What's that pesky cat doing now?' demanded Armand.

'What comes naturally,' said Kate. And smiled.

THE END

THE JOFFE BOOKS STORY

We began in 2014 when Jasper agreed to publish his mum's much-rejected romance novel and it became a bestseller.

Since then we've grown into the largest independent publisher in the UK. We're extremely proud to publish some of the very best writers in the world, including Joy Ellis, Faith Martin, Caro Ramsay, Helen Forrester, Simon Brett and Robert Goddard. Everyone at Joffe Books loves reading and we never forget that it all begins with the magic of an author telling a story.

We are proud to publish talented first-time authors, as well as established writers whose books we love introducing to a new generation of readers.

We have been shortlisted for Independent Publisher of the Year at the British Book Awards three times, in 2020, 2021 and 2022, and for the Diversity and Inclusivity Award at the Independent Publishing Awards in 2022.

We built this company with your help, and we love to hear from you, so please email us about absolutely anything bookish at feedback@joffebooks.com

If you want to receive free books every Friday and hear about all our new releases, join our mailing list: www.joffebooks.com/contact

And when you tell your friends about us, just remember: it's pronounced Joffe as in coffee or toffee!

ALSO BY VERONICA HELEY

THE ELLIE QUICKE MYSTERIES
Book 1: MURDER AT THE ALTAR
Book 2: MURDER BY POISON PEN
Book 3: MURDER OF INNOCENCE
Book 4: MURDER BY ACCIDENT
Book 5: MURDER IN THE GARDEN

THE BEA ABBOT AGENCY MYSTERIES
Book 1: A FALSE CHARITY
Book 2: A FALSE PICTURE
Book 3: A FALSE STEP
Book 4: A FALSE PRETENCE
Book 5: FALSE MONEY
Book 6: A FALSE REPORT
Book 7: A FALSE ALARM
Book 8: A FALSE DIAMOND
Book 9: A FALSE IMPRESSION
Book 10: A FALSE WALL
Book 11: A FALSE FIRE
Book 12: A FALSE PRIDE
Book 13: A FALSE ACCOUNT
Book 14: A FALSE CONCLUSION
Book 15: A FALSE FACE

Printed in Great Britain
by Amazon

55948774R00158